RUNNING OFF
RADAR

Visit us at www.boldstrokesbooks.com

By the Author

Strictly Need to Know

Running Off Radar

RUNNING OFF RADAR

by
MB Austin

2018

ISBN 13: 978-1-63555-152-5

This Trade Paperback Original Is Published By
Bold Strokes Books, Inc.
P.O. Box 249
Valley Falls, NY 12185

First Edition: July 2018

Credits
Editor: Ruth Sternglantz
Production Design: Susan Ramundo
Cover Design By Tammy Seidick

Acknowledgments

I first visited Sitka to help run a conference co-hosted by the Sitka Tribe of Alaska. The event was successful, the April weather gentle, and the food (including herring eggs, salmon heads, fry bread, and dinner at Ludvig's) memorable. But it was the way the tribal staff welcomed us and shared their sense of place that made me sad to leave and eager to return. *Gunalchéesh.*

That trip planted the seed for this work of fiction in my mind, and I felt compelled to return in order to get a host of details right. Almost all the places in this story are real, and I encourage you to visit them, especially with a guide from Tribal Tours. All of the characters are fictional, but I hope they feel real enough that you might find yourself looking for them while in Sitka.

And because publishing really is a team effort:

To the wonderful crew at Bold Strokes Books for all the work that makes each novel the best it can be,

To a host of volunteers who provided beta reader feedback, technical and military advice, language and culture guidance, and research assistance,

To each and every person who read *Strictly Need to Know* and responded with an action (verbal feedback, a formal review, recommending it to a friend or book club, getting your local library to stock it, asking for the next installment, feeding me…),

To Basha for always believing in and supporting me,

Thank you. You lift me up.

Dedication

For Basha
Always yes.

CHAPTER ONE

Rose diStephano tried not to pace. The waiting area at N1 in the Seattle-Tacoma airport was crowded with travelers headed for Sitka, Alaska. Like her, some of them must also be attending the conference on traditional foods and cultural preservation. She scanned the terminal as the gate agent announced over the PA that boarding would begin with people who needed assistance, and those traveling with small children. No one was taking toddlers to southeast Alaska on a Tuesday in April. But an elderly man with papery skin and a halo of wispy white hair was boarding, pushed by an airport attendant. And a tiny, wizened woman with burnished skin and a walker was being assisted toward the gate. The sturdy middle-aged man by her side spoke to her softly in a language Rose couldn't even guess at. Would Maji, with her polyglot's ear for languages, recognize it?

Was the incomparable, inscrutable Maji Rios still coming? Rose sighed and looked at her watch for the thousandth time since getting off her flight from California at Sea-Tac to find no familiar face meeting her there. Well, Maji *had* said she might not make it, even while confirming in a brief voicemail three weeks ago that she had booked her flight. Maybe she'd only accepted Rose's invitation out of guilt. Maybe she didn't want to date, to even try out being a couple. To explore whatever this time together might lead to. Maybe Maji didn't love her back and just wanted closure—from a comfortable distance.

The jangle of her phone broke into Rose's brooding. Maji? She tried not to be disappointed to see Bubbles's smiling face on the screen instead. Without preamble, Rose asked, "Is she there?"

"No, I was hoping she was with you. Her phone's still off," Bubbles said. Maji's closest friend had stayed in touch with Rose since befriending her the previous summer, on Long Island. Bubbles had emailed Rose an ultrasound of the baby she and her husband Rey were expecting in the fall. And called, sobbing, when she'd miscarried. Maji wasn't there for her to tell.

"Do you want me to tell her?" Rose asked. "Assuming she actually shows up."

"No, I'll do it," Bubbles replied. "And she was really pumped about the trip last time I saw her. You know she wouldn't blow you off, right? If she isn't calling, then she can't."

Where on earth could Maji be that she couldn't at least leave Rose a message? Although Rose understood that as a Select Reserve in the US Army Maji could be called up anytime, surely she would have told Rose if that happened. Or at least told her best friend and had her deliver the bad news. "Just how long has she been gone?"

Bubbles's delayed response made Rose's chest constrict. "Bubbles. Just tell me."

"Almost three weeks. That's longer than normal."

Normal? How often did this happen? "But didn't she at least tell you where she was going? Or for how long?"

"Rose, she can't. You get that, right?"

Rose sighed. "Not really. But I guess I'll know when she shows up, or doesn't. I'm not used to playing Schrödinger's cat." Realizing she'd subconsciously invoked a dead-or-alive scenario, she shuddered. "Sorry—scratch that. I'm just...unsettled."

"Look, Rose. She may be an idiot, but if she said she'd make it, she will do her best to. If she can't, try not to take it personally. Promise?"

"It's too late for that, sweetie. Gotta go." Rose disconnected and sighed again, watching the line of passengers in first class and the back of the plane file down the gangway. She got in line and shuffled her carry-on and shoulder bag with laptop, papers, and other academic paraphernalia along behind them. She thought with regret of the rolling suitcase already loaded on the plane. Certainly she'd overpacked; but going from the near-summer weather of California's central coast to chilly rain put some fear into her. So she'd followed the conference organizers' tips and found a breathable raincoat with zip-out liner and hood, tall rain boots with lug soles, and warm layers to wear from the conference center out into the muskeg, forests, and tideflats. No way would she miss learning about the local Tlingit foods by being unprepared to go outdoors.

"Passengers Huang, Rios, and Carlsbeck, report to gate N1 for boarding. Last call for Sitka passengers Huang, Rios, and Carlsbeck."

Rose took one last look around the terminal and handed her e-ticket to the gate agent. "Have a good trip," he said with a perfunctory smile.

As the flight attendant walked the aisle, reminding last-minute texters to turn off their phones and premature nappers to put their seat backs up, Rose wondered if inviting Maji on this trip had been a mistake. Maji had been painfully clear with her last July, stoically insisting that a relationship would only hurt Rose. *We'd make plans with your family or your friends, and you'd have to lie to them when I didn't show up. I'm not going to put you through that.* She'd been right about getting stood up hurting. But damn it anyway, what gave her the right to unilaterally decide what was best for both of them?

Last July Rose couldn't argue with the burdens Maji shouldered. Very scary people really had wanted to kill them, or at least kidnap her and force her cousin Angelo to do their bidding. It was a disorienting time, so far from Rose's everyday reality distanced from her Mafia relations. As Ang's teammate and closest friend, Maji had kept her promise to protect Rose from harm but had not been able to keep the physical and emotional distance she promised herself. To Rose that was not a failure to be held against her. Extraordinary though she might be, Maji was human. And if there were things about herself or her work that she couldn't share with Rose, then so be it.

But Maji held herself to a standard Rose couldn't fully grasp. She clearly felt responsible for Angelo's death, despite doing more than anyone could ask to prevent his murder. And then when the danger was over and Rose had wanted to discuss the future, Maji had given her that speech about how they couldn't have one together. *Maybe you could do it. But I don't think I could live with watching you get hurt, over and over. And blaming myself for that.* Rose knew there was love under those words, but it was buried under the rubble of Maji's fear. Rose had held out hope that by now Maji had dug her way out, but perhaps today was just the same message delivered in a new way.

Should Rose even have invited Maji on this trip? She hadn't planned to. She wouldn't even have driven up to UC Berkeley to see Maji's mother speak, without Bubbles's nagging. But when Rose had seen Maji, looking fully recovered from the previous summer's injuries in her Paragon Security uniform, all the stored-up resentment fell away. They had joked and flirted, and even talked seriously over tea in the student union. Their shared grief was clear, but not as potent as the attraction still there just under the surface. Rose would have abandoned her classes for a week to accompany Maji on the remainder of her mother's tour, had Maji only asked. But of course she didn't. Rose had been surprised to find herself inviting Maji to join her in Sitka. And then dangerously elated when Maji had not said no.

But Maji had hedged then, and now she was incommunicado. Not only had she not returned Rose's phone messages, but she didn't even call Bubbles to say she wouldn't make it. Trying not to take it personally was easier said than done. She wanted to give Maji the benefit of the doubt. Maybe something had come up. Maybe Maji would appear in Sitka, late but with a good story. Or maybe she wouldn't show at all and Rose would have to finally let go. By any standard, her attempts so far to move on seemed half-hearted. She hadn't asked anyone out, telling herself she was too busy settling in to a new town, a new college. Rose could have driven up to San Jose or even San Francisco if she'd wanted a casual liaison away from the small town watchfulness of San Ignacio. But that wasn't her style. Maji was the only stranger she had ever invited home. And though she was less physically wary for her safety than she had once been, thanks to last summer's self-defense camp and two semesters with the college jujitsu club, she just didn't want to. She was making friends at the college—and that was enough. Besides, when she had said yes to a few dates, the one nice-enough man and two perfectly attractive women she'd spent a few hours with simply paled in contrast to her memories of Maji. Until she was free of those, it wasn't fair to date anyone else.

Rose closed her eyes as the plane rumbled forward, lifting off the tarmac and circling over Puget Sound. If this was how she felt after being stood up for a trip she didn't need company on, maybe Maji was right. Maybe a future together would be too painful.

Maji watched the Seattle skyline recede, and the trees and water grow small. She sighed, feeling the sweat on her T-shirt cool as her heart rate dropped back to normal after the sprint from the security office to the gate. Maji resisted unzipping her jacket to cool down, as it was the only thing between the other passengers and her ripe body odor. She wasn't sure which day it was when she'd caught that three-minute shower, but it hadn't freshened her clothes up any. Reaching Sea-Tac on the right day was a huge relief, but waiting for her properly boxed, fully unloaded sidearm to clear security so she could board the flight had nearly snapped her last frayed nerve.

Would Rose politely but firmly tell her to piss off? She ought to. *Fucking self-fulfilling prophecies.* Anxiety over Rose's reaction to seeing her warred with exhaustion as Maji struggled to stay awake long enough to get up when the fasten seat belt sign finally went out.

The first class section's flight attendant caught her eye and smiled. Just before the free-to-wander announcement started over the PA, she replaced Maji's empty complimentary water bottle with a fresh one. "Can I get you anything else?"

Maji shook off her stupor enough to nod. Words were hard to form. Sentences? No way.

A full horizon of navy blue dress filled Maji's view, and the nameplate now uncomfortably close to Maji's face read *Tina*. When she pulled back a bit, Maji noticed the immaculate makeup, with lashes unrealistically long and dark around startlingly blue eyes. Contacts. "A snack box? Beverage?" Tina asked. The lashes blinked, the blue eyes sparkling. Flirty.

Maji pulled out a credit card and handed it over. "Food please," she said. "And water. Lots."

That was enough like sentences to give her hope. Time to find Rose. As soon as Tina turned toward the galley, Maji unbuckled herself, rose stiffly, and pulled back the curtain separating first class from the normal people.

"Which snack?" the attendant called after her.

"Both," Maji said without breaking stride. She spotted Rose in 13C, eyes closed with her head tilted against the headrest. Crouching in the aisle, she took a minute to drink in Rose's features. It was worth nearly four thousand miles of trucks, boats, and planes to see that face again. *Please don't send me home. Not yet.* Maji touched Rose's hand.

Rose startled and looked up. When she looked down and saw Maji, she smiled broadly, grasping her hand. "You made it! I didn't see you get on."

"Had to run for it. Got bumped to first class. You want to trade?" *Smooth, Rios.*

"No. I'm fine." Rose traced Maji's cheek and jaw lightly with her fingertips. "You're sunburned."

"Yeah. I...yeah. And I lost my phone—sorry."

"You didn't get my messages, then?"

"One, right before...um. Did you leave another? Change your mind?" Maji felt tears threaten. *Breathe, Rios.*

"No," Rose said, looking unsure how much she wanted to say. "I just wanted to line up lodgings. When I didn't hear back, I took a single at the dorm."

Maji knew the local college was hosting the conference in conjunction with the Sitka Tribe. It was probably good that Rose had a place of her own in case their reunion went badly. But she was hoping, well...She swallowed. "Hannah lined up a suite at a hotel, in case you needed security. She didn't mention that?"

At Rose's puzzled shake of the head, Maji plunged on. "It's big enough to share even if you want space to yourself. Or I could take the dorm if…" She couldn't assume that Rose would fall into bed with her just because she'd invited her along on a work trip. Not getting between Rose and her career was important too. "Um, unless you need to be in the dorms to get everything you want from the conference."

Rose blushed, but smiled at her warmly. "No, I don't need to. Let's settle into the hotel and see how things go."

Those big brown eyes full of light and warmth held Maji, even as she felt her calves start to cramp. "Yeah," she agreed, wincing as she unfolded herself back to standing.

Rose reached out for her. "Are you all right?"

Well, she hadn't eaten a hot meal in days, had only caught short naps for the last two, had no idea what time her body thought it was—and she stank. But she'd made the damn plane, and Rose was holding her hand, looking at her with…damn. "Sure. I just need a shower, food, and sleep. You want a snack box?"

"No, thanks," Rose replied. "I'll see you in Alaska." Maji looked down at their joined hands and nodded. She didn't want to walk away. But Rose released her hold, reassuring her with a smile. "Go."

Maji inhaled both snack boxes, drained all the water bottles lined up on her tray table, and promptly fell asleep. She startled awake at a sudden drop, along with the captain's voice over the intercom as the plane shook and shifted in the air. "Yes, folks, we're encountering a bit of turbulence. Please stay in your seats and keep your seat belts fastened. We should be on the ground in twenty or thirty minutes."

Depending on what? She could roll with uncertainty in a lot of situations, but flying wasn't one of them. To distract herself from thoughts of crashing, Maji looked out the window. The sight of small islands in a slate-blue ocean, snowcapped mountains, and an endless swath of evergreen forest took her breath. "Wow."

"First time flying in?" the man across the aisle asked, a proud smile on his face. Able to focus again after a few hours of sleep,

Maji sized him up quickly. The sandy hair and boyish good looks made him appear thirtysomething, but the creases around his eyes put him over forty. And the buzzed sides of his head would have suggested military to her, even without the American flag patch on the flight jacket he wore over a uniform.

"Yup." Maji swallowed down the snack boxes trying to rise up in her throat as the plane continued to pitch.

"Bag's in the pocket there," the man said pleasantly. "And don't worry, this is normal."

Of course it was. There were no alarms, no smoke, no spinning toward the ground. "No worries."

He chuckled. "Really. I fly Jayhawks here. This is a day in the park. And I know the captain—she's top-notch."

Still, Maji thought, anything this bouncy should come with parachutes. Not that she hoped to arrive anywhere that way again soon. In the dark. From thirty thousand feet. At least this last mission had spared her that, and the village buses had bounced along on four wheels. "What do you use Jayhawks for?" she asked, less from curiosity than to distract herself.

"Search and rescue, law enforcement, environmental disaster response." He pulled a business card from his jacket's inside pocket. "Here. Call me for an insider tour of the station."

United States Coast Guard, Air Station Sitka. Lt. Commander John T. Fitzsimmons. "Nice to meet you, Lieutenant Commander."

"Jack." Not Fitz? Whatever. He offered his hand across the aisle. "Nice to meet you, Ms. …?"

"Rios," she said, giving him a brief shake but no title correction.

"Army, right?"

Damn. She had planned to just be herself on vacation here. But there hadn't been time to go home and get her civilian ID. So she was stuck with her work identity, Sergeant Ariela Rios. And then because she was running so late, and being a Select Reserve made her active duty, they'd bumped her to first class without even asking. She sighed. "Yeah. Army Reserves now."

"Well, no need to burst Tina's bubble." He tilted his head toward the flight attendant. "She gets a little carried away with the *thank you for your service* thing. Word to the wise."

Maji blinked at him. Was he warning her off? Or was he fishing, trying to gauge her reaction? Maybe the tour offer was his equivalent of asking for her number. *Whatever, dude.* "The bump to first class was more than enough for me. I'm not looking for any favors." She set his card on the edge of her tray.

"Well," he said, "hang on to that anyway. How long you in town for?"

"Just a few days." Five, but why be precise? She thought about adding that she was here with someone, but no. Whether he was hitting on her or just being friendly, it was still none of his business.

"Ever been up in a Jayhawk?"

"No, I'm more of the Black Hawk type, I guess." They touched down, bouncing lightly and gliding smoothly to a stop. "Thanks," she added, realizing he had distracted her through the last of the turbulence.

"Happy to help," he said, giving her a wink. "But seriously. I'm in command the next few days, so I'm grounded and happy for an excuse to get out from under the paperwork. Guests are always welcome on downtime—bring a friend if you'd like."

"Sitka passengers please remain in your seats," the captain's voice said overhead. "We'll be in and out of Ketchikan before you know it."

Maji peered out the window at the glimpse of Ketchikan visible and registered houses right up to the water, a large ferry, and lots of fishing boats in the harbor. "Where's the ferry go?"

Jack leaned back to see her through the boarding group of teenage boys in matching soccer team gear. "That's the Marine Highway. Comes up from Bellingham and connects all of Southeast. Can't drive from one town to another. Or anyplace, for that matter."

Maji nodded and closed her eyes. Tina's voice woke her before she realized she had fallen asleep again. Or that she'd missed takeoff. Just as well.

"Jack? Don't fake sleep, come on." Apparently Tina knew him well too.

"Sorry," he replied. "What's up?"

"I put in for a transfer, and—"

"A transfer? What's wrong with Anchorage? What about Jasper?"

"That's what I wanted to ask you. I don't think I should take him to Seattle or LA and—"

"He'd hate LA!" All the suave in Jack's voice was gone now. Was Jasper their son? "*You'd* hate LA. And I know you're homesick. Wait—did you meet somebody already? Is that it?"

"Stop." Tina pitched her voice lower. "Just stop." Maji peeked from beneath her lashes and saw the blue tights and heels that rounded out Tina's uniform protruding into the aisle from her perch on the seat one row up. "You know I'm not even trying to meet someone until I'm legally single. Are you holding the paperwork up on purpose?"

"No! It just takes time. You could stay in Sitka till then. I wouldn't bug you, and Jasper…"

Tina sighed. "Name me three people in Sitka who don't know me. Will you take Jasper or not? He needs more runs than he's getting and…he misses you."

"Makes one of you. You don't even have to ask, T. I never wanted you to take him in the first place. Just didn't want you alone in the city."

"Right, Mr. Chivalrous. How could I forget?" The blue heels planted themselves in the aisle, and the stockinged calves went vertical in Maji's tiny slice of fake-sleep vision. "We're almost to landing."

"T, wait."

"What, Jack?" She sounded sad now, rather than angry.

"It's not too late. Nothing's final yet."

"Sure it is. Has been for a while now. We just hate to admit it."

Maji kept her eyes closed until the plane descended enough that looking out the window was irresistible. Craning to see out the windows on both sides of the plane, she gasped at the sight of mountains to the right and miles of water to the left. Just as it started to seem as if they were going to land in the deep blue, she spotted a snowcapped mountain with a scoop out of its top. "Wow," she breathed.

"That's Mount Edgecumbe," Jack volunteered.

"Wow." Fatigue was hell on her vocabulary. Hopefully when she saw Rose again shortly, she'd manage more than *yeah* and *wow*.

Maji waited in her large, cushy seat until the first twelve rows of coach had worked their way off the plane. The sight of Rose made her want to say *wow* again.

"Did you get something to eat, and a nap?" Rose asked.

Maji nodded, grateful for Rose's unstoppable kindness. "It helped. Thanks." Then she fell in behind Rose, happy just to be near her.

As she neared the exit door, someone pressed a napkin into Maji's hand. She turned to look. Tina smiled with one brow raised. "Thank you for flying with us today."

Maji nodded and stuffed the napkin into her jeans pocket without looking at it. At the baggage carousel she stood by Rose, each of them spotting for their bags. Maji's came off first, a small soft-sided bag not much bigger than the backpack over her shoulder. Rose left her carry-on with Maji, then stepped in to hoist a large suitcase off the carousel.

Rolling it back toward her, Rose asked, "What does your bag look like?"

"Like these," Maji said. "Ready?"

CHAPTER TWO

They walked out into the cool spring air to find a Tribal Tours van waiting at the curb. A pleasant looking woman in a black vest with large iridescent buttons held a sign that read, *Traditional Foods Conference.*

"That's us," Rose said.

"Sweet. Will they mind if I hitch a ride?"

Rose gestured toward the taxi driver getting out of the cab parked just in front of the van. "If they do, we'll catch a taxi." No way was Rose letting Maji out her sight again. They had a suite to share, she thought with a mix of trepidation and exhilaration. Of course there were things they need to talk about, but—

The sight of the cab driver trying to wrestle a skinny teen out of the taxi's front seat and onto the sidewalk cut off thought and movement. Rose felt Maji's hand on her arm and then the weight of her small bag, thrust against her midsection. Rose accepted it, understanding Maji wanted her hands free in case she needed to step in to help the young man.

The teen wrenched out of the driver's grasp and pulled a hunting knife from inside his jean jacket. "You can't make me go."

Maji stepped in front of the teen, motioning Rose to the man, who had stepped back at the sight of the knife.

"Simon…" the man said, raising both open hands in a calming motion. Then, "Lady—no!"

Rose took her cue and moved between Maji and the man, looking him in the eye. "She'll be fine. Are you all right?"

"I'm good. My nephew, he's just upset. His dad died recently."
He moved to go around her and Rose moved with him, a subtle
block.

"I'm so sorry," she said, trying to keep his attention on her.
"I'm Rose. And you?"

Just like at practice scenarios in camp last summer, the empathy
and redirect worked. "Nate. She really okay, your friend? He seems
calmer."

Rose turned just enough to keep an eye on both Nate and Maji,
along with the boy. Maji was now the one holding the knife, but she
was offering it back to him respectfully with two hands as if it were
a practice weapon in the dojo. Rose heard her say softly, "Beautiful
handle. You carve it?"

"My dad," the boy said, his face twisting in pain.

"They won't let you take it on the plane, of course," Maji said
in a casual tone, as if they were chatting in a café. "We could ship it
in one of those little express boxes the airports use for stuff they'd
have to confiscate." She gave the Tribal Tours driver a look, and the
woman nodded and headed inside.

Rose hadn't noticed the driver with all of her attention on Nate,
but Maji clearly had. As always, she turned strangers into members
of her team. Maji gave Rose a hint of a smile while keeping most of
her focus on the young man. "Where you headed, Simon?"

Nate opened his mouth to answer for the teen, but caught Rose's
look and waited silently. Rose relaxed her guard a bit, as Nate gave
no indication of trying to get through Maji to the boy.

"Los Anchorage," he replied with a sneer and then rolled his
eyes. "Rage City." He shrugged. "My mom's job's there."

The van driver came back out and handed the shipping box to
Maji. "Thanks," Maji said, not taking her eyes off Simon. "How bad
is Anchorage? On a scale from one to suckiest?"

The boy nearly smiled, and relaxed a notch. But as he opened
his mouth to reply, Nate spoke up. "You gotta make that plane,
Simon."

The boy held his ground, visibly charging up again. "I should
stay here. Grandma needs me."

"The Eagles will take care of her, Simon. Your mother is Raven too, and she doesn't have us in Anchorage. She needs you."

"She doesn't need me—she has a girlfriend."

"So she's got one up on you and me. But that lady's not Tlingit, eh?"

"No," Simon conceded with a frown. "She's Yup'ik."

"Then go be a good son. Finish the school year without flunking anything and you can come back here and fish with me."

Hope replaced the teen's scowl. "Really?"

"If your mom says yes, and you keep out of summer school."

"Cool."

Maji looked between them, then gave Rose a nod. They both moved from between the man and boy. Maji handed Simon the box and a twenty. "Buy the insurance, okay? I always do."

Simon looked at the box and the money. "Okay. Hey—thanks." He gave Maji a quick, awkward hug and disappeared inside, his uncle at his side. Maji waved off the van driver's profuse thanks, but accepted seats in the front of the van for Rose and herself that the driver insisted would give them the best view.

As five more people from their flight climbed in, the driver checked them off against a clipboard.

"I'm a last-minute add," Maji said to explain why she wasn't on the list. "May I pay for my ride separately?"

The driver gave her an incredulous look, then slid into her seat behind the wheel. Over her shoulder she said, "You two can ride free with me any day you're in town. Just ask for Heather. Now, where you headed?"

Maji gave her the hotel's name and felt Rose slip a hand into hers.

"With me," Rose added.

Maji turned in surprise and couldn't suppress a grin at the sparkle in Rose's eye.

As she drove, Heather volunteered the backstory on the sidewalk drama. "Simon—the boy—he lost his father just recently. The cops want to write it off as an accident, say he was intoxicated and maybe suicidal even. That's bullshit, of course. But anyway,

Simon's dad was an Eagle, like his uncle Nate. Married a Raven woman, like an Eagle is supposed to, traditionally."

"So the grandmother Simon is worried about is his mother's mother?" Rose asked. "Matrilineal," she added quietly to Maji.

"Ayuh." The driver nodded.

"Huh," Maji said. "A clan system? Sorry, I'm not an anthropologist." On nearly every mission she had to learn who was who in a community, who played well together, who was feuding. Tribal clan systems actually made that easier, if the traditional lines still held.

Heather chuckled. "Nothing to apologize for there. And yes, there are lots of clans, but you're always either from the Eagle moiety or Raven moiety. Like two umbrellas with lots of smaller groups under each one. And times like these, all the clans in the opposite moiety take care of the deceased's family."

"Is that really all you brought?" Rose asked as Heather hefted her rolling bag down from the van's rear storage. Maji hadn't let the driver take either of her small bags, keeping them between her feet as they rode. It made her press the length of her thigh against Rose's in the most pleasant way.

"Well, I had a date to go shopping with Bubbles, but then I got called out of town. And lost my phone, and ran out of time. I'll get stuff locally tomorrow." Maji looked to Heather. "There a thrift store near here?"

"White Elephant," Heather said with a nod. "Couple consignment shops too, with longer hours."

Maji looked to Rose. "What time's the conference start?"

"There's a light breakfast at eight and the plenary is at nine." If they finally got to talk, or…anything else, Rose planned to make it just in time for the opening speaker.

"But don't miss the Warming of the Hands tonight," Heather said, handing Maji a flyer.

"Thanks," Maji said and tried to hand her a twenty.

Heather gave her a skeptical look, shaking her head. "See you at Naa Kahidi at six." She smiled. "Bring your appetite."

"Clearly she doesn't know you," Rose joked, slipping an arm through Maji's as they entered the hotel lobby. It was a nice enough place, older but clearly refurbished. Some of the decor was obviously meant to evoke Alaska and the coastal tribes.

Rose observed as Maji handled getting into their room an hour before normal check-in with a combination of politeness and finesse. The desk clerk seemed impressed that Maji had booked their only suite, and offered twice to send someone to help with the bags. Or anything else they might need.

"What was that about?" Rose asked as the elevator took them to the grand height of the fifth floor, the top. In this town, the hotel stood wider and taller than almost any other building nearby. The only larger one, pointed out by Heather as she'd narrated their short drive, was the assisted living facility called the Pioneer Home.

"The suite's a little spendy, I guess." Catching sight of herself in the mirror inside the elevator, Maji grimaced. "Jesus, I look like hell."

"Not to me," Rose said. Clearly exhausted though, and perhaps a little on edge now that they were alone. "But you must be worn out. Have you been sleeping badly?"

Maji held the elevator doors open as Rose rolled her bag out. "I don't know—it's just been naps the last few days. I'm sorry to show up such a mess. It was either get cleaned and fed, and catch some rack time, or make the flight."

So Maji had gone hungry and unwashed from God only knew where, on no sleep, to arrive when she said she would. Rose felt tears prickle at the edges of her eyes. She took the card key and opened the door for them. "Let's improve that situation then."

Maji followed her in and seemed to ignore the breathtaking view out the large windows, going instead to the framed landscapes on the walls and tugging at their corners. Rose watched as she turned in a circle, scanning the room with a clinical eye, then picked up the phone on the desk in the neatly appointed office area of the suite.

"Where exactly is the safe?" Maji turned toward the hall closet as she listened to the reply. "Ah. Thanks."

When Maji dumped out her small bag on the couch, Rose eyed the metallic-looking case with two padlocks with suspicion. "Are you smuggling jewels now?"

"Not this time," Maji deadpanned, humor in her eyes. "It's my sidearm. Nearly made me miss the flight, getting through security. And now I should clean and oil it before locking it up, but I'll have to get supplies first. Oh, and"—she plucked a passport from the little pile of odd items and handed it to Rose—"sorry."

Rose opened the little blue folder and recognized Maji's photo, with her official military name under it. "Are you not on vacation then?"

"Well, I am off duty," Maji explained. "But it would be best if you called me *Ri* in public, like before. I can only travel with one passport, and I didn't have time to get home to switch them out."

So she'd also bypassed time to recover at home in order to be here as promised. Rose tried not to embarrass Maji by showing how much that meant to her. They weren't even officially unbroken up. "Or to get Alaska-appropriate clothing. What did you bring?"

Maji zipped open the modest backpack and put her nose in, pulling back with a pained look. "Nothing I can wear tonight." She looked embarrassed. "Could I borrow some clothes?"

"You get in the shower and I'll find something in there"—Rose pointed to her large bag—"that will do. Do you need...everything?"

Maji grinned sheepishly. "I try never to go commando in borrowed pants. But, yeah. I'm wearing my least ripe clothes, and I wouldn't stand near me." At Rose's laugh she added, "Thanks. I promise to shop in the morning."

While Maji washed up, Rose unpacked. The living area of the suite had no bureau and only a small coat closet, so she used the bedroom's, taking care to leave half of each drawer and plenty of hanging space free. It felt perilously like moving in together. There was bedding for the sleeper couch in the living area, but she'd wait to use it until they had a chance to talk. The idea of just falling into bed with Maji made her heart race but her head ache. Rose had counted on a return call from Maji—anytime in the past three weeks—to talk about what Maji accepting her invitation to this week in Sitka might mean.

The sound of the shower stopped and Rose fled the bedroom, leaving out some clothes that might fit Maji's shorter, less curvy frame well enough for an evening event. She looked out the picture windows at the harbor and to Sitka Sound beyond it. Curious about the curtains on the west side of the suite, she opened them and found a balcony. Out in the cool afternoon, she could see Mt. Edgecumbe, the iconic dormant volcano. The air felt fresh and soft with hints of evergreen, sea salt, and a recent rain. Rose smiled to herself. This was a gorgeous spot and she would spend her days with colleagues from interesting places, learning about things that fascinated her. And in her off-hours, whatever the two of them did or did not do this week, she would get to know the real, civilian Maji a little better. For now, that was enough.

Behind her Maji's voice called, "Rose? You still here?"

Rose turned, and the sight of Maji with one towel wrapped around her hair, and another tucked in just above her breasts, quashed her *que sera, sera* delusions.

The look on Rose's face almost drove Maji back into the refuge of the shower. She should have known better. They needed to talk, and soon. But right now she felt nearly human again, clean at last. And she couldn't get dressed until all of the wound dressings were replaced.

Rose's expression changed to concern the second she spotted the fresh bandage on Maji's arm. Or maybe it was the bruises. "How badly are you hurt?"

"All superficial. But there are two spots I can't reach. I'm sorry."

Rose ran her fingers lightly over the discolored areas around the edges of the wound dressing, and then up to Maji's sun- and wind-burned cheeks. "Stop apologizing for things you can't control. You chose to be here." She leaned in and put her lips softly on Maji's, a gift and a promise with no demands. Before Maji could lose her senses, Rose stepped back. "Now show me how to help you."

So Maji lay on her front on top of the quilt on the king-size bed while Rose gently peeled the damp medical tape and wound dressings off the chewed-up patches of skin. The one on her lower back didn't hurt much, but the strip of abrasions on the back of her right thigh stung when the air hit it. Through her own controlled breathing she heard Rose stifle a gasp.

"I don't suppose I should ask how this happened?"

"No." Maji stopped herself just before the word *sorry* popped out again.

"Well, let's let them breathe a bit. Stay there." Rose returned a moment later and began smoothing lotion over Maji's back and shoulders. Maji closed her eyes and tried to block out the images that flooded in, focusing instead on Rose's touch. But the contrast between what she'd seen over the last few weeks, the hell she'd gotten herself successfully into and back out of, and the sweetness of being with Rose in a quiet, safe, and clean place was too much. Tears leaked out and she shuddered as she opened her eyes again, staring at the bureau across the room.

"Are you all right? Should I stop?" Rose's hands paused, resting on the small of Maji's back, warm just above the towel.

"I'm just a little wiped out," Maji said, hating the wobble in her voice.

"Mm-hmm." Rose was too polite to call bullshit on her. Or too nice, maybe.

"It's been a rough few weeks. But I'll be fine. Better by the minute."

A few minutes passed as Rose moisturized her feet, her calves, her arms. "I'll let you get the rest yourself. Hand me the ointment."

Maji reached for the tube of prescription antibiotic the medics had sent her home with and passed it back to Rose without rolling over. *At least all my parts move in the right direction.* If she slept tonight, tomorrow she could go for a run, eat six meals, and get back to normal. "Don't worry about hurting me. Just glob it on."

Rose did better than that, and Maji concentrated on breathing rather than flinching. "Did you help someone?" Rose asked.

Maji smiled. Rose had some well-founded suspicions about Maji's covert work for the Army, based on what she had seen and heard last summer. But she had attended Hannah's self-defense camp too, and the core values resonated strongly with her own. Maji boiled the mission debrief down in her head, looking for a succinct answer. She had infiltrated, gotten two high value targets to a safe house, and exfiltrated without blowing her cover. And she'd handled it well enough to avoid any blowback to the villagers. So, yes. As a bonus, she'd managed to not get blown up, shot, or raped. Exfil had banged her up a bit, but nothing was broken and she hadn't cracked her skull again. "Yeah. We did."

"Good." Rose stood and pulled the far side of the bed's quilt over Maji. "Do you want me to wake you for the Warming of the Hands?"

Clean and cuddled in soft warmth, sleep was already encroaching. "I'd like to go. Just give me ten to get ready." Maji reached up and snugged a pillow under her head. Such luxury. "If I have a nightmare, don't get too close, okay?"

"Hooah, Sergeant," Rose whispered, brushing a strand of hair off Maji's face. "See you in two hours."

CHAPTER THREE

Rose's enthusiasm about attending an event hosted in the Sitka Tribe's community house was endearing. "It's a modern recreation of the traditional longhouse, of course. A great place to entertain and, I suppose, also hold ceremonies and meetings and classes. No one lives there, though, as they would have before the Europeans invaded." She squeezed Maji's hand. "I hope there's dancing."

"But they're going to feed us too, right?" Heather had intimated as much. Whatever the welcome involved, Maji hoped it started with dinner.

Rose laughed, turning them just before Totem Square Park on to Katlian Street. "Yes. Herring roe is a big deal here, and the harvest just ended. So I expect we'll get to try those. What else, I don't know."

"Well, you are all about traditional foods for the next four days, right?"

"Yes. I just don't know what's in season. I didn't do my research very well."

Maji heard the self-judgment in Rose's voice. "How many classes are you teaching?"

"Three. One intro to anthropology, one upper-level undergrad course on food and culture, and one graduate seminar. It's a small college."

"Wow. It's good you could get away at all."

Rose's thumb caressed the back of Maji's hand as she answered. "It was important to me. There are people attending that I'd have to travel abroad to meet otherwise. And…" She paused. "I wanted to see you on neutral territory. Does that make any sense?"

Maji nodded. Rose was working to build a professional life at a new college, while Maji had just wrapped up her master's degree at Columbia. Rose's family—the few left who mattered—were all in California now. Alaska would seem far enough from the worlds of career and family. "Perfect sense. I'll keep myself occupied while you work. And…I'm not making any assumptions about what you do or don't want."

Rose gave a self-deprecating laugh. "As if I knew. Honestly, I almost jumped your bones earlier. And I had a big speech ready, about taking things slow and actually getting to know each other."

"How about tonight I sleep on the couch and tomorrow we talk over breakfast and dinner? Are you free for dinner?"

Rose stopped and faced her. "Is that what you want, or what you think I want?"

"I want to make love all night and stay in bed all day tomorrow." Maji's confession earned her a deep blush from Rose and a shy smile. "But I'm seriously exhausted and you have people to meet."

"Let's play it by ear," Rose said, brushing her lips against Maji's ear. Then she turned back toward their objective for the evening. "We must be close."

Sure enough, in another half a block they saw a large, almost warehouse-like building with a signboard reading *Sheet'ka Kwaan Naa Kahidi Community House*. A few people milled about at the entry, dwarfed by the three-story wooden panels on either side of the doorway. Each panel was decorated in Tlingit designs carved into the wood, painted in red and black and pale blue.

Maji stopped, eyeing Rose's colleagues. "Is this okay?" she asked, holding their joined hands up.

"I'm delighted to be seen with you," Rose said. "But then, I'm out at work. So it's your call really. Will you get in trouble?"

Maji wished again that she were traveling under her civilian name. Joint Operations Special Command knew she was queer and didn't give an actual damn. But she'd prefer not to spend vacation dodging questions about her role in the military, or making Rose lie for her, either. Damn it, anyway. "Tell you what," she said finally, "if I get worried, I'll let you know. Until then, let's try acting like normal people."

"By holding hands in public? A lot of women would love for that to be normal."

Sadly, Rose was right. "Well, let's fake it till we make it, then. You game?"

"I'm all in," Rose replied, with a look behind the light words that made Maji suspect she meant much more than what seemed so simple on the surface. Would it ever be that simple for them?

Whatever Maji meant by *normal*, Rose wasn't ready to admit how inordinately exciting it sounded to her. That would feel like pushing, asking for something Maji had insisted she couldn't give. But as bizarre as last summer had been, the most mundane moments were the ones that always came back to her. Cooking together, talking about books, hanging out by the pool. Maji was easy to be with, whenever she laid her armor down.

Lost in thought, Rose didn't notice Javier, her friend and translator from her first trip to Peru, until he was within feet of them. "Javi!"

"Rosita!" He beamed at her and kissed her on both cheeks.

Rose kept her hold on Maji's left hand as she introduced them. "Javi, this is Ri. Ri, my friend and colleague Javier Mendez."

"Nice to meet you," Maji said.

As the two shook hands politely Rose asked, "What on earth are you doing here, Javi?"

"Following my bliss, as they say. I missed you last summer, when you canceled our trip. And then I heard such sad news about your family. I really hoped to see you again. And here you are."

Or a card would have been nice. "Oh. So are you attending the conference?"

"That's what my grant says," he replied with a wink. "But seriously, I'm really starting to get into ethnobotany. Maybe we could compare notes over a drink after this..." He waved a hand toward the sound of the crowd inside.

"Not tonight. Maybe lunch tomorrow? We could sit together then anyway."

Javi seemed to notice their joined hands for the first time. "Sure. *Mañana.* Excuse me."

As they watched him slip into the building around the short line of people waiting to get in, Maji asked, "A surprise?"

"For both of us, it seems. He's always been a bit unpredictable, though."

"Did he know how to reach you?"

"Only my work email changed. He should still have my cell number." Rose saw the wheels turning behind Maji's neutral expression. Well, it was her training to be suspicious, and she didn't know Javi like Rose did. They reached the door and received a warm welcome from a man in the familiar Tribal Tours outfit of black slacks, white shirt, and button-adorned black vest. Following his instructions, they found seats at a table in the large room inside, on the top tier in the amphitheater style setup.

Maji scanned the room, both from habit and curiosity. So this was what a longhouse looked like. The wooden walls and beams gleamed, reflecting the light from the ceiling fixtures. At the far end, behind the stage, more huge wooden carvings decorated the wall, a screen of art between them and the backstage area. The look of them was distinctive, highly stylized yet clearly evoking birds and other animals. Maji wondered which images were the Raven and Eagle of the afternoon's discussion.

Something out of sight smelled tantalizing and Maji noticed an open door at the far end of the long room, offering a glimpse of people hurriedly preparing trays of plates. And in the center of the recessed floor, a square, rock-lined fire pit waited with a neatly built arrangement of wood. Would dinner be cooked there? Or was it ceremonial? The room smelled like food, not smoke, and she didn't see where an indoor fire could vent. *Not your worry. You've ID'd all the exits, now chill out.*

As the rest of their group settled into seats, three people walked onto the stage. Holding a microphone, the short woman with graying hair introduced herself as the vice chair of the Sitka Tribe's council. "On behalf of the tribal government, thank you for coming to our land to learn. Tonight we will welcome you as we have welcomed travelers to our territory for over ten thousand years. But first, a few words from your conference hosts."

Another woman, younger and wearing a navy business suit, introduced herself as the conference organizer. She handed the mic to a tall, lanky man with a beautiful button blanket worn like a cape. He spoke a moment or more in a language Maji assumed was Tlingit. "Interesting phonology—makes me want to see some written words," she whispered to Rose.

In response, Rose smiled without taking her eyes off the speakers and gave her hand a squeeze under the table.

When he switched to English the speaker translated, "My name is Warren Paul. I am Coho Raven, L'uknax.ádi clan. We welcome you to our home tonight with the Warming of the Hands." He paused. "In the old times, we traveled thousands of miles on the sea, throughout Southeast and well beyond. Travelers always arrived tired and hungry, and often cold. A host village would warm them, feed them, and give them a place to sleep. Since it's nice out and you have lodgings, let's get right to the food." The group murmured its approval. "You all were smart to visit around herring season—we have eggs for you harvested in the subsistence manner. Who here grew up with herring eggs?" At least a dozen hands went up. "If you're from Southeast, keep those hands up." All but four went down. "Tomorrow you'll learn why Native Alaskans from as far away as Barrow share this gift of the spring. Or maybe even tonight if you take them out—but don't believe a word of those tales if you do."

The group chuckled as servers began to carry trays out, setting paper plates laden with food, bundles of plasticware in paper napkins, and paper cups in front of the guests. Teens in dance regalia carried pitchers of water and juice to the tables, performing their task with seriousness as well as care for their obviously custom-crafted clothing. Maji looked at the offerings, some recognizable to her and some not. The most obvious were a nice chunk of salmon, something that looked remarkably like macaroni salad, a small heap of tossed salad, and a lump of yellow fish roe.

Rose leaned into her, pointing her fork at the large yellow eggs. "The main attraction."

The man to Rose's right overheard and said in a good-natured tone, "If you don't like 'em, send 'em my way."

"Mighty kind of you," Maji replied, matching his tone.

"Al's all heart," a woman nearby said, nudging the man. "And all stomach."

After everyone had been served and some of the group had already dug into their suppers, Warren the Coho Raven walked back to center stage, wincing as the mic's repowering caused a squeal of feedback. "Sorry about that. I'll turn this thing off in just a minute. Now, while you enjoy the feast, I give you the Naa Kahidi Dancers."

In the expectant silence a row of dancers, from young and tiny to elderly and stout, and of all sizes and ages in between, filed onto the stage. Warren handed the mic to one of the people decked out in regalia, a fortyish woman with light brown hair and a fair complexion. She introduced herself in Tlingit and then explained, "As we like to do, we will start with an honoring dance for our veterans. What you may not all know is that the United States first peoples weren't even considered citizens until 1924. But we have served proudly to defend our home in every major conflict the US has gotten into, just like we Tlingit defended this land against the Russians, many years ago."

She called on the group to self-identify any veterans of World War II or Korea, but no one responded. At the call for Vietnam veterans, two men and one woman rose and made their way to the stage. The largest group rose when the call for anyone who served between 'Nam and 9/11 was made, with younger conference attendees rising last.

Maji felt Rose nudge her and release her hand when the dance leader called for anyone who had served since 9/11. Maji shook her head, giving Rose a frown.

Rose raised an eyebrow at her. "Go up and be honored, Sergeant."

Maji rolled her eyes but complied.

The drumming and singing began the second Maji, along with another woman and two men, found their places near the wings of the stage with the older veterans. She was glad that the dancers held her attention and the diners' as well. The few times she'd had to stand and be recognized, generally in dress uniform or in formation with her unit, she'd never felt such a visceral reaction. Was it the drumming? The voices? Or perhaps it was the sight of the people onstage, repeating for her a dance passed through centuries of generations. When her group was dismissed, she headed past the clapping audience directly to the restrooms down the hall.

Rose found her a few minutes later, patting her face dry of the cool water. Maji met her worried gaze in the mirror.

"Are you all right?"

Maji wasn't sure what the correct answer to that was. *No? Nearly? Better with you in a few hours than I have been in years?* "Depends. Is my plate still safe from Al's big heart?"

Rose wrapped her arms around Maji's waist from behind and swayed her gently, their reflections smiling. "It's ready for your big appetite. If you still have one."

Maji nearly joked again in response. But no. Rose deserved whatever honesty she could manage. "Rose…I'm not used to this."

"Being cared for?" As always, the warmth in Rose's eyes held a twinkle even when she looked serious.

"Being taken care of. I'm not good at it."

Rose brightened again. "I know. But turnabout is fair play, and even superheroes need a little TLC sometimes." She kissed the back of Maji's head and took her hand, pulling her toward the door. "Come on. Your herring eggs may be in danger—Al can only be held off for so long."

❖

Rose slipped her arm through Maji's as they walked back to the hotel, and Maji let herself bask in the at ease feeling of their being together, in public, with no worries. *Just like two normal people in love.* They talked lightly about the dances and the food, and how the sky was still light after eight p.m. in April. The small wonders and simple pleasures of travel to a new and interesting place just for fun. Standing in front of St. Michael's Cathedral, Maji intoned a few words in solemn-sounding Russian.

"Is that a prayer?"

Maji smiled. "No. It translates to, *The church is near but the road is icy; the tavern is far, but I will walk carefully.*"

"You are such a smart-ass." The fondness in Rose's voice was as good as a laugh from anyone else. Better.

"Hey, I didn't make it up. It's a well-known proverb."

"But of all the Russian proverbs you know, that's the one you picked." Rose moved to face her. "And watch it with the languages, or we might have to skip that talk tonight."

Maji felt herself flush at the memory of the last time she'd spoken multiple languages to Rose, to give herself the freedom to say things she couldn't speak otherwise. They'd slept little that night. "English-only rules are discriminatory."

Rose's eyes twinkled. "So sue me."

"What's the deal with Javi?" Maji asked, deliberately switching gears as the Spanish- and Quechua-speaking interpreter came to mind. "Has he ever acted stalkery before?"

Rose's eyes widened in surprise. "Stalkery? No. He's very much the modern Latino male feminist. Friendly, sort of casually intimate, but not...weird like that."

"Good. Still, I want you to call Hannah tonight and give her all the information you can on him."

Rose looked skeptical. "I hardly think—wait, you promised not to boss me around. We're not going back there. Ever."

"Agreed. I'm just reminding you that you promised Hannah." Angelo had asked Hannah to watch out for Rose after he was gone, until they were sure none of the angry Italian, Russian, or other organized crime groups were looking for payback.

Rose blew out a frustrated puff of air, riffling the glossy black curls on her forehead. "Fine. I'll call her right now." She dug in her purse for her phone and sat on the cathedral steps while the direct line to the head of Paragon Security rang. "Oh, Hannah, I'm sorry. What time is it there?...Yes, she's here. And she insisted I call you about an old friend who's in town also. I'm sure it's nothing, but—"

Maji paced the sidewalk while Rose spoke with her godmother. Then Rose passed her the phone. "Just bruises and scrapes," she responded to Hannah's predictable questions. Before she hung up Maji added, "Tell Bubbles I made it, okay? And...that she's right."

Stowing her phone again, Rose asked, "What's Bubbles right about?"

Maji gave Rose a hand up off the steps. "That I'm an idiot. Every time you went out with somebody, she reminded me."

"Brat," Rose responded, looking a bit pleased. Didn't matter which of them she meant. "If you really want a talk tonight, you'd better do it before we reach that posh suite with the lovely king-size bed." She took Maji's hand again and pointed them toward the hotel, now in sight just two blocks away. "And it's too chilly out here to linger, so speak now or hold your peace."

Maji gathered her thoughts. She'd practiced in her head nearly every time she was awake in transit from the mission debriefing to Sea-Tac. And still, here at go time the words got stuck. "English only?"

"*Oui.*"

"Fair enough." Maji paused, taking a long inhale. "So, I still think I was right. You had to call me Ri tonight. Who I am, what I do...it follows me. And it isn't fair to ask you to just put up with it. But..." She almost said, *I love you, so*—. "As Bubbles keeps pointing out, you should be the one to decide that, not me."

"Are you really worried that I'll decide you're not worth it?" Rose stopped and looked Maji in the eye. "You couldn't stop me from falling in love with you. And breaking up with me, no matter how noble your intentions, didn't work either. Maybe you should try being happy and see how that goes."

Maji put her hands on Rose's upper arms, to maintain the small distance she longed to close. "You have a week to figure out that I'm not worth the grief. After that you might not get rid of me. Seriously."

Rose pulled her close and a few minutes later the throaty rev of a truck engine and a hollered, "Get a room!" brought Maji back to the reality of the night sky beginning to mist on them as they kissed on the sidewalk. Fortunately they had a room.

As they entered the lobby, Rose spotted a familiar-looking woman exiting the elevator and heading toward them. The pretty features, dirty-blond ponytail, and jeans didn't add up to any of her academic acquaintances on downtime, though.

Then the woman spotted them and her face lit up as she approached. "Sergeant! What a lovely surprise."

"Um, Tina, right?" Maji asked. At the woman's nod, she added, "This is Rose."

Rose extended her hand. "Hi." Recognition dawned. "Oh, from the plane. Nice to meet you."

Tina's smile dimmed. "Yes. Well I've got to run before the sushi bar closes with my order inside. Then it's off to bed so I can be up at four. But...I'll be overnighting in Sitka again in a couple days. If you two would like to get together, maybe have a drink or something? I believe our soldier girl has my number."

Rose felt her hackles rise at the way Tina seemed to be including her in an inside joke. One that featured Maji as their common link.

"I do?" Maji asked. She didn't seem to be in on the joke either.

"You do," Rose said. "It fell out of your pocket when I picked your jeans up." Remembering the kiss imprint on the napkin with the phone number and flight attendant's name on it, she scanned Tina's now makeup-free face. "Nice shade of lipstick."

The hint of reproach in Rose's voice didn't seem to faze Tina at all. "Thank you. I think we may have similar tastes in many things. I'd love to find out, if you're interested."

Again with that mix of competition and collaboration, Rose noted. *Are you asking what I think you're asking?*

"Ah. No." Maji stepped in, as casual as if they were old friends scheduling a coffee date. "Rose isn't big on sharing. I got the impression Jack's not ready either." At Tina's wince, she added, "Sorry. I wasn't trying to eavesdrop. Are you really okay?"

"No. But I will be. And Jack, well." She shrugged, the playfulness replaced by an edge of vulnerability. "But what he wants doesn't matter one way or another anymore. And if you were listening, you'll recall I'm just looking for a little fun, at least until the papers clear." She started to move past them, then turned partway and added, "So should you two change your minds, I can promise you that much. No complications."

They stood silently until the sliding glass doors of the lobby slid shut behind Tina. Rose felt vaguely sorry for the woman. "That was weird," Rose said. She meant both Tina's game playing and Maji's ability to turn the odd conversation into something real, despite the weirdness.

Maji just gave her signature half shrug and headed for the elevators.

"Does that happen to you a lot?" Rose asked. "Strange women hitting on you, giving you their numbers?"

Maji didn't answer until their elevator arrived. "It happens once in a while. Probably not as much as it does to you."

"Me? No. I mean, I get asked out but…well, never mind."

Maji stepped into the elevator and pressed five. "Doesn't matter. I'm not interested. Rose, I haven't had a date, or a hookup, or anything, since you. I just haven't wanted to."

Rose took her hand. "You haven't missed anything. Nobody I said yes to inspired me to make a second date. I think you ruined me."

"Sorry." Maji looked serious. "For hurting you, not for making you pickier. I'll take any advantage over your hordes of admirers that I can get."

They stepped off, and Maji quickly scanned the hall, then tested the door before keying it. *Always on duty*. Maji held the door for her, but Rose paused, rather than passing through to their private space. "Wait. How do you know I don't share?" She tried for a hint of indignation but didn't think she was fooling anyone.

A smile quirked at one side of Maji's luscious lips. "Wishful thinking. Or maybe I was just projecting."

"Good. We're on the same page then." Rose pulled Maji through the door behind her, then pressed her up against it when it closed behind them.

Maji absorbed the feeling of Rose pressing against the length of her, kissing her like their connection was oxygen itself. And for the first time in months she felt whole. She ran her fingers through Rose's hair and down her back, drawing her closer, reveling in the certainty that Rose wanted her. As always when they touched, the rest of the world faded back, replaced by the scent, the sound, the taste of Rose. Oh God, the taste of her…

Rose broke their kiss, gasping. "Maji. How do you do that to me?"

"How do *I*?" Maji couldn't rein in her grin as Rose levered herself off the thigh that had insinuated itself between her legs. "I can't even control myself."

They both straightened up as Rose held her gaze. Her olive skin was flushed, her eyes soft but intense. "Does that scare you, black belt?"

"It should." Absolute mental and physical control saved her life, made it possible to save others. Maji trained hard to stay sharp and solid. And Rose could make the whole world shift under her feet with just a kiss.

"But?"

Maji struggled for the words to explain. Rose was so close, she wanted to answer with her body, to make her feel the answer through her skin. "Rose," she breathed.

"Yes?" Rose grasped her hands and stepped back. "What is it, love?"

Maji sucked in a deep, calming breath. "Love. It's love." The slow smile blossoming on Rose's face gave her the courage to go on as she gently walked her backward toward the big, cushy bed. "I thought I could get over it, when you left. And I'm sorry about—"

"Shh. No. No more *sorry*." Rose held her at arm's length as they reached the bed, still fully clothed. "Go on. After I left…"

"Nothing I did felt right. It was like I had a hole—" Her fist pressed to her sternum of its own accord, trying to rub away the bleakness. When Rose covered it with her hand, Maji rolled her eyes in embarrassment. "I know how sappy that sounds."

"All you had to do was call. Why didn't you?"

Maji forced herself to meet Rose's questioning gaze. "I didn't deserve to. And I knew you were better off without me."

"God, you are an idiot." Rose withdrew her hand. "Then why are you here?"

"You gave me another chance." Maji blinked back hot tears. "How could I say no to you again?"

Rose pulled them back onto the bed, kissing Maji hard before flipping her onto her back. Straddling Maji's hips, her hands pressing Maji's into the bedspread, Rose glared down at her. "You were scared and you ran away from me. I don't know where we're going, but I have to know that if we try you will not do that to me again. Do you understand?"

Maji nodded, pinned by the fierceness in Rose's voice and eyes. She felt her pulse pounding in her neck and at the spot where their hips met.

Rose leaned in close, her pelvis grinding into Maji's crotch as their nipples grazed each other's, their mouths inches apart. "Use your words."

"Yes."

"Yes what?"

The question eluded her, but Maji was sure of the answer. "I love you. Yes." She arched up to close the distance between them.

Rose released her hold and began stripping Maji's top off. Equally invested in shedding every stitch of fabric that stood between them and complete skin-to-skin contact, Maji shed her pants and went to work on Rose's outfit.

As she slipped Rose's slacks past her ankles, Maji slid off the bed and stood back to drink in the sight of her. Rose's body was resplendent with curves, soft and rounded in almost all the places Maji was stripped down to bone and muscle. Under the softness was strength, and over it, warm silk. Maji wanted to feel that silk with her lips, her cheeks, her palms and fingertips. To memorize every dip and rise, to know exactly what evoked which of Rose's reactions.

Maji's exploration began surely, starting at Rose's bare feet and working her way north. Paying close attention to Rose's responses was easy until the moment when Rose could reach Maji's scalp, her neck, her shoulders. Then Maji felt her focus blur, split between the feel of Rose herself and the sensation of Rose touching her. She gently pulled Rose's hands away, safely off her humming skin and toward the quilt. "I do want your hands on me, but could you wait just a little? I'm trying to…"

"What? Trying to what?" Rose sat up as Maji gathered her wits.

"To learn you." Maji kissed Rose's fingertips. "I want to know everything you like, and how to give it to you."

"There's time now," Rose assured her. "And still room for surprises."

Rose flipped Maji onto her back again, chuckling as she straddled Maji's hips. "Lesson one—don't leave my hands free if you don't want me to use them." She pressed her palms into the bed, leaning forward until her breasts brushed Maji's cheeks. "Two—take your time here. With both hands and mouth. Vary light and teasing with…"

Maji didn't wait for further instruction.

"Yes," Rose breathed, her arms busy keeping herself suspended in reach of Maji's mouth and hands. "Like that. And—oh, that too. And…um…"

Rose's hips circled near Maji's thigh, the slick heat of the brief contact making them both moan. Sensing a request, Maji slid one hand down to Rose's silky curls and cupped her firmly. "Here?"

In response, Rose pushed against Maji's hand and kissed her hard. Maji struggled against the urge to plunge inside, rubbing the base of her palm against Rose's clit instead. Rose broke the kiss with a moan, arching back. "Stop teasing. Fill me now."

The sight and sound of Rose's raw need pulled every fiber of Maji tight. She kept her eyes on Rose's face as she slipped in deep, keeping pace with her as Rose rode her hand. Witnessing Rose's pleasure took Maji to the brink of release, and she struggled to hold herself back. "Yes," she encouraged Rose. "Yes, baby. All yours."

Rose let go with a long cry, dragging Maji over the brink with her. She dropped her full weight onto Maji and they rolled onto their sides, entangled and clinging to each other.

"Yes," Rose echoed, her breath hot against Maji's neck. "Yes."

CHAPTER FOUR

Rose woke to Alaska-centric news coming from the radio by the bed. The station identified itself as KCAW, Raven Radio, which normally she would have found endearing. But she heard Maji, who had always been up before her, groan and mumble, covering her head with a pillow. So off it went. Rose slid out from under the covers before the desire to stay and cuddle could override her sensible side. *People to meet. Speakers to hear. Shower.*

Thirty minutes later, Rose congratulated herself on making the right decision as she headed for the conference center by the water. The four block walk gave her just enough time to reflect on the night, before putting on her professional face. Although they had shared a house and been together by necessity nearly twenty-four seven last summer, this was only the third night that she and Maji had put one another to sleep. The first time, Rose had invited Maji home after Maji had stepped between her and armed kidnappers. Rose had thought then that perhaps it was the sense of danger, bringing a stranger home for the first time ever, that made every touch so exciting. But then six weeks of enforced no-touching in close proximity, while they pretended Maji was Angelo's girlfriend, had wound them both up beyond all restraint. Rose barely recognized herself, unleashed and nearly unhinged with desire, the one night they spent locked alone together. With anyone but Maji, it would have been frightening. But no one had ever made her feel both so wild and so utterly safe at the same time.

And the sex they'd shared after Angelo's funeral—grief sex— felt like a whole other type of need being met. As if only the intensity of their passion could burn away the loss temporarily. Rose had found herself sobbing in cathartic release, held close within Maji's arms.

Last night she had cried too, though less dramatically. Surely tears wouldn't always ambush her like that. Rose had laughed in bed with a lover before, but the crying was new. If Maji hadn't been so tender, almost reverent, maybe she would have laughed instead. Whenever they touched, Maji acted as if Rose was the only person in the world. But this time, for the first time, Maji held her gaze and said *I love you* in plain English and with no hesitation or hint of retreat. And Rose felt the tears wash all the frustration of the past months away.

They didn't, as Rose had feared, lose much of last night's sleep. In fact, she felt so well rested there was a bounce in her step. And Maji hadn't stirred all night. But then, she had been exhausted. Maybe that was the key to moderating their hunger—emotional overload and physical exhaustion. That couldn't be how normal people in love managed, could it?

The cheery bustle of the conference center brought Rose back to the land of handshakes and polite conversation. She went through registration, shared pleasantries and introductions with a tableful of colleagues in the banquet hall, and listened attentively to the morning keynote speaker.

Javi was nowhere to be seen, Rose noted with a vague sense of relief. Maybe he was one of those academics who attended conferences more as a vacation than as an opportunity for professional development. In the field he was extremely organized and on task. But here? There was plenty to interest an ethnobotanist, if he didn't abhor conferences. Which she remembered Javi once confessing that he did. Rose set those thoughts aside during the morning's first panel. Near the end, during the question and answer period, her phone buzzed. Not once, to signal a good morning text from Maji, but repeatedly. One glance at the screen sent Rose out into the hall.

"Hannah? Is everything all right? I am so sorry about waking you last night."

"Don't be. Never hesitate to contact me," Hannah assured her. "Is Maji available? She isn't answering her phone."

Rose balked, still a little shy at how much Maji's godmother knew about their romance. "She could still be sleeping. Apparently she was up for several days in a row and she also lost her phone. She was going to pick one up today."

"Ah. Well, have her call me as soon as you see her, please."

"Sure. Is there anything I should know?"

"For now, just use caution. Don't let yourself be alone with your friend Javier. He did not secure grant funding as he told you, but he did have his travel sponsored. I'm still working on the source of the funding in order to ascertain the real purpose of his trip."

"I expect to see him at lunch. Why don't I just ask him?"

There was a pause. "Certainly find out what you can. But Rose...do not reveal your suspicions to him. Understood?"

"Yes." Rose sighed. Javi had been a good friend and a valuable colleague. Surely there was a reasonable explanation. But Hannah made her living keeping people alive and safe from harm. "And I'll send Maji your way as soon as I can. I could go wake her..."

"No. Stay with people you know—let her come to you. I'll try the hotel."

"Yes. Um...thank you for setting up the suite. It's lovely."

"Is there room for a third person, if need be?"

Rose hesitated. It wasn't like Hannah to pry, so she must have a practical reason to ask. "Yes. But why would we have company?"

"For your safety. That way Maji could remain on vacation, which I'd prefer she did. Wouldn't you?"

"When you put it that way, yes. Thank you, Hannah."

Hannah made a sound that could have been a chuckle, if Rose didn't know better. "Just send her home in a better frame of mind and we'll be even. Bye for now."

The call disconnected before Rose could ask what that meant. Perhaps Bubbles hadn't been exaggerating when she complained about Maji being short-tempered and working out like a demon to sublimate her desire to reach out to Rose. She wished Maji had just called her, or come to visit. They were making up for that lapse now, she thought with a smile.

Maji thrashed the covers off while the phone rang, insistent and annoying. "What?" she croaked out when she had it up to her ear, the right way up on the second try.

"Maji," Hannah said with a rare hint of concern bleeding through her normally implacable tone. "Are you well?"

Maji looked at the clock. Nine forty-five. "Think so. I slept like the dead. And Rose forgave me for being an idiot. Now I just need clothes and a new phone, and all's right with the world."

"Mm. We need a secure line. Get your phone first thing and call me back."

"Fuck." Would she ever get more than one night at a time with Rose? Maybe even some days?

"Don't jump to conclusions. You're still on vacation for now." With that Hannah hung up.

Maji dropped the receiver back in its cradle and headed for the bathroom. She nearly skipped the shower, since smelling like Rose was no hardship. But not everyone would enjoy that so much, so she hopped in briefly, taking care not to wet the bandages. Freshened up, Maji pulled on her jeans, which weren't clean but didn't smell much, either. All her T-shirts, on the other hand—nope. She rummaged in the bureau and picked a lightweight sweater that would look great on Rose. It fit her quite differently, loose in the bust and tight across the shoulders. Well, she'd have her windbreaker on in town.

In the living area of the suite, she found a heaping plate of eggs, potatoes, and sausages. Rose had left her enough for two people, a gentle nudge. She knew how fast Maji burned fuel and the effort it took to maintain any fat over her muscles. Maji stuck the plate in the microwave, reflecting that she must have slept through Rose showering, dressing, leaving, coming back with food, and leaving again. Amazing—and a little disconcerting.

As breakfast heated, she put coffee in the single-cup machine and started on the bowl of cut fruit, feeling pampered by the simple gesture. Bubbles was so right about her being an idiot. Hannah had held her tongue about Maji's refusal to see Rose after the danger was resolved and she'd left Long Island behind to resume her normal life as an academic. But not Bubbles. Her best friend adored Rose and never failed to point out all of her good traits. Including her unfailing thoughtfulness and natural generosity. Would it be jarring to come home from a mission to such sweetness? If so, she'd just have to learn to ride that transition with some grace. *Getting ahead of yourself, Rios.*

❖

Maji's replacement cell phone showed thirty-seven voicemails waiting. She ignored them all and sent Rose a text. *Good morning. How's the con?*

Seconds later a smiley face appeared along with the message, *Hannah says please call.*

Maji thought about sending a *ma'am, yes ma'am* back, but decided it might sound snarky to someone who used emoticons to communicate. So instead she just texted, *Will do. Lunch?*

Traditional foods, here in the banquet hall. Join us?

Hell yeah.

Hannah picked up on the first ring, on her secure line. Maji's phone was encrypted, so their conversation would be as private as any from the deserted corner of a small-town coffee shop could be. Mostly she expected to be listening, anyhow.

"Go for Rios," Maji replied to Hannah's greeting, signaling that she had moved into professional mode.

"Three things to be aware of." Hannah jumped right in, without greeting. "One, Javier Mendez was paid to travel to Sitka by a holding company. Rose is aware and agreed to not be alone with him for now. I'll update you when we know more."

"Okay." That was business for Paragon, Hannah's personal security company. Unless Angelo had dumped untraceable funds into Hannah's account—which he very well might have—Hannah was protecting Rose pro bono. Maji had avoided asking her. Last summer Hannah had promised Angelo to watch out for Rose as if she were her own. So she was family, regardless of the finances.

"Two," Hannah continued, "telecommunications in your area were disrupted eighteen days ago. This happens periodically when the underwater cable between Sitka and Seattle is damaged by fishing boats, or…submarines."

That sent an icy trickle down Maji's neck. *Whose subs?* "Okay."

"Three, the tabloids were wild with stories about Russian subs sighted off the Alaskan coast several days before the cable disruption. There were no further sightings in that area and none that we know of in your area. JSOC is making contact with the Coast Guard station in Sitka."

"I have a contact there. A friendly flyboy who offered me a ride in a Jayhawk and gave me his card on the flight up here."

"Very good—but hold off. Do you have a laptop with satellite uplink?"

"Not with me." If JSOC wanted to give her orders or an official briefing, she would need a secure internet connection. "Coasties might have a secure terminal."

"Not until we have a working agreement." Even though the Army and Coast Guard were all part of the same military, and the counterterrorism unit Maji worked for was closely tied to the work of Homeland Security, cooperation was never assumed. If Maji could have walked on to the air station and flashed her ID, told the commander what she needed and whom she was with, it would have been so simple. But Delta operators never did that, preserving their real identities even within the family of federal law enforcement and intelligence communities as well as within the larger armed forces family. So if JSOC decided to send her in for work purposes, she would wait until they told her what cover she was operating under.

"Just FYI," Maji said, "I've only got my military ID and matching passport here."

"Understood." Hannah paused. "Have you noticed anything else there that might indicate Russian activity?"

Maji thought about the young man with the knife, his father recently laid to rest. "Not exactly. A Tribal fisherman died a couple weeks ago under suspicious circumstances. Sounds like the cops wrote it off to drugs and/or suicide, but the family insists he was clean and sober and making plans."

"Hmm. Well, for today, check in on Rose. Anything else you can learn as a tourist is fine, but don't push it." Hannah paused again. "Have you checked your voicemail yet?"

"No. Which ones are critical?"

"Skip anything not from Command until you have Rose secure and your feet under you there."

That sounded like code for bad news, but nothing Maji could do anything about. Unsettling, but right now she just wanted to find Rose and make sure she was safe. And get a bead on that Javi guy. "Will do. Out?"

"Yes, and in case you do go on assignment soon, Maji...I love you. Give Rose what time you can while you have the chance."

Maji smiled to herself. "Promise. I gave her the week to decide to dump me or not. I don't plan to blow it."

"Very good. Out."

Maji put the phone away and headed for the conference center. Even from the far side of the tiny downtown, it was less than a ten minute walk. She started to jog, trying not to think about how an assignment would affect her week with Rose. For starters, Hannah would stop all direct communication with her. That firewall was Joint Special Operations Command's solution to the perceived conflict between her close personal relationship with Hannah and Hannah's role as a consultant to JSOC on the pilot program using a handful of women operators as part of Delta, the Army's covert ops unit. Maji could deal with that—she'd see Hannah again when the mission was over and they could talk about anything outside of Army work again.

But the thought of losing the next few days with Rose chafed. She'd already wasted months. If she hadn't been such a stubborn ass, she could at least have seen Rose on their school breaks. If she ruined this trip by disappearing for work, would Rose give her another chance?

Staying on vacation the rest of the week also meant she could watch Rose's back. Javi having a mystery backer was a definite red flag, and of the potential threats, Leonid Sirko rose to the top of her worry list. He'd vied for top spot in global money laundering before Angelo took him on. With an empire built on murder and extortion to inspire fear in even the toughest criminals and terrorists, he'd use anyone his enemies loved against them. For the civilian pawns he targeted, death was the easy option.

Sirko had managed to evade the wide net of roundups and arrests, thanks to powerful friends within and beyond Russia. Until he was captured, no one related to Angelo was safe. And despite having his empire gutted by Angelo's cyber coup, Sirko might have enough resources left to try for revenge. Using an old friend to spy on Rose was his style too. Last summer he'd tried using a Mafia mole, fake police, and even fake soldiers to gain access to them. Just because he didn't need Rose for leverage anymore didn't mean she was safe.

Maji broke into a run and covered the rest of the distance in only three minutes. Outside the conference center entrance, a group of people stood with their faces toward the morning sun. *Like sunflowers.* No Rose or Javi, though. She wove through the crowd milling about in the lobby and continued her search down the hallways. Switching to bodyguard mode, Maji kicked herself for not getting a program in advance and learning the layout of the building. She sighed with relief at the sight of Rose emerging from a ladies' room down the hall.

Rose smiled in response to her wave. "No time to shop yet?"

"Sorry. So far there's only been time to get my phone and talk to Hannah. Thanks for breakfast."

"Of course. And you're welcome to any clothing you need. That's a nice color on you."

"Thanks. Doesn't fit me right, though." They exchanged a look that suggested both of them liked the ways in which they were shaped differently. "Anyway...any sign of your stalker?"

Rose frowned. "He's not. I'm sure. Did Hannah learn any more?"

"Not much. When's lunch?"

Rose gave her an indulgent smile. "They're setting up right now. Shall we get you a ticket?"

At the registration table Maji opted to pay for full conference access. Until they solved the Javi riddle, best to have free rein to go wherever Rose chose to be. She wrote *Ri* on her name tag and left it at that.

"You got a full pass?" Rose asked, eyeing the colored tag hanging from the pinned-on name badge.

Maji just gave her a shrug and asked the way to the banquet hall.

Chapter Five

Maji took a seat next to Rose at a long table. The buffet had yielded a full plate of lunch, with a few things Maji had never considered edible before. The salmon heads, for instance, split and baked on a cookie sheet, were popular with the Alaskans in the crowd.

"Try that," the man behind her had said when she had hesitated to accept one.

"Will there be enough for folks who really want them?"

The woman behind the counter and the man in line behind her had exchanged a pleased look. "We have enough to share with you," the woman answered for them. So Maji accepted one, still wondering how much of it was supposed to be consumed.

At the table, Maji noted Rose was pinching chunks of roasted vegetables with her right thumb and first two fingers, eating them without a fork. Rose didn't have a baked salmon head on her plate though. Maji looked to her left, saw one, and asked, "How do I eat the salmon head?"

The woman to her left's eyes crinkled. She demonstrated, then smiled and said, "Traditional foods taste better when you eat them with your hands."

Rose, who apparently already knew that secret, chatted quietly with the man to her right. As Maji ate, she scanned the room for Javi. Rose had offered to talk with him over lunch. If he was so anxious to see her, where was he? There was something in his manner, a thin veneer of casualness over a deeper anxiety, that set her alarms off. So far he'd only lied about being here on a grant, while his real funder used a holding company to mask its identity. Which didn't necessarily mean he was on Sirko's payroll. But they did need to figure out who was behind the curtain, sooner rather than later.

Javi slipped in the door and joined the short line of people seeking seconds. Rose didn't seem to notice as he sought her out and headed for their table. Maji leaned over to alert her. "Javier on his way. Act cool."

Javi apparently hadn't gotten that memo, however. He approached from Maji's side, asking, "Are you done? May I have your seat?"

"Sorry," Maji replied. "Still working on my lunch."

The man to Rose's right pushed his chair back. "You can have mine. I have to go set up for my panel."

Rose touched the man's arm. "I'm so sorry I'll miss your talk. Will you have slides to share?"

"For you, I'll make sure they post them on the website." He fished a card from his jacket pocket and handed it to her. "Call me if you have any questions after you read them."

Rose took his card with a smile and turned her attention to Javi. "How's the conference been for you so far? Did you attend the session on mapping cultural resources?"

"Yes, very good. So much to learn, so many good contacts. You know."

They talked about nothing much until the table was almost empty, the conference center staff clearing the last of the plates and starting to wipe down tables and chairs. When it became clear that Javier wasn't going to speak freely in front of her, Maji excused herself. She wished she had a listening device to eavesdrop but settled for just walking to the back of the room, where she could keep an eye on Rose while working through the backlog of voicemails.

Hearing Rose's messages while watching her felt surreal. The undertone of disappointment in Rose's simple words triggered a pang of guilt. Even if Maji's phone had not been crushed under the tires of a truck in Luzon, she wouldn't have been able to respond. Making unencrypted calls home from the field was never safe. Once the phone was destroyed she'd felt freer, having one less link to home to have to protect.

The look on Rose's face brought her back to the present. Maji almost moved forward, but she checked the impulse. Rose was in no physical danger from Javi and was perfectly capable of holding her own while getting useful information out of him.

When Javi stood, chagrin on his face and resignation in the slope of his shoulders, he did not look around the room. Maji watched him exit the banquet room, then headed over to help Rose clear her spot at the now empty table.

"Well?"

"I thought he was a friend," Rose said, looking away. After a few seconds she took a breath and held Maji's waiting gaze. "First he tried some nonsense about this *spark* between us."

Maji held her peace. Javier could easily have been attracted to Rose, even if unrequited, and projected his feelings on her. Rose might even have reciprocated. Who knew? It wasn't her business unless it affected how Rose felt about her now. "And?"

"And I told him as gently but clearly as I could that I always saw him as a colleague and a friend, but not as more." Rose paused, an internal argument playing behind her eyes. "Javi is bi and was always very open about who he found attractive, when we traveled together. He knows I generally prefer women but can sometimes be attracted to a man."

"So he was honest with you and you reciprocated the trust. And if he wanted more than a working partnership, he didn't tell you back then." She took Rose's hand. "Did he say why he suddenly wanted to be that lucky man?"

"He gave me a bullshit line about taking me for granted before and learning about the danger I was in last summer waking him up." Rose squeezed her hand. "And about not wanting to hurt our professional relationship before. Which is when I knew for certain that he was lying."

"So he has hit on you before."

Rose shook her head. "Not so overtly. But he made it clear that if I ever became interested he'd reciprocate. Javi is serially monogamous and he likes intellectuals."

"Handy for a grad student."

Rose frowned. "I suppose. Anyway, he had the nerve to say he hadn't taken me seriously before, but since all the news stories last summer, he had taken the time to read my work. And now suddenly I'm irresistible."

Nodding, Maji gave her a sympathetic look. Rose would take the loss of trust in an old friend hard. "Any idea why he's messing with you?"

Rose shook her head. "Really, I'm as baffled as I am hurt."

"How invested are you in this afternoon's panel sessions?"

"Not as much now as I should be. What do you have in mind?"

A return to their room flashed through Maji's mind's eye, and she swallowed hard. "Shopping. I still need clothes and other essentials."

"Retail therapy." A smile washed the last traces of regret from Rose's expression. "I'd love to help."

"There's a tour at four," Rose said as they left the conference center. "I do need to go on that."

Maji nodded. "Cool. I'll go with you."

"Great," Rose replied. A fleeting doubt tagged her heart and she stopped walking. "Is this surge of togetherness because you want to spend time with me or because you're playing bodyguard again?"

Maji gave her that steady look Rose had come to realize meant she was weighing her words before speaking. "I don't play at that. But I would have stayed at the conference with you and not minded. Also, I appreciate having your fashion input. Good taste and all."

"I suppose you can't wear my things all week." Rose took her hand, glad that Maji was comfortable with the simple display of affection. "Where to first?"

An outdoor gear shop was not where Rose would have headed to look for clothing. But they did have running shoes to replace the stained pair on Maji's feet. "How long since you've had a run?"

"For fun? Weeks." Maji stood and walked in the new pair, then nested her old ones into the box. She gave it to the sales clerk to hold at the checkout counter for her.

Next Maji found socks, Carhartt jeans from the boys' section, and a T-shirt she pulled off the clearance rack with less than thirty seconds' consideration. "Be right back," she said.

While Maji changed, Rose perused the collection of dozens of T-shirts by an artist who seemed to specialize in fish themes. Some were simply beautiful, others both artistic and humorous. She smiled to herself at the graphics, wondering which Maji would find amusing if she slowed down enough to look at them.

"You know Ray Troll?" the salesclerk asked, with an optimistic lilt to her voice.

Rose shook her head. "Afraid not. Quite the thing here I take it."

"Oh, yeah. He's from Ketchikan, but you can find his work all over the country. We have one of the largest collections."

Maji's reappearance saved Rose from having to admit that she'd never before shopped anywhere that fishing was a major pastime. Or industry, come to think. Eyeing the relaxed ensemble of denim and cotton, Rose had to admit Maji looked at home in her new clothes. Cute too. Not quite butch, but definitely tomboyish. Even the artwork of fish swimming upstream looked right on her. Rose swept her hand in a top-to-bottom motion. "Is this your natural habitat?"

Maji blushed. "Pretty much, yeah. We can get some nicer things next."

"No complaints here." Rose paused. "Though I do have some ideas, if you'll indulge me."

Maji's mouth twitched at the corners. "Matching rain boots and jacket? I don't think I can pull off the colors you brought, though. We're different seasons and all."

Rose itched to tickle her. And why shouldn't she? They weren't pretending anymore to be anything they weren't. So instead of answering, she just stepped in and went for Maji's sides. She might have a six-pack under that shirt, but it wouldn't protect her from laughing.

"Hey," Maji said, dancing back away from Rose's teasing fingers. "No fair."

But Rose pursued her until Maji spun her into the little dressing room and pressed her against the wall, her hands trapped by her sides. Playfulness turned to hunger at the feel of Maji's body, and Rose met her mouth with an abandon that surprised her. She'd never made out spontaneously in a store. The semi-publicness made her both nervous and excited.

When she stepped back, Maji looked pleased and not nearly finished. "We indulge any more, they might call the cops."

Rose nodded. "Let's get whatever else is on your must list and beat it."

They tracked down the clerk, who tried admirably not to blush as Maji had her cut the tags off her new clothing and bag up her old jeans and Rose's top. At Maji's request, Rose found a few pullovers that looked like they might fit and would complement her caramel complexion. As she carried them up to the checkout area, Rose wondered where Maji had been exposed to so much sun recently. The red had faded already, but like the scrapes on Maji's back and leg, she imagined the conditions that caused it were harsh. Would she feel any better if she knew the details?

Maji met her at the checkout counter with a pack of socks, a box of Clif bars, more first aid supplies, and two items from the guns and ammo section of the store piled on top of a large box with the Xtratuf logo on it. She placed them all on the counter and tapped the box. "Will I need these on the tour?"

Rose nodded. "You might. If they're too expensive, you can always stay on the trail in your sneakers."

"Everything's returnable if you don't wear it," the man ready to ring them up added.

"Cool," Maji agreed, handing him a credit card.

While he scanned the first items and started filling the shopping bags, Maji tried on the tops Rose had selected. The first was too snug, so Rose set everything in that size aside. The next was baggy on Maji's lean frame, a poor cut for her build. Being five four with virtually no fat and muscles that showed with every movement apparently had its fashion challenges.

"Angelo was better at this than I am," Rose said and instantly regretted it. Last summer he had ordered Maji a whole wardrobe for playing the role of his girlfriend. Maji hadn't tried any of it on, yet everything fit on arrival. How well he must have known her.

"All clothing is costume," Maji said with a faraway look in her eye, more wistful than pained. She sighed. "He had a lot of practice. I didn't mean to set you up. I'm sorry."

Before Rose could argue, Maji disappeared down a nearby aisle, back into the young men's section. She returned with four PolyPro pullovers in different colors, and held them up by her face for Rose's approval. One went on with the tags removed, one into the bags, and the rest back on the racks.

They carried the box of tall rubber boots with heavy lug soles, and the bags with old clothes, new clothes, and miscellaneous gear back to the hotel. Rose had to walk briskly to keep up with Maji. "What's the rush?"

Maji slowed. "Sorry. I need a few minutes in the suite and I don't want to make us late for the tour."

Rose consulted her watch. "We have an hour and a half."

"I'll try to make it quick then. I still need a running bra and I'd like underwear too. Plus," she added as they entered the hotel lobby, "whatever idea you wanted indulged."

Rose didn't rise to the bait. If Maji indulged her again like she had in the changing room, they would miss the tour for sure. Letting them into the suite with her card key, she noted, "I'd better get my field clothes on too. Do you need a hand with something? New bandages?"

"Nope, thanks," Maji replied, heading for the entryway closet after depositing her purchases on the couch.

Rose headed to the bedroom alone and changed into jeans and a turtleneck with a light sweater. Add the Xtratufs and rain jacket that she'd brought, and she'd be ready for woods, muskeg, and tideflats. The tour that the Sitka Tribe's guides offered was promised to be tailored to the conference goers' interests in local foods. Something none of them could get from the PowerPoint presentations and discussions in the meeting rooms.

The unpleasantly familiar scent of gun cleaning oil reached Rose even before she circled the little table in the living area of the suite. Maji was already reassembling her handgun from the pieces laid out on the towel in front of her. The sight and smell made Rose back away, then crack a window. She gulped in the fresh air.

Maji looked up, concern in her eyes. "Sorry. This was overdue. Not safe the way it was."

"How safe is it now?" Rose asked, eyeing the cardboard box of ammunition. "You're not going to wear it here, are you?"

Maji got up and went over to the kitchenette sink, washed her hands, and toweled them off without looking at Rose. "I'll keep it out of sight. But since we don't know what Javier's really up to, and I don't have any backup—yeah. I'm sorry."

"You've started saying that too much again," Rose noted. "I don't want an apology—I want an explanation. Look at me, Maji."

Maji turned so Rose could see her face, but it was unreadable. "I'm a professional. Keeping people safe is what I do. Can't you just trust me on this?"

"I do trust you. With my body and my heart. But this is my life. If I need protection, I get a full say. None of this *Don't you worry your little head, ma'am* crap. You hear me?"

"Hooah," Maji breathed, looking pained. Did she really hear, understand, and agree? "Rose, the idea of you getting hurt, or worse, freaks me the hell out. Honestly, it's easier to just not talk about it. The things I see when I go to sleep, those aren't nightmares. They're memories of real people enduring horrible things. I don't think I could live with you in those images."

Rose crossed the room to hold her. Maji didn't protest. "I'm here now. And I'm fine. You know I can help if you just talk to me. What's got you rattled?"

"Could be nothing, but I feel the storm coming." Maji pulled back and held her hands, her eyes asking for understanding.

Rose nodded. "Just because Javi's acting weird?"

"No. Because someone using a holding company to mask their identity sent him here to get close to you where they thought you weren't under watch."

"Under watch? You mean the way Hannah checks in? It's hardly like I have a bodyguard at home."

"I wouldn't bet on that. I've tried to keep out of Hannah's business where you're concerned, but she did promise Angelo to keep you safe. She wouldn't be intrusive about it, but she can't do it by phone, either."

Rose stared at her. "Why wouldn't she say something?"

"If there was a threat, she would. Didn't she give you instructions about Javi?"

Yes, she had. "My God. Do you think if you weren't here, she'd have sent someone else?"

"That's my best guess. Not that I asked."

Hannah had seemed stressed when she couldn't reach Maji. "What else are you making educated guesses about?"

"Well, Javi's acting squirrelly and anxious." That was true, Rose realized, despite the breezy front he put on. Maji looked hesitant to say more but responded to Rose's expectant look. "Until we know who he's answering to, we need to assume the worst."

"Which means?"

"Sirko."

Rose let go and turned away at the name of the man she blamed for all of her family's tragedies. But…she turned back, crossing her arms across her middle. "Isn't he broke? And in jail like the rest of them?" There were so many sweeps and arrests, she'd lost track.

"If you haven't seen it on the cover of every major paper, no. It'll be huge news. As for broke, I'm sure he's hurting. But maybe not enough to keep him from revenge."

The idea sounded much worse in specific terms, from a genuinely worried Maji, than it had in general terms when Hannah started their check-in calls. "But Javi would never work for someone like that."

"Not knowingly, maybe. But think about last summer, and the kind of cunning and determination it took to keep coming after you then, on home turf even."

"Because Angelo loved me." Rose shook off the urge to blame herself. "But what is there to gain now?"

"Don't underestimate revenge as a motivator," Maji cautioned. She put a hand on Rose's bicep and squeezed gently, just a hint of comfort. "Please let me take the gun. No one will know it's there unless I have no other choice."

"Hurry up and get changed," Rose said. "We have one more store to squeeze in before the tour."

Maji opened her mouth, then shut it. She nodded and gestured at Rose's boots with a smile. "We're gonna look like the Alaska equivalent of the urban cowboy, going shopping in our foulies."

"Foulies?"

"Foul weather gear," Maji said as she slipped off her running shoes and pulled on the boots and rain jacket. "At least it's not all yellow."

"Is that what you wear on Long Island Sound?" Rose asked, intentionally distracting herself from the firearm being tucked into the holster behind Maji's back.

Maji grinned. "If you're serious about sailing, yeah. Or you have too much money and you just want to look serious."

Rose remembered watching Maji handle a little catamaran with skill. "You really enjoy sailing? We never talked about it before."

"We didn't talk about a lot of things." Maji held the door for her with a flourish. "Ask me again over supper, and I'll bore you with racing stories. Then you'll know I'm a real sailor."

Rose laughed. "Try and bore me. I dare you."

Maji got the running bra and a pack of underwear as quickly as humanly possible. "So tell me your idea. Do we still have time?"

"Really it was just something nice for dinner out. A tailored shirt or maybe a cashmere sweater. And some earrings. That's all."

Maji spotted a boutique down the block. "If we had time I'd want to hit the local thrift shop, dink around awhile." She took Rose by the hand. "But if we hurry, I bet we could get one thing nice enough for you to be seen with me tonight."

Rose seemed inclined to protest, to defend her willingness to be seen with Maji no matter what, but stopped when faced with the wager. "You want a race to find one nice top that fits, for under a hundred dollars?"

"Yep. In this shop," Maji answered, pointing at the threshold they had reached, "in ten minutes or less. Ready?"

Rose was through the door and scanning the racks before she even replied. "What do I win?"

"Whatever idea you want indulged."

Rose flushed as a smile crept across her face. "Excuse me," she called to the woman behind the counter in the back.

Twenty minutes later, they made their way arm in arm toward the conference center, hands free. "Nice of them to deliver to the hotel," Maji said.

"Nice of you to offer such a generous tip," Rose noted. "Are you rich now?"

Maji considered the question. "I have two homes to stay in and no rent. No debt. Hardly any stuff. And people always trying to feed me. Plus interest off what the IRS didn't take as gift tax. So kind of, yeah. It's weird."

Rose gave her arm a reassuring squeeze. "It's not fun? What about the Robin Hooding?" Angelo had arranged for the money he drained from the accounts of organized criminals—an estimated 3.4 trillion dollars—to be deposited into the accounts of millions of nonprofit organizations and ordinary people around the world. The money transfers weren't traceable, so the IRS gave Americans a choice for their windfalls: donate to a tax-exempt organization or keep it and pay the hefty gift tax. Rose and Maji had each received five million, and Rose had given all of hers away. In March, Maji had indicated she was going to do the same, but more slowly.

"Frankly? It's a bigger pain in the ass than I expected," Maji confessed, feeling oddly vulnerable. "How'd you decide where to donate your bundle?"

"It was quite an exercise in self-examination, actually," Rose replied. "Five million seemed like so much until I researched all the groups around the world doing work I feel strongly about."

"Addressing hunger alone could have taken billions." Maji chuckled. "'Course, I would go there."

Rose rewarded her with another arm squeeze. "Angelo was right about the lottery game. It was an excellent test of character."

"Well, I didn't play very well. I always told him I didn't need anything."

"See? Some people immediately think of the responsibility that wealth puts upon them. And others just want to self indulge."

But Maji had never wanted that kind of power, or the responsibility. She'd locked the remaining principal away and conservatively invested it. Even so, the interest was more than her pay as an active-duty sergeant had been. Probably more than Rose earned at a small university. Not the fantasy millions that bought yachts and big houses, but enough for Maji to decide whether to work or not while pursuing her PhD. "I'd really like your help figuring out what to do with the part that doesn't go to Uncle Sam. If you don't mind."

Rose stopped and looked at Maji, her head tilted a little to one side. "Me? You have Hannah, and Sal, and a Nobel laureate to advise you. What could I possibly add?"

"Hell, I could just turn the whole thing over to one of those green-investment consultants," Maji conceded. Yet she hadn't. Nor asked her godmother, father, or mother to advise her. "But I want to think about it for myself, make up my own mind. And you...you'd listen, and ask me good questions, and—"

"Make it fun?" A playful look came into Rose's eyes. "Like floating in the pool watching clouds drift by, and talking about a whole world of possibilities, without the weight of the decisions pushing you underwater?"

"Like that. But in the shallow end, please. 'Cause I'm a sinker."

Rose broke into laughter. "Come see me in California. We can lie in a hammock instead."

Chapter Six

Three Tribal Tours buses waited outside the conference center. Clusters of attendees waited on the sidewalk, ready to board and see the local sights. As before, Maji noticed some of them standing with their eyes closed, faces turned to the sun. "Sunflowers," she said, nudging Rose.

"Mm. They must be from farther north. Athabascans, Yup'ik, Inupiat—you know."

"No, I don't know. I'm not a real anthropologist—I only play one on TV," Maji countered. "What about Norwegians, or Icelanders?"

Rose gave her an I'm-humoring-you look. "One Swede and a Dane. The program has short bios for the panelists."

"Including you?"

"Of course. I may be a small fish, but I'm still in the pond." Rose looked at her suspiciously. "Why?"

"Was the lineup posted online, ahead of time?"

"Yes."

"When?"

"A month or two ago, I guess. The keynoters were announced nearly a year in advance, but not the rest of the schedule." Rose frowned. "Is this about Javi?"

Of course. "I'd like to disprove my hypothesis as much as you would, Doc. More information is always better than less."

A stout, sixtyish man with a conference lanyard sidled up to them as Maji was about to dial Hannah. "Now those would have made decent jungle boots," he said, pointing to her Xtratufs.

Maji just squinted at him. He had no way to know she'd just come from the Philippines.

"In the Mekong Delta. You know—'Nam. Sorry…you were up onstage with us, weren't you?"

Maji nodded, relaxing. The veterans' honoring dance.

"George Koreki, Notre Dame," he said, offering his hand. After a quick, strong shake he asked, "So, where are you?"

"Columbia." In linguistics, but true enough. She could walk the graduation stage in May, if she wanted the recognition for her master's degree. A quiet celebratory dinner sounded better, though.

George grunted his approval. "Good school. Do you know Gunderson? Taught physical anthropology for ages. Haven't heard anything since he retired."

"Sorry, I didn't study with him."

"Just as well—probably dead now. What about—"

Maji spotted the drivers coming out of the conference center, ready to claim their vehicles and the milling groups that had self-selected which bus or van they wanted. Javi didn't appear to be among any of them. "Excuse me," she said, heading Rose on an intercept path with Heather. "We promised that driver we'd ride with her."

Heather smiled when she saw them. "My favorite couple. I have a spot up front for you."

Maji and Rose took the seats she offered, and Maji dialed Hannah while the others filed in and filled up most of the remaining twenty or so seats. She gave Hannah the new bits of information and promptly hung up. Rose was looking at her sideways.

"What?" Maji asked.

"You're very curt when you talk shop. All shorthand, no pleasantries. I was wondering what you're like to talk with on the phone when it's just, *Hi, honey, how was your day?*"

"I wonder too. Would be nice to find out, huh?"

Heather pulled the little bus away from the curb and launched into her talk over the PA system. They stopped first at the National Historical Park, with its Totem Trail and Southeast Alaska Indian Cultural Center. The wooded path by the waterline looked perfect for a morning run, and Maji felt the itch to lace up her new shoes and get out to explore. She needed the exercise, if nothing else.

Heather told them about the history of the totem poles in the park, collected from Haida and Tlingit villages all over southeast Alaska and brought to Sitka in the early 1900s for restoration. When the park ranger met them at the visitor center and started to field the group's questions, Maji kept one eye on Rose but dropped back to speak with Heather.

"How's it going?"

Heather shrugged. "My sister finally got her boat back from the state police. Spent all day cleaning it up. But at least she can get back to work now."

"Her boat?"

"Oh, yeah—sorry. I forget you don't know who's who here. Dee and Charlie—"

"Simon's dad?"

"Right. He's our cousin. Was. Anyways, Charlie owned half the boat. Dee's been hiring out the last few days with other skippers. Not the same, but she'll make rent at least."

"Why the state police? Didn't Charlie live here in town?"

"Where he died, pulling downed cedars off the shore for the herring egg harvest, you can only get to by water. When Dee couldn't raise him by radio or phone, they sent the Coasties out to search and found him right away. Since he was dead when they got there, the troopers took their marine enforcement boat out to work the scene and bring him back."

"So did the state police field the whole investigation? Tox workup and everything?"

Heather snorted. "If you can call it an investigation. Tox screen was clean, of course, and they still won't call it a homicide." Heather paused, looking uncomfortable. "Wait. You're not a cop, are you?"

Maji's mouth twitched. "No. Definitely not."

❖

At the next stop, the Alaska Raptor Center, they saw eagles, hawks, and owls that had been injured and were being nursed back to health. Most would be released back into the wild, but two eagles that couldn't be rehabilitated were permanent residents.

"Lifers," Maji joked.

Rose smiled at her dark humor and noticed that Heather did as well. Might the driver have a crush on her girlfriend? *Her girlfriend.* That still felt too new to be true, yet too thrilling to dismiss. She watched Maji soaking in the zoologist's spiel on the center's attempts to mimic the habitats specific to each raptor.

Maji looked completely at home in rubber boots with jeans and a pullover, like she might pick up one of the five-gallon feed buckets and get to work as soon as the tourists cleared out. She could probably look at home like that just about anywhere, Rose guessed. It had something to do with being so self-contained. What Maji didn't seem to understand was why that quality drew people to her. Everyone crushed out on her in their own way—the students at the dojo, her Army buddies who called her *dude* but treated her like a sister, even Rose's grandmother, who never liked anyone if she could help it.

And women looking for a woman, like that flight attendant, probably gave her unsolicited attention all the time. Yet Maji seemed as unimpressed with the fangirls as she was with her own ability to attract them. She wanted to blend in, not stand out. Maybe that was all she meant when she suggested *acting normal.*

Maji turned and her face took on a knowing look, catching Rose watching her. Well, maybe Maji did want to stand out to some people. Lucky her. Rose's face heated, and she turned back toward the zoologist answering a question on the difference between ravens and crows. Rose raised her hand.

"Yes?"

"Raven seems to be the trickster in every culture that has them. Is there a similar sort of common mythology about eagles?"

Heather chuckled. "I'll field that one. We never let the zoologists tackle the anthropology questions." She paused. "But seriously, I can only speak for my clan, which is Raven/Frog. The best eagle stories belong to the Eagle clans, which hold the rights to tell them—our form of intellectual property law." She gave Rose and the others a few seconds to absorb that concept. "But think about what you know already. What traits do people often ascribe to eagles?"

With the question turned back to them, the group re-engaged.

"Vision," one woman suggested.

"Leadership," offered another.

"Nobility," said one of the men. "In the sense of dignity with goodness, not caste."

"You opened up an academic Pandora's box," Maji whispered to Rose, slipping close behind her in the small crowd.

Rose leaned back into her, turning her head to speak softly. "You just hate it when people say nice things about you."

"Me?" Maji's hands found Rose's waist and pressed lightly. "I don't do noble. If one of us is an eagle, it's you for sure."

Rose felt the buzz of Maji's phone against her ribs. Maji sighed and stepped outside, ahead of their group. When they headed outdoors again she was waiting for them by the bus, a distant look in her eyes.

"What's wrong?" Rose asked.

Maji glanced away, then met her gaze and held it. "I may get orders in the next day or two."

"But you're on vacation," Rose protested. "And you're still healing from your last…business trip."

"I may have been on my own time these last couple days. And hopefully I will be for the next few. But I'm always on call. Twenty-four seven, three sixty-five." There was no trace of self-pity in Maji's almost clinical tone.

Rose stared at her in silence. How was that humanly possible?

"Hannah's sending someone out to watch your back, just in case," Maji said, then winced. "Don't worry. They'll be discreet." She took Rose's hand as they followed the others to the bus. "I shouldn't have said anything, but I don't want you to think if I pull a disappearing act that it has anything to do with you, or us."

Rose crossed her arms and leaned back against the side of the bus. She kept her voice low. "I may not know much about the military, but I can't believe this is how the Reserve works."

The blankness in Maji's expression told Rose she had pushed too far. "It is for me."

"We're back on you-can't-tell-me ground, aren't we?" Rose asked.

Maji stared back toward the Raptor Center. "That's where I live. Come on, let's get on the bus before Heather makes us walk."

As she drove away from the Raptor Center, Heather announced that they would be going to the tideflats next. "We have a saying: *When the tide is out, the table is set.* Anybody want to guess what that means?"

The group chuckled, and Heather rattled off an impressive list of edibles, giving both the English and Tlingit names for geoduck, sea cucumbers, and kelp. Rose watched Maji listening intently and silently repeating the words.

By the entry sign for the Alaska Native Brotherhood Harbor, Heather flipped on the turn blinker and promised, "Our stop here will be brief and totally worth it. We're picking up a local fishing boat captain to answer your questions about the range of seafood that can be caught in deeper waters around here."

Rose noticed how Heather hesitated before turning off the bus's engine. She leaned forward to ask, "Was the captain supposed to meet us here?"

"Yeah," Heather answered. "My sister. Being late's not her style." She stood and pasted a cheerful expression on. "Ladies and gents, welcome to ANB Harbor. Feel free to step off and take a look around. But please be back in five minutes. 'Cause I will, and I have the keys!"

The first ones off the bus, Maji and Rose watched Heather stride down a gangway to a dock where mainly commercial-looking trawlers berthed.

"She's worried," Maji noted.

"I know," Rose said, glad for the validation of what she'd read into their new friend's body language. "Think we should follow her?"

Maji shook her head. "Let's just keep her in line of sight. They might need privacy."

As the others milled about, peering into the clear green water and checking out the fishing boats, they waited.

Barely two minutes later, Heather returned, worry etching her face. "She's been there. Didn't lock up, though. Could be sick. I'm going to check the restrooms."

She didn't protest when they walked beside her. The little concrete-block building showed no sign of activity, just the two entries at either end segregating visitors by gender.

"Check the men's," Maji instructed Rose as she turned the opposite direction to follow Heather into the women's section.

Rose popped her head into the men's area, feeling sheepish. "Hello?"

No one answered, and Rose saw no one by the urinals, no feet under the stalls. A scream from the other end drew her back out.

As Rose reached the other entryway, Heather emerged, stumbling as Maji pushed her out. Maji turned her, pointing across the street. "Get the police. We'll keep her safe. Go!"

Heather nodded, looking panicked but already running in the direction of the squad car parked in front of the Pioneer Saloon.

Maji turned toward Rose and locked eyes with her. "Get me a circle." When Rose nodded, remembering the move from training last summer, Maji added, "I'll bring them out. Give us space."

Maji disappeared back into the restroom. Blocking out her fears for Maji's safety, Rose ran toward her colleagues on the dock. *Get a circle.* Would anyone here know what that meant? There was no time to explain and practice. She spotted George Koreki and headed for him.

"We need help at the restroom. A woman…in trouble," Rose began.

She didn't get any further before he nodded and called out to two other middle-aged men chatting nearby. "Peters, Nowak—with me."

Rose wondered as they fell in without question if he had been a drill sergeant. "Ri went in after the woman. She wants a circle outside. You know how?"

"Just put us where you need us," he replied, breaking in to a trot. "Called 9-1-1?"

Just as Rose finished arranging the three blessedly cooperative men in a half circle outside the restroom entrance, Maji emerged. With one hand in a thumbs-up and the other pressing a finger to her lips to ask them to keep quiet, Maji paused and nodded to Rose. Rose caught the gazes of the academics to either side of her briefly, while breathing in and exhaling deliberately, modeling the relaxed and ready fence post posture. They mimicked her, their hands extended, palms forward.

Maji turned back and called into the restroom, "Coast is clear. Bring her out quick." Then she spoke to them a bit more urgently, in Russian. A repeat of last summer?

Rose took a deep breath and tried to feel her feet press into the concrete. This was no time to panic. George gave her a steadying look.

As Maji talked out a man burdened by a slumping, staggering woman, she reached out to help him. Then before he could react to the sight of the human barricade, Maji slammed the man's head backward with one palm. As it crunched against the cinder blocks, Maji yanked the woman free, pushing her toward Rose. "Now!"

Rose stepped forward and caught the woman, pulling her backward and to the outside of the circle. "Hold the line!" she heard herself bark out, as she and the woman crumpled to the ground behind them.

Everything that followed jumbled together. Sirens grew in volume, feet pounded toward them, Heather's voice screamed out, "Dee!" And as Rose cradled the semiconscious woman's head and shoulders, she caught flashes of motion through the gaps between her helpers' legs and backs. Maji's fight wasn't over.

"Police! Move aside," a deep voice bellowed. Rose's cadre shifted.

Heather knelt across from Rose, repeating Dee's name over and over, trying to get a response. "Can you hear me?"

"There's the ambulance," Rose told her, relieved to see two EMTs spilling out of the van and jogging toward them. Glancing at the black-clad police officers looming over Maji and not one but two men on the ground, Rose fought the urge to spring up and go to her.

Instead, Rose backed away from Dee, settling her gently onto the ground and making room for the EMTs. "I think those men drugged her," she told the first medic to arrive.

The pair seemed to know Heather and talked to her in reassuring tones as they efficiently got to work checking Dee for pulse, reliable breathing, and signs of injury. Rose stood and turned at last to confirm that Maji was unscathed.

Rose took in Maji kneeling on the back of one man, his arm twisted high behind him as she turned just her head to speak with one of the policemen. His partner, a woman in the same black uniform of the city police, Mirandized the already cuffed man who knelt by the wall. The male officer moved to the head of the man on the ground and tried to lift his free hand to place cuffs on him as well. The pinned man struggled, and Maji spoke to him in Russian, moving her upper body slightly. He jerked once and relaxed. As soon as he was cuffed, Maji released her grip and rocked back, stepping back and standing.

"Ri!" Rose exclaimed, moving toward her.

Maji shook her head and motioned her back, then looked to the officer, lifting both hands and placing them above her head. "I have a permitted weapon in a kidney carry holster."

Rose felt a hand on her shoulder. "Why don't we all sit over there," she heard. "Rose, right?"

She turned and saw George's name tag hanging askew. "Thanks, Dr. Koreki." The other two hovered behind him, looking pleased but concerned. "Thank you, all."

Additional sirens wailed as a black Jeep with a police logo and an Alaska State Trooper vehicle wove their way through the crowd that had gathered in the parking lot. Over by the ambulance, Rose noted, some fishermen stood protectively close as the medics loaded Dee in on a stretcher and Heather climbed in behind them.

"I'll be right with you," Rose said, patting George's shoulder and trying to project calm. She watched as the officer finished his pat down of Maji's front and sides. Without waiting for him to ask, Maji turned and faced the wall, hands still resting on her head. Rose held her breath as the officer lifted the back of Maji's jacket and withdrew the semi-automatic Rose had watched her clean only hours earlier.

"Where's the permit?" he asked in a neutral tone.

"Billfold, back right pants pocket," Maji responded. She sounded completely unruffled and didn't flinch when he plucked the little leather folder out. He opened it and started scanning her ID.

"Stand aside," came a commanding voice behind Rose. She turned and saw two imposing men in blue uniforms and trooper hats striding toward the Sitka officers. "Donna, Joe," the one in the lead said. "Give you a hand?"

"Hey Sam, Stu," the woman officer said. "One of you could watch the two in custody, that'd be great."

"Sure thing," Trooper Sam or Stu said and nodded toward Maji. "What about her?"

"She's with us." He tapped Maji on the elbow and said, "Here you go, ma'am."

Maji accepted her gun and billfold and motioned Rose to join the helpful trio of colleagues now seated at the picnic table.

Rose sat and watched Officer Joe scribble notes while Maji talked. Then Maji walked him over to the table and said, "Officer, this is Dr. Rose diStephano. She's under federal protection. You can interview her, but keep her a Jane Doe in the paper and computer record. Please."

Rose heard a *huh* from behind her, and she did not look to see if it was George or one of the other two. Hopefully Maji would fill her in before she had to speak with them again.

The local cop looked uncertain about the request. Maji's face betrayed neither anxiety nor impatience as she pulled a card from her billfold and handed it to him.

"Call the number," Maji said. "We'll be in the Tribal Tours bus when you're ready for us."

Maji gave Rose a hand up, but then stopped to shake each man's hand. To George she asked, "Army?"

"Marines," he replied.

She tried to look unimpressed. "Good enough in a pinch."

Laughter and voices rehashing the adventure provided a calming backdrop as Maji steered Rose toward the bus. "You okay?"

"Fine," Rose answered. "Shaken, but...fine. You?"

"Right as rain." When Rose stopped and looked at her sternly, Maji backpedaled. "Really fine. Just bruises. I need to make a call." At the bus door she asked, "Could you get my water bottle?"

As expected, Rose was happy to help. Maji dialed into Command while Rose stepped inside. When the operator answered she opened with, "Rios for IC. Orange."

She held while the operator put her through to whoever was incident commander on shift at the Dogpatch, her unit's twenty-four seven operations control center.

"Wyatt. Report." At the sound of her commanding officer's voice, Maji took a deep breath.

"Incident in Sitka. Two Russian mercs tried to render a fishing boat captain from the harbor. Both in custody of city PD, who will be calling to check my creds."

"Roger that. What's your condition?"

"Five by five."

"Is Doc secure?"

Maji nearly smiled at the colonel's use of Rose's call sign. That JSOC had adopted the nickname that the girls at self-defense camp created tickled her. "Yes, sir. Target appears unrelated. However, I asked the locals to keep Doc's name off record. I said she was under federal protection." Vague yet persuasive, she hoped.

"Well congratulations, Sergeant. You are now with Diplomatic Security. Tell Doc to limit how much she says about her daddy the ambassador."

Yep, that would do in a pinch. "Hooah, sir. Rios out."

Maji locked the screen and dropped the phone in her pocket, wondering if she should call Hannah next. Instead, she poked her head into the bus.

Rose held out the bottle of water, a frown creasing her brow. "That wasn't Hannah, was it?"

Maji shook her head, uncapping and drinking down half a liter before saying more. "Let's sit and chat."

They left the bus door ajar for air and watched the local police load the suspects into two vehicles. "What did those men want?"

"Don't know. They fed me bullshit, and I rolled with it. All I know for sure is they weren't after you."

Rose blinked at her. "They were Russian, weren't they? But not all Russian thugs work for you know who. Surely."

Maji put a hand on the small of Rose's back. She wished she could hold her, but now was not the time. "Of course not. Could be anything—drug deal gone bad, roofies, maybe even fishing rights or some local crap like that."

Rose looked unconvinced. "They were wearing Xtratufs and overalls."

Brand-shiny-new ones. "Exactly. And you did so well backing me up. Thank you. I want you to call Hannah and tell her everything. She'll be really proud."

Looking out at the cops still interviewing witnesses, Rose asked, "And the police? Is there anything you want me to say or not say?"

"Let's keep it simple. You're here for the conference, this was a total surprise. Stick to what you saw and heard."

"What about that federal protection business? Tell me you just made that up."

Normally Maji wouldn't tell a civilian that she was using a cover, but in this case it seemed unavoidable given Colonel Wyatt's instructions. She laughed. Either it really was funny, or she was getting punchy as the adrenaline dropped. "Officially, you are now an ambassador's daughter and I am your security detail from Diplomatic Security."

"Is that really a thing? I mean, legitimate?"

"It is indeed. But you might want to decline to discuss your father."

Rose looked unamused. Not knowing her biological father's identity had long been a sore point. But then she shook her head and sighed. "Why not. But if I have to pretend that I'm not your girlfriend again, I will not be laughing."

"Me either. How about this—we act just like we have been, and let them wonder whether we're pretending as part of a really clever cover, or if I'm actually bad at my job."

"Shh." Rose pointed at the officer approaching.

Maji gave Rose's hand a squeeze. "Call Hannah," she said and stepped down out of the bus.

Officer Donna, who seemed to be in command of the scene, reconfirmed the details Maji had given her partner. She looked satisfied and shook Maji's hand. "We have enough from the other witnesses. That'll be all for today."

Rose was off the hook, then. Good. Maji popped back in to check on her.

"Are we done?" Rose asked, looking deflated.

Time for some TLC. Maji smiled. "Yep. You think those tideflats will be here tomorrow?"

"I hope so. Right now I'd love a glass of wine and a good meal. If you're available."

"I'm all yours. Room service?"

Rose smiled. "Better. There's a place near here that's highly recommended. Though I doubt they serve breakfast for dinner."

Maji grinned at her. Eggs and anything was her comfort food of choice after a run-in. Since their first night together, when Rose had invited her home and cooked her an omelet, it had become a ritual. But not tonight. "I guess I could settle for fresh seafood—if they also have tapas."

"How did you know?" Rose's surprise was gratifying.

"There aren't that many great places to eat in this town. Everyone agrees on Ludvig's, even the cops."

"Oh. Well, I think we've earned it. And Hannah agrees."

Chapter Seven

The casual interior of Ludvig's belied its farm-to-table gourmet menu. Maji's mouth watered at the descriptions of fresh halibut with oyster mushrooms and asparagus risotto, wild Alaskan paella, grilled duck…"Want to share the black cod tips appetizer?"

Rose tilted her menu down to make eye contact across the little polished wood table. "Yes. And then I want to try everything else on the menu. We may have to eat here every night."

Maji agreed. "I'm amazed a town this size can support a place this cool. Thank you, tourists. This is exactly the kind of place I wanted to take you last summer."

"No," Rose replied. "It's the kind of place I wanted to take you. Remember, I told Ang he should take you to Brio."

Maji looked away, instinctively hiding the pain she felt at Rose's mention of her cousin Angelo. Rose, like most of the world, believed he was dead. And as Maji could never see her old teammate again, he kind of was. She didn't feel guilty, as Rose suspected, for Angelo's fate. Only for the pain it caused Rose, and his mother, and the rest of the family not now in prison. Rose's hand on hers made Maji meet her gaze again.

Rose asked, "Have you talked to someone? Hannah, Bubbles…a counselor?"

Hannah, yes. And not another soul. Only five people knew what they'd done—herself, Hannah, Tom, and Dev. And of course

Angelo, assuming he was still alive wherever he had ended up. Even JSOC didn't know what they'd pulled off, only that Angelo had managed to bankrupt most of the world's organized crime rings in one fell swoop, by stealing trillions of dollars from their electronic bank accounts. They thought he'd run a suicide mission for himself, while tricking his best friends from his Army team into helping. By now, Rose would know enough from the media to think the same. "Yes."

"Good." Thankfully, Rose didn't press further.

"How about you?"

"Oh, I've talked to Aunt Jackie and Nonna, of course," she replied, naming Angelo's mother and their shared grandmother, the formidable Benedetti matriarch.

Typical Rose, looking out for everyone else. Maji raised an eyebrow at her. "I'm sure that helps them, but what about you?"

"I saw a grief counselor for a little while, and joined the jujitsu club on campus. Talking and hitting things—you know." Rose smiled to accentuate the inside joke. "I have some very nice friends, plus Bubbles checks on me by phone."

A cheerful woman with a server's waist apron over her floor-length skirt greeted them, pouring water before leaving the little pitcher on their table. "Can I answer any questions? Get you something to drink?"

"Just water for me," Maji answered.

Rose absorbed that with barely a flicker of expression, and turned her sparkling eyes to the server. "I'd like a glass of the prosecco, please. And to know how anyone ever decides what to have, when everything sounds so delicious."

Maji watched the effect Rose's words and warmth had on the woman, and wondered not for the first time if Rose realized how potent her attractiveness was. Whether their server was married or single, gay or straight, or someplace else in the mosaic didn't matter. Any challenges on the rest of her busy shift would be cushioned by the Rose Effect.

"You'll just have to come back," the server answered, her eyes crinkling. "I'll have your prosecco right up."

When she'd headed off to the bar, Rose fixed a questioning look on Maji. "Do you ever drink?"

"Well, I am armed and kind of on high alert now."

"Yes, I've been following recent events. But that doesn't answer my question."

Well, there was a secondary Rose effect. Maji wanted to tell her everything—every stupid thing she'd ever done when she was a teenager trying to blunt her anger and insecurities with alcohol. And she wanted to admit nothing, hope Rose would see only the best in her. Rose just waited, patient but not letting her off the hook. "Well, I'm not an alcoholic," Maji started. "But I don't trust myself to make good decisions when I drink. Seems like somebody else always gets hurt, and they wouldn't have if I'd been sober."

"I suppose I shouldn't ask a black belt what kind of hurt you mean. It was impressive that you took both those men down today. And without serious injury." Rose looked both sad and sympathetic. "But surely there are times when you're really off duty and only interacting with friends."

Maji gave her a wry look. "Like the night we met? You sent me a beer."

Rose flushed at the memory, silent except for her thanks as the server placed a flute of sparkling white wine in front of her.

"Have you decided?" the woman asked, directing the question to Rose almost flirtatiously.

Rose ordered the paella to follow their cod tips, and Maji opted for the rockfish caught locally just that morning.

Rose picked up the conversation where Maji had left off. "I'll have you know, that was the first time I ever sent a stranger a drink. And you hadn't even rescued me from armed kidnappers yet."

Maji was glad Rose could joke about it now. Especially right after their run-in by the docks. "Speaking of which, you did tell Hannah how well you did, right?"

Rose flushed just a little. "Yes, and that I owed it to her training. I really never expected to have to use it. But as soon as you said *make a circle*, I knew where we were going. It's amazing, really."

"That you knew what to do, or that it worked?"

Rose laughed. "Both, I guess." As she sipped her prosecco, she reflected on how right it felt to help Maji and to put her new skills to work. Someday when Maji was out of the Army, if she chose to work for Hannah at Paragon, maybe there would be a role for her too. But she wouldn't dream of pushing Maji to think that far ahead right now. Instead she asked, "What will happen to those two men?"

"Dunno. Hopefully they'll stay in somebody else's jurisdiction. Somebody not on vacation."

Rose didn't see the humor in that. "Don't tease me with hints you can't explain. It's not fair." She sighed. "I'm sorry. I know it's not your fault. Let's just…stick to other topics."

Maji nodded her agreement as the black cod tips arrived. She speared a chunk of fish with her fork, tasted it, and groaned in appreciation.

Alone with Maji but for the increasing number of filled tables, Rose leaned in. "For tonight, nothing matters but you, and me, and being together. Agreed?"

Maji leaned in, matching her. "*D'accord.* And I can't tell you how much I appreciate that."

"Then you'll just have to show me later."

"I'll do my best." The look in Rose's eye made Maji want to skip the delicious dinner about to arrive and show her now. *Please God, no calls tonight.*

Rose looked endearingly sheepish and took another bite of black cod off the serving plate in the center of the table. She deserved all the one-on-one time Maji could give her. Maji tamped down the urge to apologize for not having done this sooner or being able to say when she'd be available again. As Rose had put it, the things Maji couldn't control. So she sat dumbly admiring Rose instead of leading her onto the minefield of discussing their future.

After savoring the morsel in silence, Rose asked, "How are your parents? Do you get to see them much?"

Well, that was a safe enough topic. "They're good. I stay at their place when I'm in the city. Papi keeps long hours at the clinic, but we hang out in the kitchen whenever he's off." Maji paused.

"And Mom's traveling less. She wanted me home for Nauruz and I kind of blew that."

The Persian New Year—the first day of spring, March 21 this year—had fallen near the beginning of Maji's recent mission. Rose wouldn't know that, or that it was also Maji's birthday. Should she tell her?

"Well, she must understand." Rose paused. "Does she actually cook for the holiday? Preparations seem quite elaborate. I went to a campus celebration one year, and the spread was sumptuous. Do you have any favorites?"

Maji let slide the fact that her parents did not know more about her work than Rose did. That her role was classified and unpredictable they understood. And the question was an obvious softball, designed to let her off the hook in classic Rose style. "Kookoo sabzi, of course. That's the omelet with all the herbs in it."

Rose smiled. "Not the sweets? The baklava or the gaz?"

"Mom keeps a tin of store-bought gaz on hand all year," Maji conceded. The nougat candies, like all versions of baklava, were too sweet for her. "But I was always more excited by the savory stuff—dolmens any day, and fesenjan. And the various kabobs, of course."

"Of course." Rose took another chunk of black cod. "Last one's yours."

Maji claimed it and moved the appetizer plate to the edge of the table. "Until I was six, I thought the whole festival was for me—the food, the gifts, the *haftseen* table. Only made sense to me, since it happened every year at my birthday."

"No—really?" Rose beamed, then looked chagrined. "Bubbles didn't tell me. I wish I'd known. I could at least have left you a nice voicemail, along with the other, whiny ones." She looked hopeful. "Come visit, and I'll make you whichever dishes you want. No— don't look like that—I'd enjoy it."

Maji knew she would. "Okay. I will." Enough focus on her. Even without work to skirt around, talking too much about herself made her squirm. "What about you? Did you associate your birthday with Halloween?"

"Not really. The fifth is far enough away, and Halloween was never that big a deal for me. Mom never got into decorating, and she certainly didn't have time for making costumes." Rose smiled at the recollection. "Gerald took me out trick or treating, while Mom scared the kids who came to our house. My friends actually were intimidated by her. I think she gets that from Nonna."

Their server reappeared, and Rose watched Maji appreciatively inhale the aroma from her plate of rockfish with wilted spinach, potatoes, and crispy onion sticks. That unabashed love of good food, even the simplest dishes, made her a pleasure to cook for. Cooking itself relaxed Rose, gave her an outlet for her creativity in lieu of art or music or other hobbies. "Oh my gosh," she exclaimed as the steaming dish of paella appeared in front of her. "Did you give me extra?"

The server blushed. "It's very good left over," she said, conceding without confessing.

"We have a microwave and fridge," Maji pointed out.

Rose couldn't suppress a grin. "If you're hungry in a few hours, there'll be some waiting for you." To the server she added, "You'd never believe how much she can eat."

The server merely cleared her throat. "Anything else I can get you?"

They sent her off with thanks, and Maji leaned in. "You burst her bubble."

"How so?" Rose knew she'd been nothing but polite and friendly. She declined a second date with anyone who treated waitstaff poorly.

"You got her hopes up and then you dashed them. No phone number on the back of the check for you." Maji's eyes said she was teasing but not really joking.

"You're the collector of phone numbers, not me. Besides, how do you know she's even...not straight?" Rose didn't care for the word queer, Maji's umbrella term. And *lesbian or bi* was too cumbersome, *that way* or *interested in women* too euphemistic for her taste.

Maji shrugged. "I just assume everyone is, until they say otherwise. But you have an effect on people that transcends orientation anyway. To meet you is to adore you."

Now it was Rose's turn to flush. "That's ridiculous. You're biased."

"No, I'm observant. And look—I'm dropping the subject. How are your mom and Gerald doing with Nonna under their roof?"

"Um...surprisingly well. I thought Mom might feel like she'd picked up at seventeen, but they both seem to accept that everyone's an adult now. Plus, Gerald dotes on Nonna, which doesn't hurt."

"Has she taken over their kitchen?"

Rose had to laugh. Maji was insightful, even if she overestimated Rose's charms. "Completely. Mom complains about gaining weight, but I think she's happier now than she has been in years."

"Good. And how's Jackie?"

"Rocking the real estate world, with a little advice from Mom now and then. Of course, Mom doesn't do repos, and Aunt Jackie has so many it's become the core of her business." Rose hesitated to point out Angelo's role in upending the Long Island housing market when he bankrupted the region's Mafia. "The FBI seized an awful lot of property, and reselling it to people with clean money is a profitable niche."

Maji nodded, her mouth pulling to one side. "I can see her taking real satisfaction in helping normal people move into houses that used to be mobbed up."

Normal people, Rose noted. What did that mean, exactly? Maji used the expression surprisingly often. And it had been some kind of code between her and Angelo. But...another time. "Speaking of mobbed up, do you know that show, *Growing up Gotti*?"

"No. A documentary on John Gotti?" Maji managed to look interested while working her way through her dinner without a pause.

Rose shook her head. "A cable TV reality show. Apparently, the cameras followed around Gotti's daughter and her three sons. And their friends, and other wives whose husbands were in prison on RICO charges."

"Please tell me nobody was stupid enough to ask Nonna to be on a reality show." Maji looked wary yet amused.

"Not until after they got Aunt Paola and Sienna signed up." Uncle Gino's wife and newly widowed daughter needed the money, she knew. Neither had careers of their own like Angelo's mother did. "Wait—it gets worse. The producers keep hounding Aunt Jackie to sign on, and now she's threatening to move to California too. As if that would help."

"It might. Reality TV is really cheap if you can keep production costs low. Units on both the East and West Coasts might be too expensive to maintain." Maji looked completely serious.

Rose blinked at her. The breadth of Maji's life experience, given her age—twenty-six now? twenty-seven?—always surprised her. "There are so many stories I want you to tell me. Why you know all the odd bits and pieces you know, where you learned things, how you know so many interesting people. How you have room in your brain for anything else, with all those languages in there."

"Most of them live in the dusty back room," Maji said, looking a tad embarrassed as she pointed to the back of her skull. "Got to pull them out and brush up when I need them. As for the rest, well—I could just be bluffing."

Maji clearly meant for her to laugh, but Rose didn't feel like it. "This isn't about your work. And I fully understand that you've seen and done things that are hard to talk about. But they're part of you, and I want to know you. Not just in the Biblical sense."

"Fair enough." Maji didn't blush at the reference to their physical intimacy. "But tonight I'd like to catch up on your life. You changed jobs, moved house and home. That's big."

The server approached to check on them. "How is everything?"

"Fabulous," Maji answered, sincere. It was a great meal, in a warm and relaxed setting, with the best company she'd shared in ages. "I'm sorry we don't have enough days here to try everything."

"Well, we're open for lunch too."

Rose sighed. "I'll never make a paella like this at home."

The thought of Rose making paella made visiting California even more enticing. If she didn't have a paella pan, Maji would bring her one.

"Another glass of wine?" the server asked Rose.

Rose shook her head and said quietly, "I don't want to be sleepy tonight."

"But we could look at the dessert menu," Maji suggested.

The server gave her a wink. "Coming right up."

"Guess she forgives me," Maji said to Rose, completely in private again. "Now, where were we? Oh, yeah, life at Bonaventure College."

"A school I'm sure you've never heard of. California has so many private colleges. It may be small, but it does offer graduate programs. Even a PhD track or two."

If Rose was angling to have Maji move there now that her master's at Columbia was complete, she would certainly look into it. She thought about the Defense Language Institute in Monterey, not too far from Rose's little town. "What's San Ignacio like?"

"Pretty nice. Quiet, a little artsy, not too conservative thanks to the college's influence. It has a couple nice restaurants, if you don't want to trek over to Monterey or up to San José. And the farmers' market runs all year."

"Sold," Maji joked. "Sounds like a good fit. Friends?"

"A few, so far. The admin coordinator for my department lives in town with her partner, and we've had some brunches and art walks and things. They finally stopped trying to set me up, thank God."

"Bad guessing at your tastes?" Maji wondered if Rose had mentioned her, if only as an ex. She shouldn't care, but she did.

Rose blushed. "Yes and no. I don't want to sound judgy, because they're lovely women, and so are their friends. But it seems that all the singles they know are part of a kink network. And I guess I'm more vanilla than I ever realized."

"Don't confuse that with boring, okay?" Maji felt her mouth twitch, despite her attempt to be sincere and reassuring. "You could never be boring."

"Thank you. And for the record, I'm open to considering anything you might enjoy." Rose held their eye contact. "I don't think I've ever trusted another person enough to say that."

Maji felt the Rose Effect kicking in, like the impact of too many shots of whiskey tossed back in a row. The sight of their server felt almost like a relief. "Give us a minute," she asked, taking the dessert menu without giving it a glance.

As soon as they were alone again, Rose gave her attention to the short list of homemade treats. "Ooh," she crooned. "The chocolate torte. They had me at *ganache*. Do you actually have room?"

"Not right now," Maji admitted. What she had was a growing need to be alone with Rose.

Rose set the menu card aside. "Social life aside, school is great. Guess who's helping with my new project on farmworkers?"

The student from last summer's camp whose family organized farm laborers came immediately to mind. "Soledad?"

Rose huffed lightly in disappointment. "Did Bubbles tell you?"

"No. It just makes sense. What's the project?"

"Come to my presentation Friday and find out. I have a PowerPoint with photos."

Maji chuckled at Rose's attempt to make light of her academic pride with self-deprecation. Then she thought of the men in custody, the worrisome sub sightings, and the riddle of Javi. And Rose named in the conference program. "I'll try."

"Good. You know, we should get the cake. For your birthday."

"Ah, I don't know. Wouldn't be the same without the songs, the dancing, the poetry…"

"Poetry?"

"Oh, yeah. Persians are huge poets, going back to the seventh century, maybe earlier." In Farsi, Maji recited the opening lines of a famous poem.

"Could you translate a little?"

"Sure, but it sounds better in Farsi, frankly."

Rose didn't press the point. "Do you have some more to recite?"

"Uh-huh." Maji remembered in a rush the effect her speaking Farsi had had on Rose last summer. She couldn't hold back a wicked smile.

Rose motioned for the server. "We need to head out," she told her, the calm in her voice betrayed by her eyes.

"I'll bring your check right over," the woman replied, starting to turn away with the final words.

"Wait!" Maji spoke up. "We need the chocolate torte with ganache—"

"To go," Rose said, beating her to the punch line while extending her credit card to the now amused server.

Maji shook her head, offering her card as well. "I got this one."

Rose snatched it from her. "Oh no. This is on me."

"Only the ganache, I hope," Maji joked.

The server accepted Rose's card with a barely suppressed smile.

CHAPTER EIGHT

They practically skipped down the sidewalk, hand in hand. Maji held the little bag of neatly wrapped paella and cake in her free hand, feeling at peace with the world. The pale colors over Mt. Edgecumbe made her realize just how leisurely a supper they had enjoyed. And yet the time had zipped by, leaving her wanting more. More talking and hearing Rose's throaty, unbridled laugh. "I could get used to this."

Rose kept her eyes on the view. "We've been lucky so far. Locals say it's normally so overcast in April that they don't notice how long the days have gotten."

"No," Maji said, pulling Rose's hand to her own belly. "This."

"Oh." Rose brushed her lips against Maji's cheek. "Me too. Let's go home."

Home. With Rose. Heaven. They turned away from the waning light to the west and headed briskly toward the hotel. Halfway there, the phone vibrated against Maji's ribs. "Damn. Hold on." She handed the food to Rose and fished it out. Hannah.

"Go for Rios."

"Maji, your credentials and a laptop will arrive in the morning, carried by Dev. He'll take watch over Rose for us. Command will call with your briefing time."

"Fuck." The word popped out before Maji could censor herself. "Sorry. Is he in transit?"

"On a redeye as we speak." Hannah's voice betrayed neither irritation nor sympathy. "Anything new, other than the apprehension of the two John Does?"

"No. Rose made you proud, of course." A niggling detail surfaced. "Wait—yes. Check out a reality TV show that's signed Paola and Sienna Benedetti. They've been after Jackie and Nonna but not Rose yet."

"Does she know the show's name or network?"

Maji called to Rose, who stood at a polite distance neither listening nor ignoring her. "What's that reality show called? Or the network?"

Rose shrugged. "I'm sorry."

Back to Hannah. "Negative."

"Well, I've got a contractor who can find out quickly. Now, about your assignment—"

"Tomorrow," Maji interrupted.

"Yes, tomorrow. But should you need to interact with anyone before you've received your orders, two things. One, you will be a special agent in Army Counterintelligence. Two, JSOC is sending two SEALs to Sitka. When you meet them, one will be there as Navy Intelligence. You two will work closely together, as would be expected."

"Roger that. And FYI, the locals think I'm Diplomatic Security. Best I could do on the spur."

"I know," Hannah replied. "That made it into the police report. Shouldn't be a problem. If the LEOs realize it was a cover, at least it's the sort they would expect counterintel to use. But since they have it in their heads that Rose is a diplomat's daughter, Dev will arrive with DS credentials. In case he needs to step out of his cover as an academic."

"Criminy, stop before I get dizzy." Hannah didn't respond to Maji's attempt at humor, so she added, "Oh, and…sorry for swearing. It's been—"

"I understand." Hannah paused. "Have you spoken to Bubbles yet?"

Maji's scalp prickled. "No. Why?"

"Check your messages, please." Now her tone betrayed a hint of frustration, which only worried Maji more. "Then talk with Rose. Good night."

Maji signed off and looked at Rose. "I have to check my messages. Now. Something's up with Bubbles."

"Yes," Rose said, taking her by the arm. "Listen while we walk."

Maji played the four messages from Bubbles. Her best friend didn't specify what was wrong, just asked her to call. And each time she sounded worse, more hollow in tone and spirit.

Maji pocketed her phone as they reached the hotel lobby. "She sounds terrible, but she doesn't say why."

Rose looked as if she might cry. "Bubbles and Rey lost the baby. She miscarried a few weeks ago."

"Aw, shit." Maji didn't know how much of Bubbles's rough past her friend had shared with Rose. But getting pregnant once had been a risk emotionally and physically—one she'd never imagined Bubbles would take, prior to meeting Rey. The loss would be crushing.

"It's been awfully hard on her," Rose acknowledged. "I didn't realize you were unaware, or I would have told you right away."

Maji nodded, at a loss for words. What kind of friend was she? Always unavailable to the people she cared about most. "What time is it in—"

"Too late to call," Rose said. "Why don't you try her in the morning? Before you go running."

And get my orders and disappear again, Maji thought. *Shit.* Could she even warn Rose of that? The SEALs were coming here. Would the mission go down in Sitka? Or was this just a stepping off point? And was she just advising, or actually being attached to their team? She pushed the rising frustration down. *Forget tomorrow. Be here, now.*

They rode up to the suite in silence. Inside, Rose turned on lights and put the food into the minifridge while Maji closed the curtains, feeling numb. She felt Rose's hands on her shoulder and turned to face her.

"Majida Ariela Kamiri Rios," Rose said, giving her a stern look laced with sweetness, "stop beating yourself up."

"It's not just that I let Bubbles down," Maji said, wanting to look away but not managing to. "I'm…this might be our last night together. Here in Sitka, I mean. Not—"

Rose put two fingers against Maji's lips. "I know. You saved a stranger today and then told Hannah what cover you used. Maybe it's best you leave now." Maji's surprise must have shown. Rose smiled gently. "We'll pick up when you're really on vacation again. And someone else will play bodyguard here. Much as you mean well, I don't want our relationship to be you in charge of me. Not in that way, anyhow."

Maji tried to reply but Rose shook her head, pressing her fingers more firmly against Maji's lips. Until tomorrow, there was nothing she could do for work or for Bubbles. But Rose was right here. *Give her a hundred percent, Rios.*

Rose took her fingers away cautiously. "You should get plenty of rest tonight. But since I may spend the rest of this trip without you, I'd like a compromise."

"Does it involve ganache?"

A smile spread across Rose's face. A delectable, wicked smile. "Mm-hmm. Also a little champagne, served with…imagination."

Rose with a full pantry at her disposal might be truly dangerous. And someday Maji hoped to face that challenge. For now, though, champagne and chocolate plus Rose's imagination? Maji met her gaze and couldn't suppress a shiver of anticipation. "Anything you have an appetite for. You're in charge."

Rose danced away from Maji's grasp and went to turn the lights off. "Open the curtains back up."

"Yes, ma'am," came the reply from Maji's silhouette across the room. A soft light from the street lamps below suffused the room, not bright but adequate to move about by.

Rose extracted the champagne and the torte from the fridge, handing the bottle to Maji. Maji accepted it without a word, then reached for Rose with her free hand, a faint smile on her shadowed features. Rose brushed her hand away, tingling at the touch. "Not yet," she said. "Open that."

While Maji worked the cork out, Rose plated the cake and found a fork. Thinking ahead, she filled a glass of water as well. Now, where to feast? The bed was large and comfy, but the light in here was perfect. "Hang on."

When she came back out of the bedroom with the comforter and a pillow in her arms, Maji was standing exactly where she'd left her by the little dining table with the champagne. "May I give you a hand?"

Rose warmed to the half-octave drop of Maji's voice. "You certainly will," Rose assured her. "Here, take an end." They folded the comforter in thirds, and laid it over the plush carpet.

"Softer than the dojo mats," Maji murmured.

Rose's pulse sped up in response. The realization she might come undone tonight the way she had in the dojo only made her more determined to take her time. She would lose herself to Maji's touch soon enough. Right now she wanted to savor her with as much awareness as she could maintain. She crossed over to the makeshift bed on the floor and lifted Maji's pullover up. Maji helped her slip it off and tossed it into the corner. Rose couldn't resist kissing her then.

The kiss alone almost derailed her plans, as Maji's hands found their way under Rose's top and along the length of her back, drawing their bodies nearly as close together as their mouths. The feel of her bra giving way brought Rose back enough to turn her head. "Stop," she whispered.

Maji froze.

The knowledge that her lover, who could disarm multiple attackers twice her size, would heed her desires at a mere word from her delighted Rose. *So this is being in charge.* Taking the lead required more restraint than she'd anticipated.

Helpfully, Maji let her arms slip away from Rose's skin. She stepped back a fraction, the tiny distance between their bodies shimmering with heat, and raised both hands in front of her bare biceps. And smiled enticingly.

Rose found her words again at last. "That's it. T-shirt off." Maji let her remove it as she bit her lower lip, watching Rose admire her arms and torso. She stood still while Rose slipped behind her and circled her arms around Maji's waist, unsnapping her new jeans.

"Um," Maji said, her voice still low but a little hoarse now, "I could probably use another shower."

Rose brushed Maji's french braid to one side, inhaling the skin at the back of her neck, then her shoulder. "You'll need one soon enough," she replied, sliding Maji's jeans down to the floor. She hadn't put on any of the underwear purchased this afternoon, and the warm scent of her arousal reached Rose. Rose felt herself dampen everywhere, a light sweat breaking out under her silk camisole in addition to the usual spots. Thirst hit her as she ran her hands over Maji's thighs, and Rose straightened back up behind her. She nipped at Maji's firm, round runner's ass, and smiled at the little noise in response. Rose pressed herself close behind Maji, only her clothing between them, and ran one hand down Maji's front, the other up to her breasts. Maji moaned as she leaned back into Rose. "God, I want you," Rose breathed into her ear before sucking on the salty skin of her neck.

"You've got me," Maji rasped back at her. "What now?"

"Water," Rose declared.

She let Maji drink first, then asked, "Grab two large towels from the bath, please."

"Uh-huh." Maji handed her the glass and disappeared briefly. Rose filled the glass, drank it down, and refilled it. She tossed her own top aside, along with her slacks and bra. The silk camisole and ridiculously wet panties she kept on—for now. She still had plans, after all.

Rose kissed Maji slowly, deeply, with their hands clasped together behind Maji's back. Touching the slight tack of Maji's abrasion, she paused. Maji opened her eyes and focused, looking a little glazed from passion. "I'm healed enough. Don't worry."

That enticing smile returned, and Rose didn't ask any more permission. Gently she pushed Maji down onto the comforter and carefully poured a trail of champagne down her etched belly. Rose kneeled by her side and licked and sucked the bubbly off Maji's skin, listening to her breathing change in response. "Want some?"

Maji eyed the bottle. "To drink? Just a little."

Rose chuckled. "I would never get you drunk and take advantage of you."

Maji propped herself up on her elbows. "Already have. You're the best drug ever."

Wishing for a glass but not wanting to move either of them, Rose tipped the bottle back, taking a mouthful. She tilted Maji's head back and gave her a drink that ended in a kiss. A contraction, sudden and fierce, surprised Rose, and she moaned, tearing her mouth away. Maji sat taller, sliding a hand into the curls at the back of Rose's head, and kissed her deeply, not releasing her until the aftershocks of the ambushing orgasm had rolled through and subsided.

"How do you know..." Rose asked, trying to catch her breath and some remnant of dignity.

Maji smiled a lopsided smile, wonder in her eyes. "You radiate pleasure. It's impossible not to ride that wave. You're incredible."

Rose felt tears starting and blinked hard. To hell with dignity. "We haven't gotten to dessert yet."

"Bring it." The dare in Maji's eyes inspired Rose to rise up off her knees, strip off the last bits of clothing, and grab the cake off the table.

"Bite?" Rose asked.

Maji looked her over. "Where?"

"Wherever I want," Rose said. She placed a dollop of ganache on each of Maji's pert little nipples, more than covering them.

"So not vanilla," Maji murmured, leaning back on her elbows again.

Rose swiped her left index finger through the thick icing and offered it to Maji, who opened her mouth, her eyes never leaving Rose's face. They both hummed as Maji sucked the ganache off Rose's finger, eyes locked. Rose pushed Maji back onto the comforter, swinging a leg over her to straddle her hips. Then she wove her fingers between Maji's, lowering herself until Maji was pinned and Rose's tongue could lick the ganache away.

Maji made little sounds as her breath grew ragged again, and Rose paused just long enough to peek at her face. Finding Maji watching her, eyes open and tuned to Rose's every touch, gave her a surge of pleasure. She levered herself up to kiss Maji, the taste of dark chocolate with cream rich between them. "Stay here," Rose said when she could pull away at last.

Maji just watched her drink down the glass of water, a mix of happiness and hunger in her expression. When Rose offered her some, Maji shook her head slowly. Apparently, all she wanted was within sight.

Rose sank down by Maji's feet. "Pillow. Please."

Maji took it from under her head and handed it over, putting her hands behind her head as if to start a set of sit-ups. Rose motioned for her to lift her hips and slid the pillow underneath. Then she stretched herself out, feeling the soft carpet against every inch of her skin on the front of her body. She peeked over Maji's hips before dipping into the glory of her glistening, swollen flesh, ripe as a fresh peach in July. And just as sweet. As Rose explored with her tongue, she heard a soft thud, and hoped it meant Maji had let her head drop, her eyes closed to release all sensations other than the ones Rose was creating.

Rose wanted to reach up and stroke Maji's taut muscles just above her tiny curls, or find her hand and grasp it tightly. But she needed one arm to prop herself up, and the other...well, she'd kept it free of chocolate for a reason. With the fingers of her right hand, she teased at Maji's opening. Maji lifted her hips in response, a soft keening sound reaching Rose's ears at the same time. Oh yes.

Rose focused her tongue and lips on Maji's clit, feeling her tense and then relax in response. Good—she was paying attention. Rose held back from pushing her too hard too quickly. Tonight was about savoring. And that teasing touch was about to change. Rose pressed two fingers smoothly inside, just a little.

"Yes. Please," Maji breathed. "Yes."

Rose slid deeper inside, reveling in the feel of silken heat and slipperiness. But Maji was so open to her, Rose curled those fingers out, slowly, and added one to their return. Maji hummed, and Rose nearly laughed with joy. Rose kept teasing Maji's clit and caressing the marvelous skin wrapped around her hand until the rhythmic moans grew nearly to a howl and Maji rose up from the comforter, shouting.

Rose kept her right hand snugly in place, but let Maji drag her up to lie half on top of her, half beside her. They kissed softly, Rose surprised to taste tears. So it wasn't just her body that responded that way to the rising tides of pleasure. "I love you," she managed between kisses.

"I know," Maji replied after a moment, stilling to look at Rose directly with bright, soft eyes. In the half-light, they looked darker than their daylight green. "*Te adoro.*"

Rose smiled and kissed her softly. "*Te amo, mi corazón.*"

Maji murmured back in what sounded to Rose like Russian.

"*Je t'aime,*" Rose whispered.

Maji gave her a dose of what Rose recognized as Hebrew in reply. "I love you," Maji said. "You've heard it in Farsi." Her next words sounded like the dinnertime poetry but stirred an older, more visceral memory. "Sound familiar?"

Rose rested her head on Maji's shoulder and traced the lines of her face with her fingers. "I thought that's what you said before." The words had ripped out of Maji that night last summer as if they hurt her. Everything that followed had been a surrender to the truth. "It's good to know, though."

"It seemed like you knew."

"I did. But you seemed so unhappy about it. Like you didn't want to."

"I didn't." Maji's hand trailed up from Rose's shoulder to her ear, where it tickled. "I wanted to protect you."

The self-mockery in Maji's tone took some of the sting from the memory. "You're a lovable idiot."

Maji repeated *I know* in several languages.

Rose sighed. "I don't want you to protect me from you."

"Even if I disappear in the middle of our week together?"

"Even if you have to go, yes. And whenever I get to see you again after this."

Maji glanced away and inhaled deeply. "Damn, we smell good. You want more champagne?"

"No. I want our bed. Would you like a shower first?"

"If you come with me."

"Sold."

CHAPTER NINE

The sky was overcast but beautiful in its own way. And Maji found the low sixties, with just a hint of a breeze, nearly ideal for running. After six or seven sound hours of sleep, she'd woken at a quarter to six and slipped out of bed. Rose needed more sleep, and Maji needed her running fix. One of the conditions of her Reserve status was that she maintain her level of fitness however she could. On Long Island, Hannah helped her keep a well-rounded regimen. But on missions she often had to sneak in exercise, as weight training and martial arts rarely fit her cover. Today she could seriously use a workout too, but the town's trails and quiet streets called to her in a way the gym never did. No matter how brief her assignment in Sitka might be, it never hurt to get the lay of the land.

The retail shops Maji passed were all closed, and no cars stopped at the traffic light locals referred to as The Light. Did they really only have one? Even the Highliner coffee shop and the fire station next to it looked asleep, no sign of the staff she knew must be inside. She reveled in the magic hour—that still time when a runner felt like she owned the whole world. Looking toward Crescent Harbor, Maji noted a few souls on the docks and a lot of empty slips. Magic hour for commercial fishing boats must be predawn here, as it was in most ports. She wondered how Heather's sister was doing today. Would she wake at her usual oh dark thirty even in the hospital, pulled by the water as Maji was by the pavement and trails? Maybe she'd even be on her vessel by now.

With that idea in mind, Maji turned west, passing the cathedral and the Community House. As she approached ANB Harbor she slowed. Maybe for once she should stick to her own lane. Problem was, all signs pointed to yesterday's shenanigans tying in to all the other weird bits of intel and intuition. In a few hours her orders might put her right back here. Why not do a little advance recon?

Down on the dock where Heather had gone in search of her sister yesterday, a small figure in a blue uniform pounded on the stern of a fishing boat, waited a beat, and headed back up toward the parking lot. A cop? No, wrong uniform.

The short, pretty woman with glossy black hair pulled back into a bun looked at her suspiciously. "Can I help you?"

"Maybe." Maji read *Taira* embroidered in white over one pocket, *US Coast Guard* over the other. "I was looking for the captain of a boat. Female, about my height, got hurt here yesterday. Do you know which boat is hers?"

"Who's asking?"

"A friend of the family."

Taira shook her head. "I've never seen you around. Want to try that one again?"

"A rider on Heather's tour bus who pitched in yesterday." Maji respected the woman's protectiveness. "Not a reporter, not a friend of the two jackasses who got arrested. I'm just here for a conference, tried to take a tour yesterday. That better?"

Taira sighed. "Yeah. But she's not down there. Might still be in the hospital. Heather will know."

"I'll check in with her later then. Thanks," Maji said, and headed farther out Katlian Street, past ANB Hall and more fishing-related businesses. The sight of Ludvig's brought back memories and kicked in Maji's appetite. Just a few miles, and then she'd enjoy a hot shower and a large breakfast. Possibly the last of either for a while.

On Halibut Point Road, the sight of a McDonald's surprised her. But the laundromat and apartment buildings reminded her that even in a place this spectacularly beautiful, not everyone was living their dream vacation. And it probably didn't feel so refreshing when short dark days brought cold rain and high winds. She wondered what it was like to be Tlingit here, surrounded by people who had come from other places to make a living on your land and didn't even recognize you. And the tourists who came looking for Russian America. Maybe when she saw Rose in California she'd get to hear her thoughts on that.

At the big grocery store that advertised twenty-four-hour shopping, fresh fish, and fresh produce, Maji popped in to use the restroom. The view from the parking lot included fishing boats, open water, and Mount Edgecumbe. She was tempted to call Rose just to tell her she was eating an apple at the grocery store with the most beautiful view in the US. Instead she pitched the core to a seagull and headed back toward town, past a large pond with eccentric moose sculptures, somewhat overreachingly named Swan Lake. Rush hour appeared to have started, because the compact cars and four-wheel-drive trucks had to yield as they navigated the traffic circle. *Could do with a second light. But then what would they call them?*

Using the map she'd locked in her mind, Maji followed Sawmill Creek Road past the cemetery. Eagles and ravens both perched in the trees, reminding her of their visit to the Raptor Center and Rose's remarks. Would Rose have such a high opinion of her when she had been briefed on all the sorts of tasks Delta took on? Not that anyone would tell her mission specifics, but even just from stories and jokes the guys did tell, her work couldn't possibly seem so simple and clean as Rose made it sound when she'd asked, *Did you help someone?*

As Maji passed the turnoff for Indian River Road, a group of mostly men in gray T-shirts and dark gym shorts passed her, heading toward the buildings visible beyond the *Public Safety Training Academy* sign. On the far side of the road another group headed in the same direction, led by a man in a red shirt. Spotting her, he waved and hollered something she didn't catch. Maji waved and kept going, still not used to how casually friendly the locals were. She'd lost count of the number of times a driver had lifted one hand off the wheel in greeting. As she crossed over Indian River mulling the oddity of small town life, the sound of feet slapping pavement behind her made her turn. The cadet's shirt clung darkly to his torso, and Maji hoped he wouldn't throw up on her.

"Can I help you?" she asked.

Sucking wind, he managed to get out, "Corporal Duncan wants to see you, ma'am. He's coming to pick you up."

Before Maji could place the name, a pickup slowed and pulled off just ahead of them. She walked up to the cab and recognized the driver as Trooper Stu. He'd been quite courteous the day before, so she just said, "Morning."

"Hey, glad I caught you. Been a weird night."

"Is the fisherwoman okay?

"Dee—yeah. Going home today. But that's the good news. Can I borrow you for a few minutes?"

Maji hesitated, fighting a reluctance to be caught by any law officer, a holdover from years of evading them as a teen. "Sure," she said at last. When he leaned over and pushed the door open, she climbed in.

"Dee will pull through fine," Stu said as he drove the short stretch back to the Academy. "You don't run a fishing boat around here if you're not tough as hell—and that goes double for women. But how are we going to protect her if we can't arrest those guys? Really fucking cheeses me off, pardon my French."

"Are you telling me they aren't in custody?"

"No. That's the bad news. Some guy came with diplomatic passports, insisted the SPD let them out. I guess they called somebody, who called somebody, who said yeah, diplomatic immunity."

"How long ago?"

"Twenty, maybe thirty minutes ago. Thought you'd want to know, being in Diplomatic Security and all. And if you could, maybe help us keep an eye out for them too."

Maji nodded. "Sure. Thanks. How far's the police station? I'd like to see the booking reports, photos if possible."

"I can do you one better. Come in—I'll hook you in via my desktop."

Maji followed him inside and accepted both water and coffee while he got the Sitka Police Department on his desk phone and computer screen. The officer on speakerphone was no happier about the situation and was willing to share the photos of the men's passports, as well as security footage of the man who had brought them to the station to expedite his friends' release.

Tom. Maji made sure her face betrayed no sign that she recognized her Delta teammate on the grainy video. She had heard he was attempting to infiltrate what was left of Sirko's network but had hoped for his sake that some other operative beat him to it. Not that she'd wish that on any of the guys in Delta. To prove himself worthy of Sirko's trust, who knew what kind of pain he'd had to inflict? Her nightmares might be hellish, but she could still face herself while awake. If Tom was here springing those two thugs, two things were clear: Sirko was the man behind this curtain, and Tom wasn't about to give up his cover and head home. She wondered if JSOC had any way for her to connect with him, without putting him at risk.

"Right?" Stu asked.

"I'm sorry. What?"

"I said, shitty way for them to repay us for saving their asses. These are the same guys that Maydayed out on the Sound a couple weeks ago. Coast Guard hauled them out, even salvaged their boat."

"They came in by boat?" Not a plane or the ferry. Or a sub. "What kind?"

"Fishing trawler registered to some holding company up on the Bering Strait," Officer Joe replied over the speaker. "Didn't say anything about diplomatic immunity then. What kind of official state business has you sport fishing and shanghaiing women?"

Stu shook his head. "You know they'll never tell us. And they probably won't pay the salvage fees, either. Diplomats." He spat the last word out like an epithet.

"Not real ones," Joe corrected. "Just some corporate goons in bed with the Politburo, or whatever it's called now. I think they got sent to scout out a factory site. They've been all over the old industrial park since…when did the cable go down?"

"Sixth. No, fifth. Yeah, the fifth. Anyway, can we get them out of town, or what?"

"You know the rules, Stu. No harassing or intimidating or interfering with…whatever they get up to that's legal." There was a pregnant pause on the line. "Doesn't mean we can't keep a close eye on them, though."

"Thanks," Maji said. "Can you print me out their passport scans?"

"Sure," Joe replied. He typed as they listened, seeming to be talking more to himself than them. "Ruslan Anasenko, coming through. Oleg Petrov, transmitting." The printer by Stu's desk started to spit a page out. "You want the third guy too? The one who sprung them?"

"Yes, please." Hallelujah for professional courtesy. "Also any updates you have, should you spot them around town the next few days. Please."

"Roger that. I trust you'll return the courtesy. If you see them or your people, you know, have any information to share. From Interpol or whatnot." The printer continued spitting out pages as Joe spoke. "Just watch your six, okay? They know they have immunity, remember."

Maji wasn't sure what these two guys thought Diplomatic Security did beyond protective duty. But their instincts were solid and she admired their willingness to pool resources. "Roger that," she echoed. "Will not approach without backup."

Stu dropped Maji at a little parking area by the trailhead for the Sitka National Historical Park. "About a dozen totem poles in there, pretty cool stuff. Just stay on the trail, or the devil's club will scratch you up good."

"Thanks." She climbed out and headed toward the trail. As Stu pulled back on to Sawmill Creek Drive, a little bus with *The Ride* on its side pulled in. The driver gave her a wave, and she waved back before plunging into the forest.

Maji glanced at the trail map and skipped the close loop, crossing a footbridge over the Indian River instead. She wanted a few minutes under the green canopy, a chance to digest this bombshell and get her game face on. Rose might be up by now, and there was still Bubbles to call. The pounded earth of the trail felt soft underfoot, compared to the hard road and sidewalks of town. Where the Indian River fed into the Sound, the tree line thinned and she saw trailer homes on the far side, beyond the park's boundary. She smiled to herself and added them to the list of mundane structures with the best view in the country—more to tell Rose about.

Sparing just a glance at the totem poles interspersed along the looping trail, Maji noticed the quickly passing view at eye level, the lush growth and the chunks of giant old fallen logs now covered with moss and ferns. A fishy smell let her know the pebbled beach was near, as well as the main entrance to the park. She slowed as the beach came into view, not wanting to scare off the host of seagulls and tiny pipers eating from the rocks and pools. Apparently, *When the tide is out, the table is set* applied just as much to wildlife as to humans.

At the turnaround by the Visitor Center, the bus sat idling with the same friendly guy at the wheel. Maji jogged up and asked, "You heading into town?"

"Sure am. Hop on."

"Um, how many minutes to someplace near Crescent Harbor?"

"About seven. But I got to load everybody first." The driver nodded toward someone behind Maji, and she turned to see an old woman with a walker being helped slowly forward by a younger woman.

"Think I'll race you, thanks," Maji said and started following the road along the water toward town. She could see the harbor in the distance, so no worries about getting lost. And the thought of Rose getting up and dressed and leaving the hotel on her own made her put on some speed.

Maji reached the hotel seven minutes later, barely registering the quaint stone churches and lovely houses with water views along the way. Maybe her assignment would be a quick consult, and she could stroll around the historic sights and photo ops later with Rose. Yeah, and maybe Bubbles wouldn't care that she'd been AWOL when she needed her support. She sighed and checked her watch. Just a few minutes left to call.

Rose woke alone and rolled to Maji's side of the bed to peer at the clock. The radio alarm clicked on to KCAW in the middle of the weather forecast. Dry and climate-controlled in the conference center, she thought to herself. Rose stretched and clicked the news off, inhaling the scent of sex on the sheets. Another shower was in order. Maybe she could fit one in and grab two plates of breakfast from the complimentary buffet before Maji returned from her run. That could become a nice *normal* routine, making breakfast for her early morning runner. She made a mental note to ask Maji if she kept this schedule all year or only in the warmer months. Rose found a robe on the floor and slipped it on, walking barefoot into the living area.

She spotted Maji standing out on the little balcony with the view of Mt. Edgecumbe, the door closed and muting the sound of her voice. Had work reached her already today? Would she leave now? Rose pushed back against the apprehension that welled up, tightening her chest and making her breaths shallow. She didn't want fear or sorrow to overshadow their time together, whether it was only a few hours more or stretched to a few more days.

As if feeling Rose's presence, Maji turned and gave her a little wave, then a *hold on* signal. She slid the door open and held the phone out. "Bubbles wants to say hi."

"I told you she'd make it," Bubbles said by way of hello. She sounded happier than Rose had heard her in weeks.

"No, you didn't."

"Well, I hoped she would," Bubbles countered, undeterred as usual by mere facts. "You really did take her back, right?"

Rose laughed. "She admitted to being an idiot, and I accepted her apology." Rose eyed Maji, who looked a little uncomfortable at being talked about. "So what does that make me?"

"Happy?" Bubbles suggested.

Rose slipped an arm around Maji's middle. "Yes. Really, truly happy. Thank you."

"Hey, I'll tell the brat she's an idiot anytime you need me to." There was a clatter in the background. "Gotta go. I'm back at work, and it's FUBAR as usual. Love you."

"Love you too," Rose said, just before Bubbles hung up on her. She handed the phone back to Maji. "She sounds so much better. Is it for real?"

The look on Maji's face was guarded. "She's been through worse. She'll be okay, but it would be great if you'd check in every couple days, if you can."

"Because you're going to be out of touch again?"

"No. Maybe? But either way, she needs you." Maji eyed Rose almost warily. "Did you ever get to meet Rey?"

Rose felt a flare of anger. "You know I did—and didn't know it." Bubbles's husband, an FBI agent, had managed never to be available for social occasions last summer, or even for Angelo's funeral. Later, when Bubbles emailed a photo of the two of them, Rose understood why. She had recognized Rey as the caterer for the big party at the Benedetti estate. Clearly he had been undercover, spying on her family. She sighed. "I'm sorry. Of course you couldn't tell me."

Maji gave her a sideways squeeze. "I'm glad you know now. You didn't tell Bubbles, did you?"

"No. I did not. Bubbles didn't mention it, so I assumed she doesn't know. Though she does talk about his work in general."

Maji nodded. "I hope they let him transfer soon. Undercover work is too hard on a family."

Rose sensed that they weren't talking about just their friends anymore. Well, she hadn't been up long enough to play the *What can I ask?* game with any patience. "I'm showering. Join me?"

That seemed to jolt Maji from the funk she was heading into. She hesitated, then grinned. "Do you have time?"

Rose felt a flare again, but not anger this time. "I do if you do. It's still early."

"Yeah." A flash of regret swept the grin away. "I was trying to let you sleep in."

"Well, sometime try waking me up instead. I think I'd like that."

"As you wish," Maji replied, stripping off her fleece top as she headed for the bathroom. Rose remembered their shower together the night before and quickened her step.

Chapter Ten

When they left the hotel, Maji realized she was about to hand Rose over to someone else's protection. She would trust Dev with her own life, and Rose had a valid point about the power dynamic, but still. She just plain didn't want Rose out of her sight.

"Did your orders come this morning?" Rose asked, clearly not having forgotten either.

Maji shook her head. "Not yet. Soon. And then…I might not get to say good-bye."

"Oh." Rose stopped abruptly and kissed her, right there as they stood. When she let Maji go, Rose stepped back. "Just in case," she said, looking slightly embarrassed.

"Just in case," Maji echoed, collecting her wits back up off the sidewalk.

Rose held out her hand, waited for Maji to take it, and started toward the conference center again. "How was your run? Tell me about it."

Maji was happy to accept the diversion from the myriad things she couldn't discuss. "This is a great town for running. I wanted woods, so I headed back to the totem trail."

"Lovely."

"Yeah. Every way you look it's gorgeous. I passed a McDonald's with the best view in the country, and stopped in at the grocery store with the best view in the country. Oh, and there's a trailer park here with—wait for it—"

"The best view in the country," Rose chimed in, laughing. "I was thinking the same thing yesterday about the conference center. No wonder the tourists flock here."

Maji thought of her stop at the Academy. She would absolutely tell Dev. Should she worry Rose? Well, she did have a right to know, to be part of her own protection. "Um, I also stopped in at the state police. I have bad news."

"Oh no—Heather's sister?" Rose stopped midstride and turned to her.

"Fine. Doing great, they said. But the guys who assaulted her are out on the street again."

"What? How could they?"

"Diplomatic immunity. Now, it doesn't necessarily have anything to do with you, and I don't want you to worry…"

Rose glared at her. "Do not patronize me. Spit it out."

"My money's on Sirko. He has the juice to send guys here with protection like that. And the cops can't touch them unless they actually see them in the act of trying to hurt someone. It's a fucked-up situation, but it is the law."

"That's terrible. But I don't even know Heather's sister. He can't want revenge on her too. It makes no sense at all to me. Does it to you?"

Odds are it will soon. For now, she could answer honestly. "Nope. Just my gut. Of course, Hannah's checking on who owns the holding company that sent Javi here to bug you. Maybe that will rule Sirko out." *For you, at least.* "I really hate to leave you now, besides just missing out on our chance at normal people time."

"I know." Rose walked on, rubbing Maji's hand. They crossed at the light, which now had a few cars to obey it. Rose stopped again. "What is it you think normal people do?"

Maji laughed in surprise. It was a serious question, but at least a happy one. Hang out without worrying about mobsters, wander the street on vacation without a gun. "Um, cook together and watch TV? Sleep late, laugh at the Sunday comics?"

"Oh. I'm sure we can manage that. But even if I have to keep up the non-normal hiding and fighting sorts of things, I find I don't mind them so much when you do them with me."

Maji struggled for words. "I don't know what to say."

"Then don't. What did you do after the police ruined your day?"

"Then I headed back most ricky-tick." She caught the slip into Army lingo. "Sorry. In a hurry. Anyway, the streets in Sitka aren't on a proper grid, but I've just about learned my way around. Got home by dead reckoning."

"Dead what?"

"Reckoning. It's a sailing term, means navigating by known landmarks."

"Ah. You forgot to bore me with sailing stories last night."

Rose clearly wanted to lift her spirits, so Maji played along. "Nah. I realized they were actually fascinating stories, but if I unraveled all my yarns at once you'd have nothing left to look forward to."

The conference center loomed just across the street. "Then it's a good thing you saved them for next time," Rose said.

Maji's spirits soared, knowing Rose had faith they would have a next time. "Yeah, I'm crafty that way."

"Crafty like a raven," Rose replied with a smile.

Inside, Maji left a message for Dev at the registration desk and tagged along to Rose's morning session. The first speaker had the curtains closed, eliminating the stunning view of mountains and water. Within minutes, Maji's head bobbed forward. "Just go ahead and lay your head down," Rose whispered.

"Poke me if I snore," Maji mumbled back at her.

An hour later the panel sessions changed over, and they milled about getting coffee and cookies in the lobby. Once again, no sign of Javier. Whatever his purpose here, it didn't appear related to his academic career. Maybe he'd gone. *Then Dev will get the vacation I came for.* Well, better that than confronting an actual threat to Rose. *Get over yourself, Rios.*

They settled into another meeting room, Maji feeling more alert and less grumpy. The speaker, a woman who identified herself as Tlingit, was quite entertaining. Her slides had lots of photos and her wit was dry, catching the audience off guard. Showing off a clever coloring book used to teach children the words for local sea creatures, she even got the academics to listen and repeat some of them after her.

The door at the back of the room creaked open, and Maji turned to see if Javier was finally showing up. Instead, there was her old teammate Dev, looking handsome as ever but also incongruously nerdy. She almost laughed at the sweater vest. The glasses were a nice touch too. And a diffident air replaced his normal self-confidence. He might be a regular-issue Reserve now, but she had to hand it to him—he could still inhabit a cover. Hannah had made a wise call, hiring him on. Maji scribbled a note and passed it to Rose. "My replacement is here now. You don't know him. He'll introduce himself to us."

Rose read the note, her brow wrinkling. Then she turned and spotted Dev, who saw them and raised a hand in greeting. At the change in speakers up at the podium, he slipped into the open seat next to Rose.

"Hello," she said, offering her hand. "I'm Rose."

He shook her hand enthusiastically, squinting at her name badge. "Yes, yes—Dr. diStephano! I so look forward to your talk tomorrow." Then he blushed, which looked totally wrong on Dev but just right on this adorable professor. "So sorry. Prabhu Dev, from Allahabad University."

"In India?" Maji asked, leaning across Rose to join the conversation. His accent strongly suggested the answer was *yes*, and his bronzed skin and shiny black hair supported the impression. Even in his cover role, it was hard to mask how pretty he was. His looks drew a little more attention than was prudent in most field assignments. But nobody was perfect.

"Yes, I am an Indian. Ha-ha. The kind Columbus thought he found. And now here I am, in your Indian Country, far from home."

The final presenter got his PowerPoint working properly, and twenty minutes later they worked their way out to the hall together. "It's so good to see you," Rose said sincerely. "How is your family?"

"Very well, thank you," Dev said with his consistent accent and a little head bob to go with it. He turned to Maji. "And for you, I have something to give," he said earnestly. "At registration. Under your name."

"Thank you, Dr. Dev," Maji replied. "Do you have everything you need for the conference?" Like a photo of Javier, for instance. And a heads-up about Tom and the not-pretend Sirko thugs. She handed him one set of the passport scans.

"Yes, yes. All set." He pocketed the papers and shook her hand a little too vigorously to be one of the cool kids. "Come back and see us if you can."

"Thanks. You can bet on it." To Rose she added, "I'll try to call, no matter what."

Rose looked like she wanted to say more or kiss her good-bye again. "Do what you can."

As promised, the women at registration had the expensive, high-tech, encrypted and satellite-enabled laptop under their folding table, out of sight beneath the white tablecloth. In its fuchsia neoprene carrying case, it looked anything but military issue. Maji thanked the staff for watching it and headed back to the hotel to find out just what her assignment might entail.

With the curtains drawn, she set up the connection and paced around the suite. If she didn't open the files and get her assignment, could she stay on vacation? No. Hannah would call, or worse, Colonel Wyatt. Besides, she needed to get her head in the game, not miss a chance to finally track down Sirko. He'd eluded JSOC and Interpol long enough. If he regained power, Angelo's sacrifice was wasted. If Sirko could run half the world's money laundering before, who would stop him now? He'd instigate more civil wars and terrorist campaigns, just for profit. And with enough resources again, Maji hated to think what action Sirko might take against Angelo's family.

The brief was mercifully spare: Conduct reconnaissance locally and coordinate with the two SEALs who would be taking point—Lieutenants Green and Kim. Coordinate with the Coast Guard to the extent needed to gain their cooperation. As usual, she could not say outright that she represented the Army's counterterrorism unit. Letting them think she was from counterintelligence gave her enough basis for sharing intel and taking action if needed. The SEALs would give her no problems. They were quiet professionals, like Delta operators, and had teamwork in their DNA. All they would need to be clear on was how to plug her in to help get the job done.

First operational step: Go out to the Coast Guard station on Japonski Island, a little ways past the airport, and meet up. They were due in before noon Alaska time, which gave her barely enough time to review the support files and get her ass out there. After that, she would act on her own discretion, doing recon as she saw fit. That was the beauty of being a Delta operator—JSOC set the mission objectives, but you got to decide how best to achieve them.

When Maji infiltrated a community in order to obtain intel or extract a high value target, her cover generally dictated how she dressed, what she ate, where she slept, and all the other little details of daily life. This time, she had to step back and decide what it meant to the mission that she'd come here on vacation, with a girlfriend. She'd already met a lot of people in this tiny fishbowl. They might naturally ask questions about the work she was doing or her girlfriend's reaction, or both. And if so, how would Sgt. Rios, CI Special Agent, keep her private life private? She was allowed to have one, after all. Sort of.

Delta operators, all male except for the seven females in her pilot, were encouraged to marry, to have families. But only with women who could handle the normal stress of life with a soldier, as well as the unpredictability of life with an operator. When Colonel Wyatt had learned that Maji was dating his daughter—another lifetime ago, it seemed—he'd nearly kicked Maji out of the program. It wasn't that Johnni couldn't keep a secret, for children raised in the tight circle of Delta operations learned early and well how to lie about what their fathers did for the Army. And Wyatt had come to terms with his daughter's sexuality as well as her disinclination toward military life. Which had made him certain there would be heartbreak for at least one woman. And a heartbroken operator was a liability.

Ultimately, Johnni had broken up with Ri without ever being formally told that she was an operator. Being involved with a soldier just couldn't work with her off-base life of art and freedom, she'd said. But Maji suspected the real reason was that Johnni had astutely put the pieces together. And Maji could never ask her if that was true. She never even told Johnni her real name, staying *Ri* throughout their tumultuous six months as a couple.

Maji shook off the past and opened the background briefing. She blinked at the news articles on the screen. Local coverage of Dee's co-captain Charlie Shakely's death, plus some conspiracy website's article on the Russian sub sightings. And several on telecom cable repairs in this area over the last few years. Nothing obvious linked the three together.

But the accompanying analyst's report seemed plausible. One, Sirko had the connections to the Ukrainian military to get ahold of a sub in exchange for something of value to them. Two, subs had been used all throughout the Cold War to tap those submerged marine cables. In fact, everyone in counterterrorism and the intelligence agencies knew this form of eavesdropping was still common. Maji would hate to be the English-speaking grunt who had to sift through all the data and communications for any tidbits relevant to national security. Maybe a computer did the initial legwork—Angelo would know. She shook that thought away. Three, the analyst noted, Charlie and Dee's fishing boat was found in an area that roughly overlapped where the local sub sighting was reported. However, why its crew would feel the need to go after and kill the fisherman, even if he had spotted them, was not discussed. Simply resubmerging and running off radar for a while would have been a more typical response if they'd seen him as a threat at all. Could his death have been an accident? The report didn't indicate whether the boat showed signs of a collision.

Maji pushed back from the table and stood, frustrated. All she knew now was what she had already figured out on her own. Well, maybe by the time the SEALs touched down there would be something more to go on. If Tom could find a way to get any intel to JSOC, that would save them so much time and guesswork. But if he needed to run silent to stay safe, she'd forgive him making them work the puzzle themselves.

Packing the laptop to travel, Maji found the interior pocket of the soft case and drew out its contents. Her badge looked impressive, and the card with her title and home office contact information equally real. If anyone called the number on her card, they would reach a live human being who answered with the right division name. Colonel Wyatt, or whoever was staffing the operations center on that shift, would take the call and behave in a way that would reinforce her cover.

Sometimes the game of pretend was as simple as when she'd been a kid, swapping names at school to confuse a substitute teacher. But sometimes it took an elaborate network to make sure her cover held. When she was dropped into a hostile country, literally falling out of the sky and hiking into a strange town on her own, that network played a life or death role. But here, working in partnership with other parts of the military and local LEOs? These were the times she wished she could just walk in, explain she was Delta, and get on with the work.

❖

Walking over the O'Connell Bridge from town to Japonski Island, Maji felt like she was walking away from Rose. Which was silly. Rose was so understanding, so sweet in the way she held out the promise of a future without demanding any details about how and when Maji would deliver it. Low expectations—the key to happiness. She looked across Sitka Sound to the snowcapped hills under a clear blue sky and envied whoever was driving the little motorboat that zipped toward the private island in the middle distance. That's where she should be, with Rose. Not walking away.

A taxi slowed down alongside her. Maji startled and realized just how caught up in her own thoughts she had been. Not good.

The window rolled down revealing a familiar face. The worried uncle from the airport. *Nate.* "Need a lift?"

"No, thanks," she answered. "Short walk, gorgeous day." Now that the clouds had lifted it virtually sparkled.

"Amen, sister." He pulled ahead of her with a friendly wave, disappearing over the bridge's arc.

Be here, now, Rios. She picked up her pace, feeling the sunshine again. Mind on her destination, eyes on her surroundings.

As she started to pass Sealing Cove Harbor, she spotted the taxi again. Nate leaned against the hood, arms crossed over his belly, looking relaxed. "Gorgeous day, ennit?"

"So I hear." She met his deadpan affability with the same. Clearly he had something on his mind. Pushing him wouldn't help, though. "Too nice to pick up tourists?"

Nate gestured toward the airport farther down the road. "They don't get far by foot. Except you," he said. "Collected any cool knives lately?"

"Not for days. How's Simon?"

He didn't ask how she knew his nephew's name. In a town this size, and with the Tribal members a tight community within the larger community, she'd have been stunned if he and Heather hadn't talked. "Back to school, doing okay. Put the right bait on the hook, I guess."

"I'm glad to hear it."

"Dee's out of the hospital too. Going to be fine, looks like."

Maji wondered if he knew yet that the men who put her in the hospital were back on the streets. She wasn't going to be the one to bring it up first. Let him speak his mind. "Heather said Dee just got the boat back, that it was half Charlie's. That make it half yours now?"

"Nope."

Maji looked at her watch. If he wasn't going to share what he'd stopped to talk about, she had SEALs to meet.

"I should let you go then," Nate said, looking awkward. "Give you a ride? Make up the time? On me, since I waylaid you."

She was curious, despite herself. "Sure."

"Where to?" he asked as soon as she'd closed the door and buckled up.

"Coast Guard station."

He pulled the car back on to the two-lane road with a *hmm* his only comment. They rode in silence past the airport. Overhead, a large orange and white helicopter with the iconic Coast Guard striping descended smoothly toward the airstrip beyond the commercial area.

"Ever been up in one of those?" Nate asked.

Maji decided Black Hawks didn't count, despite the similarities. "Nope. You?"

"Just once. Coasties pulled me and Charlie out of the Sound, up by Admiral."

"And you haven't wanted to go up, just for fun?"

Nate didn't answer. Didn't even shake his head, just slowed as the Air Station Sitka sign came into view. He put the cab in park twenty yards from the gatehouse. Maji glanced over her shoulder at the empty stretch of road behind them but didn't make a move to get out.

"Coasties went out the day Charlie died, you know." He said it casually, looking ahead at the station.

"Yeah?"

He turned in his seat to look at her, one hand draped on the steering wheel. "Yeah. Some Russian guys made a distress call. Couple hours before Dee sent them out after Charlie, and not too far either."

Not too far from where his body was found, she knew he meant. "You get a lot of Russians around here?"

Nate shook his head. "Not these days. Think they could be the same guys, then?"

"I really wouldn't know. I was just in the right place, right time to lend a hand."

"You're handy that way," he acknowledged. "Could be handy with the cops. Folks at the harbor said they listened to you."

Ah. "Only about how I do my job. Not about how they should do theirs."

He nodded silently. "Charlie didn't kill himself. And he wasn't careless. He cared about living, about his family."

"I'm sure you're right." Maji opened the door, wishing she had something more to offer. She hopped out and shut the door, then leaned on the edge of the open window. "If I find a way to help, I will."

He nodded again. "I know."

By the time Maji realized there was no sentry in the gatehouse and dialed the number provided next to the wall phone, Nate had executed a neat U-turn and headed back toward the airport.

Chapter Eleven

I brought you gifts," Dev said as they stood in the buffet line for lunch in the banquet hall. A large screen and podium in the front of the room waited for the keynote speaker.

Rose glanced uncertainly at him. "Really?"

"A lovely bracelet and an elegant pin. They will look just right with your outfit. Good colors for you, Professor." Dev's voice sounded so different with the Indian accent, softer with the inflections. "Let me show you."

"Here? Now?"

"Why wait?" He pulled both items, each in its own small gift box, from the pocket of his sweater vest. The line was slow, with each person helping themselves to a plate, cutlery, and the sandwich makings and salad. Why wait, indeed. Rose took the larger box and opened it. "Ooh! A shambhala bracelet. It is lovely." Woven leather strands linked the seven beads. "Are these the chakra colors?"

"Very good." Dev nodded and smiled graciously. It was unsettling, the difference in his manner. Like Maji when she laid on her Brooklyn accent and Latina city-girl clothes last summer, becoming Ri in looks and attitude. Dev raised his eyes and held her gaze. "To better track how you are doing, at any given time."

"Oh, how clever." At least it was more attractive than the tracking device she had worn last summer. "And the pin?"

"Ah, yes," he said, opening the other box. They shuffled forward, one person closer to lunch. "Quan Yin listens to the sorrows of the world, they say."

Rose let him pin the little carved figure up near her collar. Not the best placement for fashion, but she'd trust his judgment on where a listening device should go. "I assume you keep your ears open too. Anthropologists are professional listeners, in a way."

"Oh yes. No matter where we go, we are alike that way." He gave her a regretful look. "I do hope you'll excuse me if I don't sit with you just now. I am expecting a Skype call from my wife, and the time difference is so tricky."

Rose knew that was just an excuse, a way to create space so that Javi might approach her and speak freely. But the mention of his wife reminded her that Dev was in there, that he and his family on the East Coast were old friends of Maji. And Angelo. So she gave him a genuine smile. "Your wife! Of course you must. How is she? And your children?" She avoided using Mira's name, or calling out his two real daughters. Who knew how deep this playacting went for him?

They reached the buffet table, and Dev waved her ahead. "Kids are kids. My wife wants me home—the girls just want presents on my return."

Rose saw a harried-looking arrival burst through the door and scan until he spotted her. "Oh, look," she said. "My friend Javi."

To her surprise, Dev turned abruptly and waved at him. Javi headed for them, ignoring the line to their rear.

"You must be Javier," Dev said, handing him a plate. Rose heard a murmur of disapproval behind her, but no outright objections. "Dr. Dev, from Allahabad. Dr. diStephano speaks highly of you."

Javi looked momentarily startled, then gave Rose a grateful look. "Someone is too kind. Great sessions this morning, no?"

"I learned something from both," Rose answered. "How was the botany track?"

"Don't know. I overslept," he admitted. "Think I must be fighting off a bug." He dropped sliced meat and cheese on to his plate distractedly and added a pile of lettuce on top. "But who could stand to miss this?"

Rose laughed. "I guess we can't have traditional foods every day. Unless this counts as the traditional food of American academic conferences."

"Ah, there is my Rosita. Friends?"

"Of course, Javi. Let's sit and catch up." *And you can tell me why you're really here.*

Dev vanished into the crowd. Rose suspected he'd find a spot where he could listen in and also see the two of them. That Javi could pose a threat to her still seemed implausible, almost offensive. But she had learned to respect the caution of her protectors—no, her friends. Last summer, Dev had acted with Tom as Aunt Jackie's bodyguard, putting up with inexcusable rudeness from her family without a word of complaint. And he'd used his field medic skills to help Maji, when he wasn't giving her grief like a real brother. Maybe that, and not his almost comical charade, was what felt odd. She wanted to embrace him like an old friend but had to treat him like a foreign colleague. This business of maintaining a cover would never feel right, even if she only had to play the role of herself.

Javi pulled out a chair for her and she took it, giving him a mocking look. "I thought chivalry was unfeminist."

"My head knows that." He took the seat next to her. "But my family training says to make gestures to show contrition. I was insincere with you and I am sorry, Rose."

"Where did all that romance nonsense come from, Javi? And please don't insult me with it again. We both know better."

Javier's face went through a series of contortions, speaking in place of words. "It's so awkward. They coached me to soften you up, insisted I try even though it made no sense. And then of course you were mad at me. Not that it couldn't have been true. You, me…"

The appeasing body language and cajoling face left Rose flat. "*They* who?"

Javi straightened up at Rose's decisive tone, the one she used in the field on the rare occasion when she needed to remind him who was in charge of her fieldwork. "The producers of *Mobbed Up*. You know, that stupid TV show?"

"No, I don't follow much TV." But she could guess. "Are they the ones that want my cousin Sienna and aunt Paola for a new reality show about Mafia wives or whatever?"

He nodded. "They really want you. To class it up, they said. They already blew it with your other *tía*, the realtor. And your *abuela*..."

Rose had to laugh at the face he made. Nonna's version of their attempt to woo her to television celebrity no doubt downplayed how caustic she could be with people she didn't like. Nonna did not suffer fools—she made sure they suffered. "Oh God, Javi, my family is a living telenovela." She sombered. "But you couldn't really think I would want anything to do with reality TV? It's dreadful."

"I know, I know. I told them. But Rosita"—he paused, blushing—"I needed the money. They offered to fly me up and pay me by the day to hang out with you. And persuade you to see the glorious opportunity to be one of those people who is famous for nothing. They pay me even if you say no, as of course you will. Just please, don't rush."

"Oh, I see. The longer you stay, the more you earn?"

Javi nodded. "My student loans are killing me. This could really help." He smiled, his usual enthusiasm for travel breaking through. "Sitka is very nice too. I rode the bus all over yesterday, for only five dollars. Such a beautiful land. So different, eh?"

Yes, it was different from the Andes, in so many ways. Rose nodded. "It's a temperate rain forest, you know. Hard to believe, so far north. Did you go on the tour yesterday?"

And with that, they were off into shared territory like old friends. Rose might not trust him again as a colleague in remote villages, but here they could at least talk. She barely noticed the boring lunch disappear between stories.

When Jack collected Maji from the entry point, handing her visitor badge over like he was delighted to see her, she wasn't too surprised. Someone at his level would serve as liaison to other branches of the military. He was probably the official link to the state and local police, as well. She wondered how much he knew about yesterday's incident at the harbor.

They strode briskly toward the air station offices, his steps long and hers quick to keep up. "How long have you been stationed here, Lieutenant Commander?"

"Jack. Except in front of the crew—you know." He slowed a fraction. "Going on seven years. Took a two year rotation and fell in love. You know."

She didn't. "Sure. And before that?"

"Air Force. Always been a helo jockey, from the Osprey and Pave Low to the Pave Hawk. Flew my share of combat support, including some search and rescue. Wasn't until Katrina I got to see what saving civilians was like. You want to do that full-time, Coast Guard's your home. And it's been a damn good one."

That explained a bit—his easy self-confidence, secure in his boyish good looks and the charisma of authority. Today he wore a flight suit, rather than a Coast Guard uniform suitable for giving tours and doing paperwork. Too much of that probably came with his fill-in commander role for his liking. "Did you go up today?"

Jack turned his head to grace her with a conspiratorial smile. "I was hoping to log some hours. But then I got word of your visit—no offense—and a couple of squids coming in too. No offense to the Navy. I've seen SEALs work up close, and I wouldn't cross them."

"So you're a flyboy with nothing against squids. Noted." She wondered how far to push. "You don't think Army Intelligence is an oxymoron, do you?"

He chuckled. "Not when it's counterintel. Seriously, though, I got nothing against anybody who's here to work as a team. And you impressed our local LEOs yesterday."

"So you coordinate with the local LEOs some?"

"Sure."

"Excellent. You know anything about two guys they arrested at the harbor?" *Like what they were up to the day they Maydayed.* "Or about the woman they were after?"

Jack stopped at the door to the lunchroom, which was labeled in true nautical fashion *The Galley*, and held the door for her. Maji sensed his manners were both automatic and a chance to gather his thoughts. Interesting. "That why we're blessed with visitors today?"

Fishing. "I'll have to defer the briefing to the Navy. Just thought you might have some insight, being dialed in here."

"Well, my opinion's free and comes with a money back guarantee." When she only gave him a weak smile for that, he redirected her to the self-serve food area. "Grab whatever you like, and I'll tell you a story."

They sat in a corner, away from the few tables full of Coasties in their working blues. Hungrier than she realized, Maji tucked in. Jack smiled at her. "Air stations draw the best food service specialists."

"Really?'

"Sure. They get to work above deck, as it were, with a view and solid ground. And they get to sleep at home with their families every night. The cooks we get rock big-time. How's the pulled pork?"

"It rocks. Big-time." Maji pulled on the iced tea in her cup, sucking down half through the straw. "Tell me that story, Jack."

"Oh, right." His amiability never faltered. Maybe he hadn't been trying to distract her. "Well, the woman is Deanne Davis, co-owner of a fishing boat there at ANB Harbor. Native gal, troubled, I guess you could say."

Maji held her peace while he paused to down a bite of food.

"She and her co-captain are both ex-addicts. Were, in Charlie's case. Everybody thought he was doing well until a couple weeks back when he died. A real waste. Decent guy, good crew boss, but well—you know. Demons caught up to him, I guess."

A convenient guess. "How so?"

"Well, he went out alone for herring eggs. That's not unusual, gathering subsistence from your own private area. You know any mushroom hunters?"

She shook her head and kept chewing.

"Well, they're notoriously secretive about where they find sought-after mushrooms. Anyway, herring eggs and Natives can be like that. Everybody has their favorite spots, and they only pass the secrets down through their families."

"So he was out alone."

"And had an accident. State troopers thought maybe suicide, given how high the rates are here, among Native folks and addicts especially. But his family doesn't buy that, and I'm with them. He was on a good path, as they say."

"What about the co-captain? Deanne."

Jack shook his head, looking regretful. "Might have been too big a blow for her. Time off work is dangerous for people trying to stay clean, and she was really tight with Charlie. Like a sister and brother."

"Not a couple, then?"

Jack smiled, then packed it away. "He wasn't her type, if you get my meaning. Part of her troubles, frankly." He registered her raised brow. "Oh, not like that. She could be a rainbow unicorn and I'd say right on, sister. But this is a small town, and even smaller if you're Native. Last woman she got involved with dumped her hard, with big public drama. So I figure you mix grief and a little shame, plus a baseline of lonely, and maybe she made some bad choices with the help of those two Russian guys."

"Russians, huh?"

"What? Oh, yeah. We get the ones with money here sometimes. Sport fishing and being a general pain in the ass. Police had to let them go, you know. Some diplomatic immunity bullshit."

"Fuck. So they're just back out on the street?"

"Yep. That's why I got a call, and a fax with photos, like an APB. Any of my crew sees them, we let the LEOs know. Can't have those jackasses assaulting our women, no matter whose protection they may have."

Maji slurped the rest of her tea, waiting to see if Jack volunteered any more information. She assumed he knew they were from the boat rescued by his crew, if not him.

"You should try the pie," he said instead. "If you still have room."

She had cleaned her plate of the substantial lunch. "I always have room for pie. Do we have time?"

"There's always time for pie," he quipped back. Looking at his watch, he added, "And a quick tour, if we hustle. Get your coffee to go."

She did, and they made quick work of their pie. Between bites, Maji said, "I heard you rescued some Russian sport fishers recently."

"Oh, yeah, we had a call a couple weeks back. Saved the crew, all four."

"Were these two jackasses," she asked, using his word, "from that crew?"

He looked pensive. "Dunno. I'd have to check the log. Good question."

She wondered if he knew the answer already. She stood. "Let's hit that tour."

As they headed outside toward the aircraft hangars, Maji sucked in a lungful of clean, cool air. "I can see why you'd want to stay here." She supposed it wasn't the Coast Guard station with the best view in the world, but it must be up there.

He chuckled. "It grows on you fast, Ariela."

"Jack." Maji stopped walking and waited for him to turn and come back to her. "I will answer to Rios, Ri, or Sergeant. Clear?"

He looked torn between chagrin and amusement. "Aye, aye, Sarge. I'm that way about Fitz, myself."

"Aye, aye, Lieutenant Commander."

The hangar where they housed and maintained the aircraft looked like a large, clean, and well-lit warehouse inside. Outside, just like a warehouse. From the threshold of the twenty-foot roll-up door, Jack proudly pointed out the perpetual safety checks and maintenance being conducted on the high-tech flying machines. "We may only have three Jayhawks, but they are all the latest models. And for every hour of flight time, they get four back here."

He strode over to the closest one, which had a mechanic working inside it. "Our avionics techs do double duty as flight crew, so they make sure every bird is a hundred and ten percent ready for liftoff. Isn't that right, AET Taira?"

"Aye, aye, Lieutenant Commander," came the voice of the woman Maji could now see was elbow-deep in a tangle of cables pulled up through an opening in the floor inside the helicopter.

"Can our guest peek inside without getting in your way?" Jack asked.

"Back here's off limits, sir. She's welcome to the cockpit."

Jack gestured to the door nearest them. "Climb in."

Maji swung the door wide and clambered up into the seat on the right side of the cockpit. She took care not to knock the stick or move any other steering tools, in case they were connected to AET Taira's work. The console between them, full of knobs and switches that made her consciously keep her hands and elbows tucked in, made her nervous too. And then there was the bewildering set of digital screens on the dash. How could the pilots keep up with it all? "Never been up front before," she admitted to Jack when he slid into the seat on her left.

"And now you're pilot. Best yet, you've got me for your copilot."

She gave him a look. "I thought God was my copilot. Or is that *dog*?"

A chuckle from the back deflected whatever comeback Jack was working up. "Okay, AET Taira, tell us what's special about this model helo."

"The Coast Guard upgrades the standard JH-60 model Sikorsky so it can fly three hundred miles out, remain on scene for search and rescue up to forty-five minutes, and fly back three hundred miles, all on one tank of fuel," she recited without looking up from her task.

Maji thought the delicate tangle in her latex-clad hands looked too sensitive to risk distractions, so she turned to Jack for follow-up. "Impressive. With what sort of payload, sir?"

"Outgoing crew of four: pilot, copilot, flight mechanic, and the rescue swimmer. Coming back in, up to six more adult-size people." He paused. "AET Taira's one of my best flight mechs. Best on avionics too. Puts in more hours than any other crew member here, and we've got over a hundred. That's why they call her OT, right, Liv?"

"No, Fitz. Lazy people just call me by my initials." She looked up from her work and met Maji's gaze, giving no indication that she recognized her from their run-in on the dock. "Olivia Taira. And you are?"

"Sorry," Jack jumped in. "Sergeant Rios, Army. Gonna have a couple Navy visitors shortly too."

"What'd we do this time?"

"They'll have to tell me before I can tell you," he replied. Maji was impressed with how much they treated each other as peers, despite the considerable gap in rank.

AET Taira smiled faintly. "Bet you'll be glad when the brass gets back. We'll keep a helo on standby for you." With that, she went back to her task.

Jack glanced at his watch and looked surprised. "Time to go."

Maji caught something muttered from the diligent crewmember as she climbed out. Sounded like *sense of urgency*. Well, hers was motivated by wanting out of that snug cockpit. And then by jogging after Jack, who was already crossing back through the open door into the sunshine.

Jack detoured them toward another building on their way to the airstrip. "Gimme your cup."

She handed her empty coffee cup to him and stood aside while he popped in through the door, then back out empty-handed. "Hey," she said. "Restroom?"

He held the door for her. "Far side. Make it quick."

"Nice gym," she said on her return. "Now do we have to double-time?"

"Yep." He set a relaxed pace, however, which Maji's full belly thanked him for. "We have a hell of a CrossFit team here. Sent a crew to regionals in Portland last fall."

Maji had noticed the corkboard with announcements, including the Workout of the Day. "The WOD's not one of my favorites. I'd rather do burpees than power cleans."

"Said nobody ever!" Jack laughed, then looked at her sideways. "Really? Well, you can always scale them."

"Nah, I'd just pick a different WOD. Or make up my own. Actually, I could use a workout. Too many rest days lately."

He nodded and slowed to a walk, looking relieved that the little plane on the horizon had not yet landed. "You find any downtime while you're here, be my guest. There's towels and PT clothes in the locker rooms."

"Thanks. Open twenty-four seven?"

He gave her a broad smile. "Just like the rest of this place. Semper paratus." Always ready—the Coast Guard motto.

Maji looked forward to the SEALs deplaning and filling her in on just what she needed to be ready for.

CHAPTER TWELVE

The first SEAL off the little plane would blend in fine in Sitka, once he stowed away the two large bags he carried over his shoulders. He looked Asian, like a lot of the fishing boat crew in town. Lt. James Kim, she guessed. Kim was dressed in outdoorsy civilian clothes, with a little shaggy mustache and close-cropped black hair. SEALs, like all Special Operations personnel, came in a variety of sizes and styles, the better to blend in. So chances were he was her liaison for the covert side of this op.

The guy behind him, on the other hand, wouldn't easily blend in anywhere. Lt. Kris Green was a tall, lanky Billy Idol wannabe in blue camo and shades. That spiky blond hair would stand out anywhere and be hard to forget in a town this size. Maji waited to get a better look at him, and when the lead guy started down the steps she did a double take. *Holy crap.* Kris—probably short for Kristina—shouldered the same amount of gear as her partner, with equal ease, and scanned the area with confidence before starting down the short set of steps. Suddenly the uniform made sense—if she was here under cover of being Navy Intel. The Navy, like the Army, had yet to publicly acknowledge their pilot use of female operators. *Way to hide in plain sight, Amazon.*

Not completely hiding her smile, Maji caught the woman's eye and gave her a small nod. The woman removed her sunglasses and let her eyes scan first Maji and then Jack, returning finally to Maji. Her mouth turned up as she nodded back.

Jack stepped forward to greet the pair. "Lieutenant Commander Fitzsimmons," he announced with a smile, offering his hand first to the man. "Welcome to Sitka, Lieutenant Kim." After a quick shake, he extended his hand to Green. "And you must be the analyst."

Green gave him a perfunctory shake. "Must be." She looked at Maji. "And you're Rios. An honor, ma'am."

"Lieutenants Green and Kim," Maji replied, trying not to look unsettled. "My orders are to assist you. Shall we go discuss how?"

"I've got two empty commanders' offices for you," Jack said, not appearing to have absorbed the *honor* comment at all. "Coffee, on the way?"

The SEALs passed on the offer and followed Jack into an ordinary looking office building. They all trotted up the stairs, pausing at the top to take in the hallway lined with framed photos and awards. Maji wondered if it was as weird for her two counterparts as it was for her, to see so much recognition out in the open. Not that the Coasties didn't deserve it. But when a special ops team pulled off a mission, zero fanfare was considered a sign of success.

"Need anything while you're here? Sweatshirt, hat, souvenir?" Jack asked, pointing toward the gift shop as they strode by it. When they reached the borrowed office and Lt. Kim dismissed him, Jack took the dismissal in stride. "I'll be two doors down, buried in paperwork. Holler if you need anything. I mean it—anything."

The surprises continued as the two SEALs dropped their gear on the office floor, pulled out handheld RF detectors, and started sweeping the room for bugs. They divided the work efficiently and with a minimum of words.

"Is that SOP?" Maji asked.

Lt. Kim shook his head. "We'll bring you up to speed shortly."

Two minutes later they conferred silently, and Lt. Green gave a nod. "Room's clean. Sorry about earlier," she added. "I assumed everyone knows who you are. Hope I didn't jam you up."

Maji laid her laptop on the large office's round tabletop. "No harm, no foul. Nothing Jack couldn't learn by Googling my name. Current news never mentions me, so he probably doesn't remember."

"Well, we never forget our own." Lt. Kim's statement sounded casual, the way any guy on her team would have stated something deeply felt. Her brothers in arms were funny that way. "And if we get a shot at Sirko, I'm psyched to have you on our team."

And it was nice to have a team. Even if she barely knew them. SEALs, unlike the assets she'd been given for support on her last few missions, were 100 percent reliable. Delta and SEALs had different strengths and training, but they saw each other as two branches of the same outfit. "Likewise. Bring me up to speed."

"Our working assumption is Sirko," Green started, sounding like an analyst. "Cryptology and HUMINT both point to him."

Maji wondered if their human intelligence source was Tom. And if they knew him as his Dmitry persona or by his real identity. For now, she just nodded.

"Sirko had an admiral in the Northern Fleet in his pocket before the crash," Kim chimed in. "The comm we've been able to intercept suggests the same admiral is sheltering Sirko now. And providing a Navy sub."

"The kind they use for tapping the underwater telecomm cables?" Maji asked. "Isn't this a little far south?" The Bering Sea would be a lot safer for that type of task.

"Yes indeed. But we don't think data is the target." Green paused, running a hand through her platinum flattop. "Now, this part is theory. Historical accounts tell us that when the Americans ran the first cables from Sitka to Seattle, they used lead sinkers—standard practice."

"In the 1980s," Kim continued, "a new cable was laid along the same route to provide better capacity, as the old one started to deteriorate. This time around, a contractor we now know had connections to Sirko did the work. And we think some of those weights were *gold*, not lead."

Maji nearly laughed. "Seriously? An underwater savings account? There are easier places to hide money."

"Yeah, but not as secure," Green rebutted. "Sirko's really big on that. Probably why Khodorov's dead and he's not."

Good point. Maji had long thought Sirko more dangerous, because he ran his operation less like a business and more like a covert ops unit. She wondered if they knew he'd used a surveillance drone on her team last summer. And a sub in broad daylight in Long Island Sound. Again she just nodded. "So what does it take to fish a bunch of gold weights out of Sitka Sound?"

"Well, you could snag the cable and pull it up, like they do now and then when there's a repair to be made. But you'd need a cable ship, and a whole lot of looking the other way from local authorities."

"Because?"

"Usually, if they pull cable up off the ocean floor, it's just to make a line repair above the water level and drop it back down. That wouldn't get you very many of those weights back. Plus all the attention you'd draw."

Maji nodded again. "They're small and dispersed, then. So you need a way to collect them while staying out of sight. But naval subs run nearly blind, and it's not like they have arms to grab with even if they could do the spotting."

"Correct. But they can deploy a single-person sub with capacity to metal detect and to grab small objects," Kim said.

"Okay, so you spit a few bots out of the big sub, and they pick up these gold weights. Can they carry them?"

"Not really," Lt. Green admitted. "The sub could certainly drive a mother lode back home to Russia. But the bots, as you call them, couldn't really load the weights onto it even if the sub stayed stationary long enough. Mostly likely they deployed one or two minisubs to mark the cable and then brought them back aboard before getting the hell back out of American waters."

"So you can't hang around in a big-ass military sub or an easily recognizable cable boat. How about a nice, nondescript fishing trawler right around the tail end of a crazy commercial season? Would that work?"

Lt. Kim did not smile. "I'm glad you work for our side. Yes, it would. And to save you the next question, we have the trawler that we think they used." He paused. "It's up on a cradle at a boatyard out Sawmill Creek Road, but it's been stripped. So we may be too late."

"Then why are they still in town?" Maji wondered aloud. "Something must have gone wrong." *Maybe something Tom orchestrated, even.* "You know about the Mayday? Coast Guard to the rescue. And then two of the same crew tried to kidnap a local fishing boat captain yesterday, got arrested, and got released by invoking diplomatic immunity."

Lt. Green frowned. "Hadn't heard that last bit yet. Makes sense, though. Same Navy contacts to loan Sirko a sub would also be networked into the top of the government."

"There is a little good news." Maji pulled the scans of Oleg, Ruslan, and Dmitry/Tom up on her laptop screen and turned it so they could see. "These two are bona fide mercs. But the third"—she enlarged Tom's passport photo—"is one of ours. Call sign *Thumb*."

"That would have been nice to know yesterday," Lt. Green said, her voice flat.

"Agreed. But it was a surprise to my command too, when I told them this morning." Maji paused. She didn't want to insult them, but most SEALs didn't work covert at the same level as Delta. "Thumb's silence is strategic. It indicates he doesn't believe Sirko trusts him enough not to monitor his communications. Given Sirko's penchant for spycraft, I'd run off radar too. Especially if I'd just ruined my assignment to get the gold, and wrecked the trawler in the process. The grab attempt at ANB Harbor suggests a little panic. And Thumb springing those jackasses from jail shows Sirko has at least let him live to clean up the mess."

"So you won't try and make contact?" Green asked.

Maji shook her head. "Thumb already put himself on our radar by bailing those two out and using a passport to do it. If and when he can risk sharing intel, he'll come to us."

"Rescue report said there were four crew on the Russian trawler. Now we can identify three of them. What odds would you lay that Sirko is number four?" Kim asked.

Lt. Green gave him an incredulous look, but held her tongue. Maji guessed he was the one on the team who ran every possible hypothetical. And it must be worth putting up with some patently ridiculous ideas. Like that one.

"Exactly zero to none. Sirko is holed up someplace safe, running this op by remote control. Thumb probably hasn't even been allowed to meet him in person yet. Like Green said, there's a reason Sirko is the last man standing."

"Probably so," Kim agreed. "Still wish we had a way to signal your guy that he's got support in town now."

"Oh, I bet he knows. Since I apprehended his two guys, my name's in the police report."

Lt. Green set her coffee mug down with an audible thump on the tabletop. "You what?"

"Shouldn't have assumed what your brief included. Sorry." Maji thought about where to start and what to include. "I came to Sitka on leave, arrived Tuesday. Minutes off the plane, I met a taxi driver whose brother got killed a few weeks ago. The brother's body was found close to where Sirko's crew were when they called the Mayday in. Cops aren't looking into it, but my gut says the fisherman got too close and saw too much." Maji paused and sipped her now-cool coffee. "The dead fisherman's boat had just been released from evidence when the mercs tried to grab the co-owner."

Kim listened in silence, arms folded over his chest. Green leaned forward. "Where's that guy now? Have you talked to him?"

Maji shook her head. "He's a woman, Captain Deanne Davis. Locals say she got out of the hospital this morning, doing okay."

"Is she secured?" Kim asked, reaching for his phone.

"Don't know. State and local police have eyes on the street for the mercs, might be keeping an eye on her too. Oh, and they asked Jack to share the photos with his crew, alert them of any sightings."

"Shit." Kim frowned and dialed. "You off the ferry yet? Good, stand by for directions." He looked to Maji. "Know where she lives?"

Maji shook her head. "No, but her boat's at ANB Harbor, just across the strait near the base of the bridge. Relay that and I'll get you options." She pulled Nate's business card out of her pocket and dialed him.

He answered on the second ring. "Nate's Taxi. Always on time, never rushed."

"Hey, it's Ri," she said. "Do you know where I can find Dee?"

"On her boat, most likely. The *Eagle Song*. What's up?"

"The police let those two guys out. I'm sending a couple friends to check on her."

"Holy mother. For real?" At her silence, Nate added, "I'm going to check her house."

Maji jotted down the address and promised to call with an update as soon as her friends checked the harbor.

"Hey, Ri?" He paused. "They find her and she's okay, tell them not to freak her out, okay? Maybe keep a little distance?"

"Understood. Just a normal day, unless it can't be."

They hung up and Maji filled the two SEALs in. Kim gave orders to two team leaders to check the home and boat, staying off Dee's radar unless called into action. When he hung up he gave her a faint smile. "The rest of our platoon is driving off the Alaska Marine Highway as we speak."

"You have fourteen SEALs arriving on one ferry?" Maji tried to keep the concern from her tone, but it registered on Lt. Green's face.

"Yes, Sergeant. Driving big rigs with US Navy stenciled on the side," she said.

"Kris."

Green flicked a glance at Lt. Kim. "Sorry. Three fire teams, driving two Jeeps and a Subaru. Gear is hidden, and they look like eco-tourists, complete with kayaks and mountain bikes. Feel better?"

"You have my complete confidence, Lieutenants." Maji hoped they were going resource-heavy just to be on the safe side, and not because they expected this mission to require that much muscle.

Lt. Green gave a look that suggested she could read Maji's thoughts. "Pays to be a winner."

"And the only easy day was yesterday, right?" Maji replied with another patented SEAL saying. She couldn't resist the small poke—it was a sibling impulse.

"Yesterday you didn't have a team," Green replied. "Today we'll crush it."

"Speaking of yesterday…" Maji paused, loathe to admit what came next. "I told the LEOs on scene that I was Diplomatic Security. Spur-of-the-moment cover."

Lt. Green raised one platinum-blond brow. "Why?"

"I came to town for Rose diStephano. She's here for a conference. I handed her protection off today." If they assumed she was freelancing on her time off, so be it.

"Who's she?" Lt. Kim asked.

"Benedetti's cousin," Lt. Green replied, then looked to Maji. "Right, Sergeant Rios?"

Maji nodded. "Ri." She had a feeling Green had a whole database of names and faces in her brain, like a true analyst. Probably knew all the members of Angelo's team by name and call sign. Including Dev. "And Dev Goldberg, also from Team Benedetti and now with Paragon Security, took the protection detail. Rose has a shadow up here, an old friend acting squirrelly. No clear link to Sirko confirmed, but my gut says Code Red."

"Lots of dots, not enough connections," Lt. Kim said. Maji got the sense he enjoyed a puzzle. "Thanks for the heads-up."

Lt. Green fixed Maji with a look, as if sizing up either her capacity or her willingness to do what she was about to ask. "We need to do some setup here. As you've probably guessed, we think someone who works at the air station is working for Sirko."

"Intentionally, unwittingly, or under duress?"

Green raised an eyebrow. "We'll work on narrowing down the candidates now we have access to the station's logs and duty rosters. Could be a while until we're ready to flush out our quarry, but I'd like you here when we map out the plan. Think you could run down that boat captain, get some intel, and reconvene tonight?"

"Happy to." She exchanged cell numbers with Green and Kim. "You don't have a tracker for me, do you? In case."

Lt. Kim looked surprised. "Sure. We brought a bunch." He exchanged a look with Lt. Green, who gave him a bare hint of a nod.

While Kim dug the trackers out of his gear bag, Maji found a hard copy of the scans of Ruslan, Oleg, and Dmitry's passports and ran off a few copies. She handed them to Green, who put a set each into three envelopes.

"Leave these with the ANB harbormaster," Green instructed. That fire teams A, B, and C would pick them up went unsaid.

As Maji attached transponders to her pants and watch, a knock sounded on the closed door. On Green's and Kim's nods, she opened it. "Hey, Jack. You have a spare vehicle here?"

"Um, my Jeep's a short walk, about a mile to Coastie housing." Seeing her surprise he added, "Service vehicles are all out right now. Hang on." He dialed his cell phone. "Hey. You go to town yet? Great. Meet Rios out front in two."

"Thanks," Maji said, brushing past him. "What am I looking for?"

"AET Taira in a white pickup with the signature stripe. Don't let her driving scare you. She *can* see over the wheel."

❖

Out front, Maji saw what he meant. AET Taira was standing next to the driver's door, talking to a woman who seemed to be making her blush. The flirty woman wasn't more than five eight, but Taira had to tilt her head to look up at her. Maji put her at five one.

"Hey," Maji said to the two. Then to Taira, "Hope I'm not inconveniencing you."

"Not if you introduce her to Billy Idol," the taller woman said with a grin. Maji assumed she meant Lt. Green.

"Abby…" There was real warning in Taira's voice.

"I think she's in the no-go zone," Maji replied. By now Jack would have issued some sort of standard notice that the station had visitors on classified business. More would not be said, and station staff would be expected to not ask.

"Just your type, OT," Abby persisted. "Completely unavailable."

Maji's frayed patience snapped. "We need to get going. Now." She climbed in as AET Taira and her friend exchanged a hasty good-bye.

"Sorry," Taira said with a hint of chagrin and a rev of the powerful engine. She pulled smoothly onto the drive and glanced over at Maji. "I really need to make a quick stop. For Jack, um, the Lieutenant Commander."

"Seriously?"

Taira exhaled. "Ten minutes max. His dog just flew in, and I said I'd drop him home."

"Jasper can ride with us to town. Drop him home after."

"Really?" Taira looked surprised but pleased. "He'd like that."

At the airport, they left the pickup at the curb and headed straight for the baggage carousel. Nearby, the taxidermied bears in glass display cases still looked ready to devour tourists. As did the woman holding Jasper by his leash. *Tina.*

"Oh, shit," Maji heard the Coastie by her side say softly.

"Hey, Tina," Maji said warmly, moving ahead to reach the woman and dog first. She knelt and put a hand out to Jasper, who sniffed her in a friendly way but stayed seated. "Aren't you a good boy?" She looked up toward Tina. "You really trained him well."

Tina looked ready to cry, her anger transformed. "I suppose I should be glad he sent you." She spoke over Maji's head.

"He'll be happier here," Taira responded, ignoring the reference to Jack while nodding toward the dog. Jasper's tail wagged while his eyes were fixed on her, Maji forgotten.

Maji got up and stepped back, making room for the reunion. As soon as she did, Jasper surged forward.

"Ah!" Taira said, raising one hand in a signal to halt. Jasper froze and sat again. "Good boy," she said, unfolding one palm to reveal a treat. With a series of hand commands only, she led him through a paw shake, a lie down, and a roll over before he sat and received the treat on top of his nose. With a small flick and snap, it was gone.

Taira ruffled his ears and accepted the leash. "Good consistency," she said to Tina. Maji almost expected to see her pull out a people treat.

"Just go," Tina said.

Taira nodded and pivoted away, the dog heeling smartly by her flank.

"I'll be right out," Maji called to her retreating back. She turned to Tina, who looked ready to crumble, and took a step toward her.

Tina waved her away, stepping back and sinking down onto the edge of the empty carousel. Maji sat near but not touching her as Tina pulled out a tissue and blew her nose. "Fuck." She sniffed. "No, I'm not okay. So don't ask. What are you doing here anyway?"

"Took a tour of the air station. Hitched a ride back, and it came with a detour."

Tina sat straighter, pulling herself together. "Lucky you. Well, I have another flight. Enjoy your stay."

Maji stood and Tina rose as well, smoothing her skirt down. "Safe travels," Maji said.

"You too," Tina replied, blinking as she tried but failed to smile.

Chapter Thirteen

"Y ou train dogs, huh?" Maji asked as they pulled away from the airport.

AET Taira nodded. "Where to?"

"ANB Harbor."

"Really? Is Dee back?"

Cognizant that the entire air station crew was under suspicion at the moment, and that Taira hadn't clued her boss to the fact that she and Maji had met earlier while both looking for Dee, Maji weighed her words. "I don't know yet. Why?"

"She's a friend. That's why."

"So call her up and check in," Maji suggested.

Taira flushed. "Okay, we're more like acquaintances. But I still care about her." She hesitated. "She's in some kind of trouble, right?"

"Not with me. I'd like to protect her. And I'm really short on good information." When Taira took that at face value, Maji asked, "What can you tell me about her?"

"Um, a little, I guess. I see her sometimes at local events. And I try to stop by, the days she sells fish off the back of her boat." Taira paused. "She seems pretty shy."

Troubled, Maji recalled Jack saying. "Has her behavior changed since Charlie's death?"

"I don't know. She's always been quiet. She did dance at the memorial, which was different. I didn't know she could. She's not in the Naa Kahidi Dancers, that's for sure."

"No fights you know of?"

"What? No. Not since she dumped Tina, and that was like a year ago. And I would have pushed her off the dock too. If I was Dee."

Tina? Jack left that detail out. What else had he edited in his ex's defense? "Really. Why?"

"Tina dated Dee for months and conveniently forgot to tell her she was married. I don't care if you're separated, or finding yourself, or whatever. You don't do that."

"Did Jack know?" Could be motivation for colluding with out-of-town thugs. A stretch, certainly. But she'd mention it to Lt. Kim, the idea man.

"Uh, you know, you'd have to ask him. We're close—but not that close."

"Fair enough. Did Dee seem to be over the drama, doing okay before Charlie died?"

"I guess. She took her mom to bingo at the ANB hall every week, and stayed sober. But she's always hard to read."

Maji took a leap as the harbor came into sight. "That why you haven't asked her out?"

"Jesus, you sound like Abby now," Taira complained, flushing. She pulled into a spot by the harbormaster's office.

Maji didn't wait for her to cut the engine. "Thanks for the lift," she said and slid out.

After stopping in the office to drop the envelopes off and get direction to the *Eagle Song*'s slip, Maji headed for the docks. She scanned the parking lot for a gaggle of buff guys with an SUV and kayaks trying to blend in. But if the SEALs had arrived, they had taken overwatch farther away. Then Maji spotted Taira at the bottom of the ramp, heading for Dee's boat. *Damn it.* She jogged down the ramp carefully, mindful not to catch her toes on the nonskid strips. As she approached Dee's dock, Maji recognized her boat as a troller, from the tall poles on either side of the cabin, now pointing to the sky. There were similar fishing vessels on Long Island Sound, quite different from the motor yachts and pleasure trawlers also popular in both locales.

Maji caught up to Taira by the stern of the *Eagle Song*, her head cocked to one side, listening. Maji stopped and honed in on the sound. There was a string of expletives followed by, "Maybe you'll tell me the depth if I put you on a line and drop you in!"

Taira's face lit up with pleasure. She motioned for Maji to wait, then banged on the hull in a clear greeting rhythm.

"What?" came the voice from inside the cabin.

"Permission to come aboard?" Taira called out.

The salon doors leading into the cabin cracked open and an angry face appeared. Maji recognized a fierce kind of beauty to her features, a passion missing when Dee had been drugged and staggering.

When Dee recognized Olivia Taira, her expression transformed. Surprise turned almost to fear before composure wiped the slate clean. "Hey, Liv. Howzit?"

"All good here. You need a loving touch on that depth finder?"

Dee looked like she wanted to disappear back inside. But she blinked and swallowed and said, "If you've got a minute, sure." She pushed the salon doors wide and stepped into the cockpit.

Taira scrambled up and into the cockpit, and Maji grabbed a side rail and swung herself on board. She landed carefully, mindful of how slippery the gutting floor could be even after a day or two at the dock.

"Who the hell are you?" Dee asked as if just noticing her.

Taira grinned and swept a hand in Maji's direction. "Didn't you know? This is what a guardian angel looks like." At Dee's blank look, she added, "Sergeant Rios saved your ass yesterday. Checking up on you today."

"Hey," Maji said, keeping a straight face. "Nate said you might be here."

Dee looked down at her waterproof overalls and battered Xtratufs. "Guess I'm predictable."

"You've got a business to run," Taira said. She gestured toward the salon. "May I?"

Dee blushed. "Yeah. Thanks."

When Taira had slipped inside, Dee closed the cabin doors and turned back to Maji. "What do you want?"

"To know what happened yesterday. What those men wanted, what they said. Anything you can tell me, really."

Dee squinted warily at her. "You some kind of cop?"

"Army counterintelligence." To defer any questions that might generate, Maji added, "You do know those guys were released, right?"

Dee sighed. "Yeah, I heard. What'd you want to know, again?"

"Anything you know about those guys, starting with when you first met them."

Dee snorted. "We didn't exactly get introduced. I was in the head up on land, getting ready to show-and-tell for the tourists, when they walked right in. Told them they were on the wrong side, and it just gets fuzzy from there."

"Never seen them before?"

Dee shook her head.

"And they didn't say anything before they drugged you?" Depending on what the Russians had used, Maji knew she might not remember it even if there had been an extended conversation.

Dee frowned. "They did. I just…it's all garbled in my head. Maybe it was Russian. They wanted something—I remember that. One grabbed me, and I hit him. Why would they talk to me in Russian?"

Maji expected they had spoken to her in English and to each other in Russian. The brain would conflate the two in hindsight, unscrambling events as she cleared the toxins from her system. Or maybe never bringing the memory back in focus. "Don't worry about it. If something comes back to you, I'd appreciate it if you'd call."

"Why? What can you do?"

The cabin doors opened, and Taira emerged. "All good. That'll be seventy-three dollars." Seeing Dee's face react, she smiled. "Kidding." To Maji, she asked, "You need a ride back?"

"No, thanks."

Maji made no move to leave, and Taira scrambled back over the railing onto the dock. When she turned to wave good-bye, Maji saw the two women connect briefly across the distance, before Dee glanced away.

"Thanks," Dee said, looking at her feet before turning her eyes back to Taira on the dock. "See you at bingo?"

"Not this week. Night shift." Taira gave them a conciliatory smile and a little wave and headed back toward her truck.

Maji watched Dee's eyes follow the petite Coastie. "Charlie went missing the day a sport fishing boat Maydayed, right?"

"Yeah. Coasties to the rescue, like always."

"Well, those two guys who assaulted you were also crew on that boat."

Dee processed that information in silence, her widened eyes the only change in her studiously impassive face. "You think they killed Charlie?"

Maji shook her head. "No idea, really. But I don't like coincidences. Intuition says whatever they were doing the day Charlie died is connected to them coming after you yesterday."

"Well, that's better than some bullshit about Charlie doing drugs and falling in. As if." Her face hid none of her contempt for the idea or the people who proposed it.

"I can't bring Charlie back. And I can't promise we'll end up with good answers, or justice. But if you help, I'll try. And you will be in some danger—but not alone."

Dee's expression changed to disbelief, then almost to amusement. "Wow. You sell on commission?"

"Well, you don't get rich on a soldier's pay."

Holding the cabin door open, Dee shook her head. "Screw it. Come on in."

Maji stepped around the nets, traps, and lines in the wide, flat cockpit of the troller and walked into the structure that served as wheelhouse and salon combined, the main cabin above deck. Beyond the pilot's wheel and nav station by the forward-viewing windows, a passage led into a forward cabin tucked into the boat's bow. Dee ducked under the lintel and disappeared below with practiced movements, not inviting Maji to follow.

"Has anybody been on board, that you can tell?" Maji asked, projecting her voice. "Taken anything?"

"Nope," Dee's voice came back at her. "Cops tore the place up, left dusting prints on everything. Since then it's been like I left it after cleaning up."

Looking around the neat cabin, the papers squared away at the navigator's desk and the single cup and plate drying on the rack by the galley's little sink, Maji reckoned the woman would know. "What about other places Charlie used? Storage? A truck? His home?"

"Nope." Dee stepped back up into the salon, ducking by habit as she did so. "We shared all three. I'd know."

Huh. Maji would have sworn that AET Taira was the captain's type. "You were a couple?"

"Couple of fools with a boat loan between us." She squinted, then sighed. "Look, I got errands. You can come if you do what I tell you."

"Anybody getting hurt?"

Dee laughed for the first time and her face transformed. "Talked to death, maybe. Can you shut up around old people?"

"I'm game."

Dee drove the big diesel truck to the back of the Community House. In the large commercial kitchen, three chest coolers sat on the floor. "Grab one end."

Maji took a handle and hefted her half out the door and onto the truck, impressed with the other woman's strength. Dee was about her height, barely five six with a boost from her boots' rugged soles. Fishing would require upper body strength, of course.

They loaded the first cooler in silence and went back in for the next. As the back door banged behind them, Heather popped in from the service entry. "Dee, you got time to wash down a van with me—" She stopped and cocked her head in surprise at the sight of Maji. "Hey, Ri. She sucker you into the elder run?"

"Looks like."

Dee shrugged. "She wants to ask me questions. Got to pay to play."

"What kind of questions?" Heather's gentle teasing came to a screeching halt.

"About those guys. And Charlie."

Heather crossed her arms, taking a stance Maji thought must run in the family. If stubbornness was a matrilineal trait, she bet their father won few arguments. "I heard those guys were back on the street. Maybe you shouldn't be out."

"I've never hid from assholes before. Why start now?" A flicker of a smile crossed Dee's face. "Besides, I got a guardian angel with me."

Heather looked torn. "Mom's not going to like it."

"Then don't tell her." Dee took a cooler handle, looked to Maji, and nodded.

Maji wasn't about to get into whatever family politics lay beneath the exchange. If it didn't lead her closer to Sirko, it wasn't any of her business. She grasped the other handle and lifted in time with Dee.

Heather was still in the kitchen when they came back for the third and last chest. "Hey, you and Rose should come for dinner tonight. Mom wants to meet you two."

"Way to sell it," Dee said to her sister. "You don't have to," she added to Maji.

"No, I'd like to. Thanks. I'll ask Rose." She would love that, especially if they let her help in the kitchen. If today's search took Maji back to Japonski Island instead, at least one of them could enjoy some normal people time.

Dee drove several miles out Sawmill Creek Road, Maji quietly letting her pay attention to the road. After turning up a smaller road into the hills, and then onto a rutted trail, Dee glanced sideways. "Well? Aren't you going to ask me anything?"

"Okay. Tell me about Charlie." Maji intentionally left the question wide open.

A minute went by. "He was alone that day. I had the flu, so he took the boat out by himself. Wanted to harvest one last haul of herring eggs before they were all gone."

Maji kept her eyes on Dee's profile. "How do you harvest the eggs?"

"Depends. Most commercial boats take them from kelp out in open water, then sell it with the eggs attached to the Japanese. Serious money. But we follow the old way, put hemlock trees into the water at the shoreline. Then you go out in your skiff, pull the branches up. Charlie had his favorite spots. Hardly anybody but me knew where."

"What about your boat?" The Coast Guard had located it in their search.

"He used it to tow the skiff out, get more branches in one run. Charlie always promised a big haul, and a lot of people depended on him to deliver."

Charlie's big troller with the little skiff reminded Maji of the big sub with the little subs. And the Russian trawler waiting on the surface. Could they have used the *Eagle Song* instead, with or without Charlie's agreement? No—the Russian trawler had made it to dry dock for salvage. So why would they have bothered? And if Charlie had stayed at a distance, why would they have paid him any mind? Not questions Dee could answer.

Then Maji remembered that Green and Kim had said the sub would have been gone before the cable pulling started. But what if it had come up and bumped the *Eagle Song*? Surely that would leave a dent. "Where'd the Coast Guard find your boat? And in what condition?"

Dee pulled up to a weather-beaten one-story house in a clearing. She cut the motor and turned to face Maji. "Anchored, safe and sound, in the next cove over from Charlie's secret spot. Like he meant to come back soon."

Okay, so not whacked by a sub then. "And the skiff? Where is it now?"

"On a trailer in Mom's driveway. I told Nate he could use it for a while."

If it had been her friend's boat and she didn't need it urgently, Maji wouldn't have wanted to see the reminder either. "Could I take a look at it?"

Dee shrugged. "Sure. Before supper."

Maji waited quietly in the living room of the little house while Dee helped an old woman stash large, paper-wrapped parcels in her fridge and freezer. Their words were soft, Dee's tone mild and respectful. When she asked the old woman a question, she called her Auntie.

Across from Maji, an old man dozed in an overstuffed recliner tilted back to elevate his feet. His eyes opened to see her watching him. "Knew you'd be out today," he said. "Like clockwork."

Maji nodded, adding a small Dee-like smile. Either his eyesight was poor, or she wasn't the first tagalong helper Dee had brought on her regular runs. The elder fiddled with a clear plastic tube that came around his face and settled under his nose, then leaned over and poked something by the side of his chair. A humming started up and he closed his eyes, inhaling. *Oxygen.* Breathing, food, and love—life's essentials.

Dee came back into the living room followed by Auntie, and motioned with her head toward the door. Maji rose and preceded her down the front steps. She stopped by the truck and watched as Dee turned back, catching Auntie before she closed the front door. "Call if you need a ride to the doctor," she said.

The old woman smiled and kissed Dee on her forehead, level with her face as the younger woman stood one step down. "You know it."

The next few stops went about the same, with some bits of conversation and offers of coffee added in. Dee was gracious with all the elders but didn't linger at any one house, always mentioning the other deliveries still to be made. Her beneficiaries seemed to understand her urgency and take it without offense.

As they pulled away from a house with several small children in addition to the adults, Maji asked, "How many households does your program feed?"

Dee frowned. "We deliver a share of the harvest to all the Tribe members who can't fish or hunt for themselves anymore, or have a family member here who can. It's not charity, you know. The elders are part of our Tlingit family. We take care of each other." She sighed. "Heather explains it better."

"Nah, I get it," Maji replied. She thought of the surrogate grandmother in Brighton Beach who taught her Russian and how to make dishes from home. Maji smiled at the thought of cabbage rolls as traditional food. Mrs. K never asked her to work in return but did praise Maji when she carried the groceries, cleaned the kitchen, and otherwise helped out. Mrs. K asked for help without apology, told stories of her girlhood in Russia, and gave plenty of unsolicited advice. Maji could only imagine what that would have been like if she'd been Russian herself and looking to an elder to teach her who she was and where she came from. Growing up with only her parents in this country, Maji couldn't quite stretch her imagination to being part of a community that had stayed in one place for ten thousand years, like Heather had told them on the tour. "Nobody seems to mind that I'm tagging along."

Dee shrugged. "You're with me. If I don't introduce you, you must not need any explanation, eh? But you can bet there'll be some talk later."

The last home they visited sat up on a bluff, with a sweeping view of Sitka Sound from the front lawn. It was much larger than the rest, with a stone foundation and two stories. Big enough for several families, Maji thought. When they entered she learned why. Around her, two teens, a seven- or eight-year-old, and three toddlers worked on homework and after-school snacks. For the toddlers most of the energy went into squealing and playing with the food, which kept the kid with the shoulder-length hair and a paperback busy trying to keep them from throwing food at each other. Controlled chaos with a happy undercurrent.

The teens looked up from their schoolbooks to eye Maji with the studied indifference of adolescents. She gave them an up-nod of acknowledgment, and they blushed before returning to their homework.

"You two," the middle-aged woman told them, "go help Dee with the coolers. Take the freezer bags out. Don't try to lift that thing when it's full. Hear me?"

They nodded and loped out.

"This is Ri," Dee told her. "Came to town for that food conference. Helped me out at the harbor, and um, I invited her to see how this works."

The woman smiled after them. "I'm Charlotte," she said to Maji. "And you saw all of this lot at the Community House, with the Naa Kahidi Dancers."

"Oh, yeah," Maji replied, remembering how tiny the little toddler had seemed, bouncing to the rhythm of the music. The older kids followed actual steps, with equal enthusiasm. "They must practice a lot. The older ones."

Charlotte looked both pleased and proud. "And they get to travel too, to competitions. Not as much time on the Highway as if they played sports, but bigger trips. It's good, seeing the world a bit. Where you from?"

"New York City," Maji replied.

Charlotte shuddered. "Anchorage is too big for me. Do you like it?"

"Nettie's in the living room," Dee announced from the kitchen doorway. "She wants to tell you something." To Charlotte she asked, "You want these in the chest freezer?"

Maji left them in the kitchen. In the living room, she spotted a tiny, ancient woman in a rocking chair by the picture window. Maji crouched in front of her, palms on her knees. "Hi. You wanted to see me?"

Nettie looked her over, then gazed out the window. Maji wondered how much she could see out there at her age. Which could be eighty or a hundred and twenty-two. She must be the first of the four generations under this expansive roof. Finally, Nettie nodded to herself. "I seen that sub."

Maji bore Dee's advice in mind and waited for the elder to talk in her own way and pace. The story she got was long and meandered through time and place. Someplace back an indeterminate number of generations were Aleut relatives who hunted sea otters under duress for the Russians, when Baranov and the Russian American Company colonized as much of the west coast of Alaska and the towns of Southeast as they could to profit from the pelts prized as soft gold.

Maji knew from Heather's tour about the 1804 battle for Sitka, when the Russians brought hundreds of Aleut down in kayaks alongside their cannon-bearing tall ship. And that Sitka remained the capital of Russian America until the US brokered a deal to buy the territory from Russia in 1867. Seward's Folly, as the papers of the day called it, turned out to be a huge score when mineral gold was discovered, and later petroleum—black gold.

"Down here," Nettie said, "some of the Russian sailors ran off and married into the Tlingit. Their children were raised in the clans of their mothers, but with Russian last names, like me." She paused. "But the ones that come down later didn't want to be part of our families. They just wanted to party with our girls, drive around their big boats, show off their money. My nephew, he left the sawmill to work for that man, but he didn't like the way he used the women, so he was going to tell about the gold. When I saw that sub out there, I knew he was back. And sure enough, he killed Charlie. Kills anyone gets in his way."

Maji waited until she was sure the old woman had shared what was on her mind and then tried a couple questions to pry out why Nettie connected a long-ago death with the recent one. All that approach yielded was a lecture on fish camp and the importance of teaching young people traditional skills and values before they get too old to leave. "They have to feel how they belong to this place, or they'll leave us. Move away or get into booze and drugs. Either way."

Or sometimes they stayed and got killed, like Charlie, Maji thought. *Move on, Rios.*

❖

On the trip back to the Community House to return the coolers, Dee asked, "You make any sense of Nettie's story?"

"A little. I get that she saw a sub. I take it a sighting down here is big news?"

"Big news anywhere, if you think it's Russian. We might have intermarried a long time back, but nobody forgets they enslaved the Aleut and made them hunt the sea otters almost to extinction. Or how they took what wasn't theirs down here."

"You know, Heather mentioned that on the tour. What I don't get, though is…how?" Maji struggled to reframe that. "I mean, that's a hell of a long way to travel in kayaks, plus fight for somebody you hate already."

"Oldest trick in the book. Russians pretended to be just traders at first. But then kidnapping the women was cheaper than paying for otter pelts, and got them soldiers too. Even the toughest warrior can't let his wife and kids get killed."

"Ouch." A technique still popular today. Maji recalled how Sirko had gotten Ricky to betray his father-in-law the Mafia boss last summer, just by threatening his parents. *History always fucking repeating itself.* "Nettie mentioned Charlie's death like it was a repeat of older history. Something about a nephew and Russian party boats. I couldn't follow that part so well. Any ideas?"

"Sure. Back in the eighties, a handful of rich Soviets came down here a few summers in a row. Huge boats, played at fishing but…well, nobody talks about it much now."

"Drugs, sex, and rock 'n' roll?"

"Like that. Guns too, I hear. The cops didn't do anything, maybe got paid off. Maybe didn't care."

Maji waited. When Dee's silence stretched out, she prompted, "Nettie's nephew cared, though?"

"Oh, yeah. His girlfriend got pregnant. Wilbur—the nephew—had been working for the rich guy, wouldn't talk about what he was doing for him. Stayed on the boat and partied some nights, until the thing with his girlfriend. Then he went to the cops and said that one of the crew had raped her. They blew him off, so he told them about messing with the new cable lines too. Thought that would get the Russians in trouble, but they laughed at him. New cables worked fine. Accused him of being a druggie and a bad loser."

Maji hoped today's police relations were better, but she could see why the community might harbor a grudge. "You happen to know who Wilbur was working for?"

Dee shook her head. "I could find out. Older folks know—they just don't talk about it."

"Well, Nettie seemed sure the same guy was back." *And there are different ways of knowing.*

"Why would any of them come back after all this time?" Dee asked. "And why mess with me?"

"Dunno. You're connected to Charlie. And what if, whatever they left behind down there, he saw them pulling it up and putting it on their trawler?"

Dee smacked a hand on the steering wheel. "He said there was a boat out in the channel, just sitting. He was going to check if they were okay, after he got his haul in. If they were still there."

"How'd he contact you? Cell phone?"

"No—coverage is too patchy, especially when the cable goes out like that. They have to move satellites around, and calls drop worse than normal. We keep a radio in the house, ship to shore."

"Could anyone else have heard what he told you?"

"Sure, if they were monitoring the channels. Other boats, the Coast Guard. But if it's not a Mayday, nobody pays the noise much mind. We're busy out there."

Maji made a mental note to mention this to Lt. Green. "Okay. But say you brought a load of something valuable into the harbor and needed to offload it."

"Something you wanted to send to Russia, or what?"

"Maybe. Or just get out of town before the law came looking."

"Well, you're not going far by land. The road goes seven miles in either direction. And the only highway here's the Marine Highway—the state ferry. You could put a truck on that though and take it to Bellingham."

"What about air?"

"Depends on what this sunken treasure is. Can't fly commercial to Russia from here, so even if you could put it on a freight plane, you'd have to send it to the US."

"And a private plane would need a flight plan logged, I suppose," Maji said, thinking out loud.

"Plus be able to handle the size and weight. You take a floatplane out of here, it's got to be balanced. And have enough lift and range. Go down in the Bering Sea and you're dead."

Maji knew the SEALs had probably worked through all the likely scenarios, factoring the gold's weight and volume and what it might be packed in. She could see why the Russians had planned to use a trawler. Fishing boats, under many countries' flags, would be in this area around herring season. It wouldn't be so hard to slip away with a cargo that looked like lead weights and make a slow, safe run across the International Marine Boundary Line. Even if you were stopped for some reason, a search wouldn't turn up the kinds of contraband that anyone's navy or law enforcement would be looking for. "How hard would it be to steal a boat, this time of year?"

Dee laughed. "Jeez, I dunno, Officer, I always joyride in the summer."

"Seriously. A private boat would still be the best transport—the safest and most direct route to eastern Russia." *And if mine were up in dry dock, I'd hide my loot until I could transfer it to another. One not traceable to me.*

"Must be interesting, thinking like a crook," Dee muttered, not looking over at Maji. She backed the truck up by the kitchen door at the rear of the Community House. When the engine had stuttered to a halt, Dee turned and looked at Maji with a surprising intensity. "Herring season puts everybody into high gear. And in this harbor, we all look out for each other. Plus we have alarms and GPS on our boats, so we'd know pretty quick if one went missing."

"What about a pleasure craft? There's some pretty cush trawlers in Crescent Harbor. Would their owners be as vigilant?" People who could afford a something-million-dollar boat just for fun didn't always use them often, or pay as much attention. Maji'd stuck to cars and sailboats in her wayward youth, but she'd noticed what all her options were in New York harbors.

Dee clucked. "Maybe. Hard to figure what rich people do."

"Could you buy a reliable trawler in the middle of herring season?" Proof of ownership would help you stay off the radar too, if you had a trip to make across the boundary seas.

"Mm, unlikely." Dee paused. "I could ask around though."

"No. I can take care of that. You're better off away from the harbors and your normal contacts and routines, for now."

Dee opened her door, got out, and slammed it. When Maji closed hers and looked over the roof, Dee glared at her. "I'm not running, I'm not hiding. They come for me again, I'll be ready."

CHAPTER FOURTEEN

Rose stepped into the cool, clear air the afternoon had brought with it and felt no reluctance to leave the stuffy conference rooms. Dev had stuck to her the rest of the day, except when he slipped into the hallway during presentations to make phone calls. The presentations inspired him to doze off. Like Maji. Rose recalled Angelo joking about the sleep patterns of combat vets, about how they could conk out anywhere, anytime—except at bedtime.

Catching a few minutes here and there, he'd explained, became a habit to carry one over for times when sleeping in shifts was required. Or when the job at hand kept you up for days in a row. It bothered her that the duties of Maji's work, whatever they were, wore on her body and, at the same time, made her feel she needed to apologize for any little inconvenience her condition caused Rose. Especially when Rose knew in her heart that someone's life was saved, or at least improved, by the cost Maji paid. She turned to speak with Dev about supper.

But Dev stepped abruptly between her and the curb, standing taller and wider as a throaty pickup pulled up in front of them. Around his one-man blockade, Rose watched the passenger window slide down and Maji grin at them. "Is there a doctor in the house?"

Maji hopped out without waiting for a reply and held the door ajar, motioning Rose to get in. "Want to cook dinner with a Tlingit family?"

"Really?" Rose glanced into the truck and recognized the woman from the marina incident. Heather's sister? She looked much better. Not friendly, exactly, but well.

Maji nodded, looking pleased with herself. "Hop up. I'll be right there."

Rose climbed in, aware of Maji talking with Dev in low tones on the sidewalk. "Hi. I'm Rose."

"Yep. Deanne. Well, Dee." She didn't take her hands off the wheel, just looked past Rose as if to make sure Maji didn't disappear and leave her obliged to make conversation.

Fortunately for both of them, Maji climbed in a moment later. "Okay," she said and closed the truck door behind her. The lengths of their thighs pressed against each other.

Maji didn't ask about her day and had probably just gotten the scoop on Javi from Dev. Rose didn't want to ask about what the Army had or hadn't assigned her to do, especially not in front of a stranger. So instead she asked, "Is your day over?"

Maji slid one hand under Rose's, on top of her thigh, and their fingers laced together as if they always did. "Probably not. But Heather invited us for dinner, and it seemed rude to refuse. I'm not up on Tlingit culture, but I'm guessing hospitality's a thing, yeah?"

"Yep," Dee replied. "And Mom's venison stew and fry bread is a can't miss."

Rose hadn't thought Maji was asking her expert opinion as an anthropologist. Still, it felt odd to be in the middle of such a familiar exchange between her lover and a woman she'd only seen once before. Needing hospitalization. "How are you feeling, Dee?"

Dee's profile was blank, like Maji's when she had lots of thoughts and no intention of sharing them. "Not too bad. Good enough to work."

Her tone didn't invite further inquiry, so Rose just squeezed Maji's hand and enjoyed the view from the truck in their shared quiet. They passed landmarks that seemed familiar after only a few days, the cathedral and Castle Hill, Naa Kahidi Community House and ANB Harbor. And Ludvig's, which Rose resolved she would return to before she left Sitka, whether Maji could join her or not. Just a few minutes later, they pulled up at a two-story home that looked like the others near it—except for the art. Nearly all of the side facing the street was covered in carvings. Rose suspected they were decorative boards, like the much larger ones outside the Community House. Other than a sort of symmetry fitting them into the slope of the roof's eaves and around the front door and windows, they were a gloriously unmatched collection. Rose recognized some of the birds and animals. "Wow."

Dee turned the truck off and made a clucking sound. "That's Nate for you."

"You met Nate at the airport," Maji reminded her. She opened the passenger door and slid out, waiting to give Rose a hand down. "Simon's uncle."

Dee didn't wait for them as they walked around the front of the truck, heading for the house. She paused though, when Maji called, "Hey!" and pointed at the metal boat on the trailer in the driveway.

"Knock yourself out," Dee said, and proceeded up the stairs into the house.

Rose followed Maji to the metal-hulled boat and watched her climb up onto the trailer to look inside. "Can I help?"

"No, thanks—I'll just be a sec," Maji answered without lifting her head or shoulders. Then she swung a leg up over the side and was lost to Rose's view. Shuffling sounds of items being moved around and a metallic *thunk* followed. Maji's head popped up. "Actually, can you lend me a hand?"

Rose reached up and offered a steadying arm as Maji climbed back out onto the trailer's edge. She hopped the last foot down onto the grassy drive, and something in her jacket clunked. Rose hoped it wasn't her gun and...something else. "Success?"

"Maybe." Maji took Rose in, seeming to return from somewhere else as their eyes met. "I missed you today. Like ten whole hours or whatever. Is that stupid?"

Rose wrapped her fingers around the lapels of Maji's jacket, prepared to answer with a kiss. "Can't be. I missed you too."

As she pulled Maji toward her, the front door banged open. "Hey, you—oh. Sorry."

They turned toward Heather, both smiling sheepishly. "Hi," Rose said. "Thanks for inviting us."

Heather moved her eyes from the horizon back to her guests in the driveway. "Dee just left you out here?" She shook her head as if her sister's ways were unfathomable. "Come on in, already. Meet the family."

❖

Maji followed Rose and Heather into the house, feeling a bit self-conscious of the weight in her jacket pocket. Inside, three small children played on the floor of a comfortable living room, their toys spread across the large braided rug in the room's center. "Watch your step," Heather warned.

The smallest child, barely walking, held her hands out to Heather. She scooped her up and nuzzled her neck. "This is Kyla, my younger." She extended a hand over the middle-size child. "And Danny, also mine. And Tristan, Nate's pride and joy." To the kids, she said, "This is Auntie Rose and Auntie Ri."

Maji noticed just a tiny ripple of surprise on Rose's face. "Hi," Rose said, crouching by Danny, who looked out at her from behind a screen of bangs. "What a lovely drawing."

Danny looked down, shy with strangers maybe. Maji took a knee. "Ooh," she said. "Like the carvings outside. Did you do those too?"

The shy girl or boy shook their head, a little smile peeking out.

Maji looked to Tristan, whom she guessed to be eight or nine. "Must be you then."

"My dad," he corrected, sounding proud of Nate's artistry.

"But you're learning from him, yeah?"

He nodded seriously, then flinched to avoid Kyla's feet as she squirmed her way out of Heather's grip.

"Hi," Maji said to her, eye to eye. When the little girl grabbed a crayon off the carpet and held it out to her, Maji held both palms flat, ready to receive. "*Gunalchéesh*," she said, recalling the word for thank you.

"Gunalchéesh," Rose repeated, accepting her crayon with a beaming smile. Her pronunciation was a tad off.

Danny stifled a giggle.

"That's not it," Maji said with mock indignation. "It's *goo-nal-teeth*. Right?"

That earned her a real giggle, and a conspiratorial smile from Tristan as well.

"No?" Maji said, trying to sound earnest. "Um, *gumball cheeks*?" She stuck her tongue in one cheek, like she had a gumball tucked in there.

The two kids dissolved in giggles, and Heather said, "Okay, you two. You can coach our guests after supper. Pick up your toys and go wash your hands."

"Dinner smells fabulous," Rose said, taking her cue to stand back up. "May I help with anything?"

Heather smiled. "Watch what you offer. This way."

They followed her into the eat-in kitchen, where an older woman who looked more like Heather than Dee stood over an electric fryer, her hands and apron white with flour.

"Mom," Heather said, "this is Rose, and Ri. Ri caught those guys."

"Couldn't have without Rose," Maji corrected. "Hi, Mrs. Davis." She held her hand out, undeterred by the flour.

Mrs. Davis grabbed her by the shoulders and planted a kiss on Maji's forehead. She let her go and turned toward Rose. "You too," she declared, and gave Rose the same treatment. "And I'm Mom to all my kids' friends. Including you now."

Rose flushed, looking embarrassed by the woman's gratitude but also pleased. Maji realized that it was the first time Rose had used her training to help a stranger and then had to deal with the thank-you part. "I'm just glad we could help."

"Where is Dee?" Maji asked Heather. "I need a word with her."

Heather nodded to the back door and the yard beyond it. "With Nate, in his studio."

A narrow path led directly to a single-story outbuilding covered in carved panels like the front of the house. Quite an advertisement for a carver. The door was ajar, so Maji knocked on the frame.

Dee looked up from a shop stool by the far wall and nodded to her to come in. Nate continued working, humming as he guided a tiny chisel. He leaned in close to the pale wood, long brown hair pulled back in a ponytail, a pair of glasses pushed up above his forehead. Maji leaned a hip against a tool cabinet on the near side of the room and waited to speak until he stopped. When he straightened up, rolled his shoulders, and stretched the kinks from his back, she noticed his T-shirt. In the center of his chest, an old photo showed the legendary Apache chief Geronimo with three warriors, each holding a rifle. Above it were the words *Homeland Security*, and below, *Fighting Terrorism since 1492*.

Can't argue with that. Maji just said, "Ayup." She noticed Dee's mouth twitch, one of her few tells. "Found something in the skiff. You got a minute?"

Dee nodded and stepped into the yard with her. Maji pulled out one of the two weights and held it out in her palm. "What is this?"

"Looks like a big sinker. Too small to stabilize the boat, too big to cast for a sport fish. That was in the skiff?"

Maji nodded. "Two of them. Lead, right?" At Dee's nod, she handed it over.

"Whoo!" Dee said, her arm dropping before she adjusted to the unexpected density. "Not lead. So? What do you think then?"

Maji was tempted to joke that they'd hit gold. But that wasn't so funny anymore, and besides, more information was not likely to make Dee safer. "I think I better send it for analysis. Thanks."

Dee stood a few seconds, looking like she wanted to ask more. Then she shrugged and went back into the studio. Maji walked out of earshot.

On the second ring, her Navy counterpart answered, "Go for Green."

"Rios here. I found two weights in Charlie Shakely's skiff. Look like lead but way too heavy, and the boat's co-captain doesn't recognize them. You want 'em?"

"Hell, yeah. You got wheels?"

"No. I could call a cab. Or jog. I'm only four or five miles away." And hungry.

"Well, they're safe, right? We're going to break for dinner soon and I can come pick you up then. Sit tight."

"Yeah. Need my twenty?" They all used the same radio codes, regardless of the day's tech. Which right now was the GPS tracker Maji wore. She wondered how precise it was.

"I'm showing three forty-two Spruce Street."

Very precise indeed. "I'll be out front."

❖

Rose put the salad bowl on the table, which Tristan and Danny had set for six. That was as many chairs as could squeeze around, and she wondered if the children would eat in the living room. The two too large for laps, anyway. "It's really sweet of you to have us," she said to Heather.

"No," Heather said with a smile, "it's good of you to let us thank you in some way. It's not much, but it is from the heart."

"Hmm." Rose absorbed that, along with being made an honorary auntie. Feeding visitors might be traditional hospitality, but that was lifesaving special. "Is Dee really okay?"

Heather laughed. "She's back to normal. Wish she'd be happy, instead."

"Hey, yeah—why be normal, when you can be happy?" Nate said as he stepped into the kitchen.

Maji and Dee followed him in. Mom insisted that Maji and Rose serve themselves first, so they ladled stew from the Crockpot into their bowls and each grabbed a warm puff of fry bread from the plate by the stove.

"Thank you so much for supper," Maji said as the others served themselves. "I have to run in ten minutes or so, but I'm really glad to be here."

"Well, get eating, then," Mom said, looking more amused than alarmed by the quick exit.

Maji nodded and dug in. She chewed and groaned, unabashedly blissed out.

Rose smiled and caught Heather's eye. "That's normal, and happy."

The family ate for several minutes with almost no conversation. Rose found the quiet amiable, and quite restful compared to family dinners with the Benedettis. "Will you be back soon?"

Maji shook her head and swallowed, rising and heading for the Crockpot. "Don't wait up." She leaned down by Dee and asked quietly, "Could you see Rose safely home, on your way?"

Dee looked surprised, but nodded. "Sure."

"What kind of work do you do, Ri?" Mom asked Maji.

"I'm with the Army," she answered, sounding matter of fact. "I have a badge," she added for the benefit of Tristan, who had come back into the kitchen for seconds. "You want to see?"

Tristan looked hopefully to his father, who nodded. Maji pulled it off her waistband and handed it to the boy.

"Cool," Tristan said. "What's Counterintelligence?"

"Military intelligence," Maji said with a totally straight face, "is an oxymoron. If you work against the morons, then you are in counterintel."

Nate and Dee both snorted.

Tristan squinted at her, not getting the joke. "Come on."

"Okay," Maji conceded. "I get information on people who try to get information on the United States. Sometimes they work for other countries, sometimes for organized crime, or even terrorists."

"Like spy versus spy?"

"Just like that, but much less fun."

Tristan disappeared back to the living room with the fry bread and a story to share.

"So," Nate said, "you reckon Charlie caught those guys spying?"

Maji's expression was so neutral, even Rose couldn't guess her thoughts. "Too soon to say. Myself, I'm hoping whatever they're up to is worth a terrorism charge. Then if we can collar them before they leave town, we get to keep them. No more catch and release bullshit with diplomatic immunity."

"Oh, yeah," Dee said before Nate could respond. "Mom, you remember who Wilbur Fred was working for when he got killed?"

Mom's faced clouded over. "Trouble, that's who." She sighed. "Circus. Something like that. They said he turned the harbor into a circus and treated us like animals. New year, same shit." She looked to see if the kids had noticed. "Sorry. Name sounded like circus."

Sirko. Rose choked and felt Maji's hand caressing her back. Small comfort.

"Thanks, that helps," Maji said. She drank down the last of her water and laid her napkin on the table. "Gunalchéesh," she said with proper pronunciation and hand gestures.

Nate eyed Maji. "So, what kind of Native are you?"

"Urban." She gave him a look to show she was kidding. "I'm from Brooklyn—a native New Yorker."

Nate looked serious. "Urban Indians got it rough. Know they come from someplace, from some people. Maybe they hear some stories, but they don't get to sit with their elders, go out and learn from the aunts and uncles. Don't learn the foods, the songs, the ceremonies. How can they know who they are?"

Maji took a beat to absorb that. "I guess I never thought of myself that way. My father's one quarter Mapuche, and I don't have any clue what that means. Except Central America's full of intermarriages, like up here."

"Huh. What part the Mapuche from then?"

"Chile. One of several indigenous peoples still trying to resist going totally Euro. Unlike the folks on my mother's side, who were desert nomads way back. But in the generations before her time, the family started pretending they'd always lived in cities."

Nate nodded, eyes focused past her. "Around here we say, you're either one hundred percent Tlingit, or not at all. Whoever your folks are, you have to choose the life."

"Yeah. Well, I don't know enough to choose, so maybe I am an urban Indian after all." Maji raised an eyebrow at him. "Doesn't suck as bad as you made it sound."

"Give it time," Nate deadpanned.

Rose waited to see if anyone would laugh. When no one did, she just told Maji, "Be careful."

Maji turned down three offers of a ride and let herself out the front, stopping to chat briefly with the kids. She hadn't asked to hold the toddler, but Rose had caught her making faces across the table. Kyla seemed to find her equally entertaining.

Rose was about to clear her dishes away when Mom caught her by surprise. "You and Ri live together? Like a couple?"

Dee glowered. "Mom."

"What? That's a friendly question. Don't take it personal." To Rose she added, "We don't get many women like you around here. Tourists, maybe—I don't know. But not friends."

Heather chuckled. "You're being reverse anthropologized. I'm sorry."

"It's fine. Only fair, I guess." To Mom she answered, "No. We're just dating."

"Why? Don't you want to settle down?"

"Mom…" Dee tried again.

Rose gave her a reassuring look. "I'm Italian. Questions and opinions are always like this"—she slid the fingers of one hand through the other, into fenceposts—"and there's no escaping them." She returned her attention to Mom. "Yes, I do want to settle down. And I am in love with Ri. But we live on different coasts, and her job may be a problem for a while. So…we'll see."

Mom took her hand. "Where there's a will, there's a way. Hang in there."

Rose sensed there was some underlying tension, even when Mom let the subject go and left to help Heather with the kids. What their drama had to do with her and Ri, she wasn't sure and didn't plan to ask.

As Rose and Dee were washing up, Heather came back into the kitchen. "They've got Mom reading them *Clifford the Big Red Dog* on repeat," Heather said, picking up a towel to help Rose with the drying.

Dee didn't look up from the sudsy dishpan. "Nate's back on the mask. Middle of a tricky bit, he says."

"Mom doesn't mind. She'd be tickled if you and Nate brought her more kids."

"Well, maybe Nate will come through for her."

The dourness in Dee's voice struck Rose as a deep-seated unhappiness.

"My mother's going to have to wait a while too," she offered in consolation. Not that her mother ever pushed, but Rose had heard her own biological clock ticking for several years now. Too early for that discussion with Maji...

"You could date a single mom," Heather said, startling Rose. "Oh, sorry, I meant Dee, not you."

"Like that's going to happen," Dee said. "The only women who come to Sitka to stay are already paired up. And I'm not moving."

"All the more reason you should ask that Liv out. You know you want to." Heather turned to Rose. "There's this woman who comes to buy the day's catch off Dee's boat, once a week like clockwork. Cute as a bug, and part Haida too."

"What? No, she's Okinawan. I mean, Hawaiian, but from some special group of Japanese people."

Heather snapped her dish towel in Dee's direction. "Only on her mother's side. You're going to eavesdrop, you should listen closer. Or God forbid, talk to her."

Dee stared into the dishpan. "Why? She'll just get transferred anyway. To Hawaii or someplace."

"She's already been stationed there. She asked for Sitka to get close enough to meet her father's people. She even went to Celebration last summer."

"Really?" Dee sounded hopeful, but then shook her head. "Won't last. She won't want to stay here, and I can't leave."

Heather sighed. "You'll never know what she wants if you don't talk to her. Which is a shame, because she's really nice—and she likes you."

"She'll get over it," Dee said. She went over to the coffeemaker on the counter and started puttering, conversation closed. Rose hung her dish towel over the back of a kitchen chair to dry.

"It's your life, Dee," Heather said, breaking the impasse. "You can't use your old excuse of hurting Mom anymore. She wants you to be happy, and so does anybody else who really matters."

She paused, while her sister looked out the window at nothing in particular. "What's the worst that could happen? She says no—you're off the hook."

Dee just stalked out the back door. They heard her say, "Coffee's on." If Nate replied, Rose couldn't hear it.

"Now she can hang out and not talk, for a while." Heather gave Rose a wry smile. "I'm sorry. I shouldn't have pushed her like that. Charlie couldn't talk her into trying again either, and now he's gone."

Rose inhaled the scent of brewing coffee. "I'm so sorry." She thought of her breakup with Gayle, and Angelo's death. What if Maji hadn't happened in between? "Bad relationships can hurt for a long time, even without grief on top."

Heather went to the archway between the kitchen and living room and listened. Seeming satisfied with the quiet, she came back and pulled coffee mugs from the cabinet. "I don't know I'd call it a relationship. Tina snuck around with her, never came to church or bingo or the dances, never met Mom or me. Shouldn't have been a surprise when Dee found out she was married to that Coastie."

Tina the flight attendant? Could be. "This is too small a town to think you can keep a secret, isn't it?"

"Specially if you grew up here. But I guess this Tina thought she was in love too. At least, that's what she said when she showed up at Dee's boat, trying to make it right. Charlie had to keep Dee from tossing her in the water, right down on the docks in front of God and everybody."

Rose could imagine the painful scene. "So much for secrets."

"Worst coming-out party ever," Heather agreed.

Rose blinked, not sure how to digest this revelation. "Tina was her first?"

Heather shrugged. "I don't know, really. Dee's only started opening up since she got sober. But this isn't the easiest place to be gay, Tlingit or not. Puts you in a fishbowl, at the very least."

"Is that why your mother gave me the third degree?" Rose asked.

Heather nodded. "She never understood why Dee and Charlie didn't get married, living together and owning a boat together, and all. But I could never talk Dee into coming out. She was so sure that Mom would turn her away, or she'd lose her church friends if she didn't. Something bad either way. Course, she was right to be scared, given what happened."

"When the public breakup blew the lid off?"

"Yep. Mom was furious with those two, went on about white people, and perverts, and no values. It wasn't pretty. But she was just worried about Dee, really."

"All mothers worry about their kids' happiness. And I suppose it's already hard enough to live in two worlds, even here with so much cultural support."

"She's coming around, though. Mom wouldn't get up in your business like that if she didn't want to find some hope."

"Hope?"

"Yeah. To see that Dee could have a normal, happy life if she found the right person."

There was that *normal* again. "I guess that's what we all want. And your money's on this Liv?"

"She's not ashamed of who she is. No sneaking around. She'd be proud to be seen with Dee—I'm sure of it. Dee deserves someone who treats her right."

Maybe that was the right kind of normal to hope for. "Yes," Rose agreed. "She does."

CHAPTER FIFTEEN

Careful not to show her reluctance, Maji let Lt. Green drive her away from the cozy home of extended family and soul-warming food. "Did you get dinner?"

Green shook her head. "No, I need to pick something up. What stays open around here?"

It was getting dim out. After eight already. "There's a burger joint on Katlian. Will that do?"

"Yeah. Jimmy's hitting the cafeteria, but he's got Jack stuck to him. We should talk privately."

So they didn't trust Jack. He seemed okay to her, but she knew better than most how much a person could hide in plain sight. "You think the Lieutenant Commander could be the Russians' man on the inside? On what basis?"

"He's just on the short list for now. Everybody who responded to the Mayday from the Russian trawler is."

"Okay. Who's everybody?"

"Pilot, copilot, the air mech, and the rescue swimmer. Jack, Captain Jamie Manning, AET Olivia Taira, and AST Dan Rivera. Any or all of them might have seen something, might know where the gold went, or might have been contacted by Sirko's agents afterward."

"That's a lot of mights. All this on the theory that the rescue included securing the gold?"

"That's the working hypothesis," Green confirmed. She didn't sound satisfied, however, and Maji empathized.

"Next left's Katlian," Maji said. "Look for the homemade billboard of a burger and fries on your right in about two blocks."

"Jeez, Rios. How long you been in town?"

"Couple days. I always learn where the food is, first order of business."

Green laughed. "Spoken like an operator." She glanced over. "Sorry. I know better than to fish."

"Good." Maji spotted the sign and pointed. "That's it."

Maji passed on ordering a second supper. The stew and fry bread would keep her going for at least three hours, and then she had the Clif bars in her pocket if nothing else was on hand. She bought a small shake and a bottle of water, mostly to be polite while her teammate ate.

"Sure that's all you want?" Green asked between bites.

"The Davis family fed us plenty, thanks. And fed me some solid intel, as well."

Green glanced about, appearing to gauge the distance between them and the few other diners. "Report."

"Historically, Russians and Tlingits are not great allies, except for a few who married into the Tribe and a couple priests who were nice enough. But nobody forgets the home invasion, the enslaved Aleuts, the kidnapped women. I talked to an elder, a woman maybe eighty or ninety, who saw the sub and immediately remembered an asshole raising hell here in town in the eighties." Maji slurped her shake. "At dinner, Deanne Davis's mother confirmed that asshole the elder meant was Sirko. And a Tlingit guy working for him got killed after talking about how Sirko was messing with the new cable drop. Plus a rape allegation. Anyway, his death was ruled an accident, much like Charlie Shakely's."

"And I suppose the family thinks history is repeating itself or something?"

"If by that you mean outsiders come in and abuse the locals, who have no legal recourse for their losses. It's not a repeat so much as the same song, new verse."

Green took her time wiping her mouth and hands on the paper napkin. If she gave her any snark about going native, Maji was ready. Instead, Green just said, "So I take it you don't think Captain Charlie's death was accidental."

"Nope. Charlie radioed Dee, who was home with the flu that afternoon. Told her about a trawler in the channel near his secret herring egg harvest spot, acting weird. Planned to go over and check on it if it was still there when he had his haul in."

Lt. Green raised one platinum brow. "And he died with those two weights that are too heavy to be lead in his skiff." She took the last bite of her burger. "Can I see the sinkers?" Green asked around a mouthful of burger. She ate like a soldier on duty, or a cop on break. Fast enough to not go hungry if a call came in, slow enough to not get sick if running was called for.

Maji set one weight on the table and slid it over. "Feels about twice as heavy as it should if it was lead. But it looks like the real deal, doesn't it? Would be a clever way to hide…another metal that doesn't rust." She glanced around and confirmed that she could have safely yelled *gold* in here. "Dee—Deanne Davis, the half owner of the fishing boat—confirms they don't use anything like this and she hadn't seen it before. Charlie used the skiff that day to carry the harvest from shore to their full-size fishing boat." She paused. "He was found on shore, right?"

Green nodded. "In the shallows, caught on some branches. Postmortem said he broke his neck prior to getting waterlogged by the tide."

"Who found him?"

"Coast Guard sent out a search at daybreak and spotted the fishing boat right where Dee thought he would anchor it. They brought it in and turned it over to the state police to look for evidence." Green stopped talking long enough to get another mouthful down, along with some soda. "Coasties left the body to the state police, since he was clearly dead and it was their scene to examine."

"So the skiff might have been towed back with the coroner," Maji said, thinking aloud.

Green nodded, chewing the last of her fries. "And nobody who knew what this was saw it," she agreed, following Maji's train of thought. She smiled. "Now we know what they look like."

"Very portable, except for the weight. How many do you think they managed to collect?"

Green collected up her food wrappers, crushing them into a little ball on the plastic tray. "Won't know that until we find the stash. Assuming it's still here in town."

"It must be," Maji said, voicing her suspicions at last. "And they don't know where it is. If they did, what would they want with Dee?"

"Valid point, if Charlie's death is actually related. Let's go look at the rescue logs from that day."

When they found Lt. Kim in the communications center, Jack was nowhere in sight. The night shift radio monitor sat quietly reading a paperback, apparently ignoring them. Just the same, they moved to the empty office that had repeatedly been swept for bugs and found to be clean. Green handed him the sinker. "Fill her in."

"There was definitely a sub in these waters during the time window of the cable damage. And we've confirmed it's gone now. We think they took the minisubs back with them, leaving just the trawler behind. If they got most of these"—Kim waved the gold sinker like it weighed less than lead—"we might be looking at fifty million worth, in US dollar equivalent."

But usable anywhere, in any economy, Maji thought. "Not huge, but worth the trip."

"Big enough now, thanks to Robin Hood." Kim referred to Angelo as the media did, because he had stolen trillions from international crime networks' digital bank accounts and redistributed the funds to individuals and groups all over the world. "With the banking crackdown finally in play, hard currency is the only way to restore power to the big players. Those with access to subs and such."

"How many transport routes can you track? Ferry, private boats, air."

"Based on encrypted transmissions we've cracked so far, we're ninety percent sure the payload's still in town. Question is where and when they'll try and move it."

"Searching planes, trucks, and boats on the ground right now would take a lot of hands. How much can your platoon cover?" In teams of two, three, or four, she supposed.

Kim smiled to himself and gave Green a nod. She picked up the briefing. "ANB Harbor had a visit from a pump-out service today. Every vessel's had a metal detector with a gold sensor close enough to ping if she's got more than a class ring on board. Tomorrow our crew will hit Crescent Harbor and move in wider circles from there."

"Are you checking trucks big enough to haul freight onto the Alaska Marine Highway ferry?" Maji asked.

"Can't search every vehicle in the area," Green conceded. "But we've started screening all cars and trucks as they load on, in case they got smart and broke the payload into lighter chunks. And we have operators on board in case anybody drives on with cargo that pings. They'll be suitably welcomed when they drive off, either farther up the Inside Passage or down in Bellingham."

"What about air?" Small planes were unlikely, for the reasons she and Dee had discussed. "Any chance they have somebody working at the commercial freight business here?"

"Low probability, but we've got someone there in case," Green replied. "Which is all well and good, but if it's hidden in a building someplace or up in the hills, we've got no way to narrow the field yet."

"If the mercs are hanging around town instead of moving the gold, what's the holdup? Charlie died nearly two weeks ago," Maji pointed out. "And if it's not on the *Eagle Song*, what did those guys want with Dee?"

Green looked to Kim. "Rios thinks the Russians lost the payload somehow, with a tie in to Charlie Shakely's death."

Kim did not dismiss that option. "Be mighty handy if Thumb could tell us."

"I'll check in at Command, see if I'm cleared to reach out or if they've gotten word." Maji wished she could offer more, but ruining

Tom's long game wasn't worth getting one piece of intel from him if they could figure this out themselves. "But in the meantime, I'd like to see the search and rescue logs myself."

"We'll do you one better. There's video."

"Thank you for the ride." Rose looked at Dee's profile as the quiet woman drove, handling the big truck like it was her second home. There was a woman out there who would treasure this view, the chance to ride shotgun. If it wasn't this Liv that Heather had her hopes set on, it would be another. Rose had faith but she didn't know how to communicate it.

"Sure," Dee said. "And I guess I never said thanks. For jumping in with Ri against those guys. Heather told me what you did, how you got people to help. How'd you know to do that?"

Rose smiled to herself. "Training. Last summer, I went to a camp that Ri was helping to teach. Self-defense, first aid, that sort of thing. We practiced a scenario very much like this, a made-up scene with attackers, a victim, and bystanders. I never expected to have to use it in real life. Funny."

"Ha-ha?"

Rose chuckled. "No. Funny that it worked so well when it mattered. I'm a big believer in practice, though." After a quiet lull, she ventured, "I have a presentation tomorrow and I haven't tested it out at all. I was planning to try it on Ri tonight."

"You have to talk in front of a group? And you don't know what you're going to say?"

"Well, I have my slides ready and I know my material—it's my own project, after all. But I'm nervous about how it will sound to some of my audience."

"Why?"

"Well, anthropology's changed over the years. We're not just outsiders looking in." Like visitors at a zoo. "Now some of us are involved in the issues we study—we take sides, we advocate. And for older, more conservative academics, that seems radical."

Rose hated that old racist put-down, *going native*. "I disagree, but there are risks when you insert yourself into problems you don't understand. For one, you risk imposing your own values on the very people you're supposed to be learning about."

"The new imperialism, huh?" Dee smiled. "Engineering companies always come up to Alaska, wanting to sell us solutions that don't fit our climate, our culture. To problems they don't understand. Big money, though."

Rose blinked. "Like that, I suppose. But I know what my work is for, and I try to behave like an ally rather than a co-opter. I just don't know if I'm presenting the project in a way that shows that. In thirty minutes, plus Q and A."

"Well, how hard could that be?" Dee's flat tone revealed the dry wit that clearly ran in her family.

"I'm just nervous, really. Most of the people at this conference either have tenure and lots of articles published, or they come from communities that are doing their own work to preserve culture through traditional foods."

Dee drove in silence the last few blocks. After she parked the truck in the hotel's lot, she turned to Rose. "I could listen if you wanted. Not like an academic, or as the voice of the Tlingit or anything. Just as me."

"Really? You don't have to be up at three a.m. to fish? I don't want to impose."

"Yeah, you're pretty clear on that." Dee's mouth quirked in that almost smile. "And don't worry. I'm lying low until Ri catches the bad guys. Or something."

Rose felt a swell of pride at Dee's faith in Maji. "Okay, then. Thank you."

❖

Rose opened the door and heard a rustling from the couch as she turned on the light. She spun, ready to defend herself and Dee from an intruder. "Dev. What the hell?"

"So sorry to alarm you," he said, in character as Professor Dev. "I was just—"

"Skip it. She's a friend, and Ri trusts her. Dev, this is Dee, Dee, Dev."

"Hi," he said, taking a quick scan of Dee's work clothes. "You with the conference?"

"Nope."

"I'm going to make some tea. You two sit down." Rose used a tone she borrowed from the Benedetti women. They sat. Who to explain first? She looked at the tea sampler in the little tray by the electric kettle on the kitchenette counter. "Here, pick what you like."

Dee accepted the sampler and drew out a foil-wrapped bag, handing the collection to Dev. She watched him warily but didn't volunteer any information.

"Dev, Dee is the woman those two men tried to drag away yesterday at the harbor. She's been helping Ri today. So...not a threat."

Dev nodded. "Glad you're okay."

"You her bodyguard?" Dee looked to Rose without waiting for his answer. "Wait. I heard you were an ambassador's kid or something like that."

Rose shook her head. "Not quite." But simpler than the truth. Maybe she should have stuck with it. "No, my cousin pissed off a whole lot of criminals a few months ago. All of Angelo's survivors have security while things cool off."

"Angelo the Robin Hood guy? That's your cousin?" Dee asked.

Rose turned and poured three mugs full of steaming water. She opened a tea bag and started her cup steeping while the pain subsided. Sometimes that look of sympathy was just too hard. "Yes."

Dev got up and took the other two mugs, setting one in front of Dee. Then he pulled a third chair out from the little table and touched Rose's arm.

Dee studied him. "You his friend too? And Ri?"

Dev nodded. "We all served together."

"But now you're a bodyguard and she's spy-versus-spy. Asking all about Russian subs and smuggling buried treasure."

"Really?" Dev replied. "She told you all that?"

Dee bristled at his tone. "She needed my help to talk to folks who know things here. Getting her some stories wasn't hard, and it seemed to help."

"All the stories lead back to a Russian nogoodnik whose name sounds like *circus*," Rose said. She wasn't sure how much Maji would want her to say about Sirko, since she hadn't herself.

Dev's eyebrows lifted. "And what's this Russian guy want around here?"

"Something heavy that the Russians would kill Charlie for and try to smuggle home," Dee said. After a long pause she added, "That's all I know."

Rose hadn't seen that flavor of unrest on Dee's face before, and it made her stomach knot. What was Maji doing? Was she really going up against Sirko again? She could hear Angelo's voice from last summer, saying, *This guy's really starting to bug me.* The memory brought tears.

"Hey," Dee said, touching her hand. "She's not working alone, you know. And she must think you're safe with this guy." She looked Dev over. "You're Indian-Indian, huh?"

He smiled. "My folks are. I'm just Indian-American. As opposed to American Indian."

Dee laughed.

"Finally, someone who likes that joke," Rose said, collecting herself. "Would you still like to hear my presentation?"

Chapter Sixteen

Maji pulled earphones down over her head so she wouldn't disturb the soldiers quietly working at their posts inside the incident command room. They had given her one of the large screens and set up the video log for her. Not realizing that Coast Guard helos recorded every mission, she was a bit amazed to see and hear what the pilot did. The picture was a little grainy, the colors slightly washed-out, but then the date and time stamp in the upper left corner showed it was March and the skies on the approach to the trawler *Arkhangel* hung heavy with clouds.

The helo approached under the cloud ceiling, rapidly honing in on the boat as Jack's voice relayed their status back to the IC. Hovering some distance back, Jack noted the ship's list to starboard and hailed the captain on the radio. His voice was clear and reassuring, in contrast to the near panic in the heavily accented seaman's voice. The captain seemed equally worried about losing his boat as losing his life or his crew. Jack promised that a boat was coming out, and if they could keep the trawler afloat safely it would be hauled into port for repairs.

In under a minute, everyone agreed the helo would deploy its rescue swimmer onto the stern deck of the boat. If the swimmer couldn't help them stop the leak, the crew would don their gumby suits and prepare to get in the water for airlift.

The view stayed on the rear of the boat, now under the hovering helo, but the voices changed. Maji recognized AET Taira's voice telling the pilots each step of preparation to lower the swimmer down. When a female voice responded with the go-ahead, Maji realized copilot Jamie Manning was female. Nice. The swimmer, Dan Rivera, landed on the stern deck and unhooked the cable, which AET Taira guided back up into the helo.

While she listened to the swimmer update the flight crew on his efforts to find the leak, close the open valve causing it, and pump out the submerged holds, Maji admired the teamwork involved. Every member of the crew was totally on task but sounded relaxed. Each person could focus on their own contribution, confident in the others' abilities.

Ten minutes later, the swimmer got back into the sling and AET Taira's voice relayed his ascent back into the helo cabin. With the tow ship only minutes away, Jack bid the trawler captain farewell over the radio and turned the helo toward home. Seconds later the video feed stopped.

Maji took off her headphones, still thinking about the team. People who worked like that together did not betray each other for money. This mission, fully documented and time-stamped second by second, didn't hold any secrets. She looked around the room of screens and maps, chart tables, and computers. Every blue-uniformed soldier watched a weather broadcast or a radar screen, or listened to a muted radio channel monitoring for distress calls. Not one played on their cell phone, or gossiped, or told stories to pass the time. She was sure they let off steam elsewhere, but in here it was all quiet vigilance.

As Maji surveyed the room, she spotted Lt. Green in the doorway, leaning one shoulder against the frame. Green flashed Maji a brief smile of acknowledgment, and with a nod to follow her out, she turned and disappeared into the hallway. Maji blinked under the fluorescent lights outside and strode after Green, now turning left into the commander's office.

"Well, Rios?" Green leaned one hip against the desk that Lt. Kim sat behind. He looked up from his laptop to hear Maji's response.

"Please tell me all four crew members cleared whatever checks you ran."

"Rivera got behind on child support once, but caught up years ago. Taira has so many speeding tickets even USAA won't insure her. Manning had an arrest a few years back, but won on self-defense. Jack's squeaky clean. And nobody's got odd bank deposits, or worrisome web searches, or known associations with bad guys."

"Good. Is there video for the search for Charlie too?"

Kim nodded. "It's sad, frankly. Totally professional, but you can hear the pain when they realized there was no way to help him. These guys live to save, and they count the losses."

"So others may live," Maji reflected. The rescue swimmer's creed didn't seem at all trite, in light of the risks she'd watched them take. On an easy day. "Did they cover the whole search?"

Kim shook his head. "They went right where the co-captain thought the *Eagle Song* would be, then to the nearby coves. Spotted the skiff, then the body. Dropped the swimmer onto the beach, confirmed death."

"Did they stay on the scene?"

Green frowned. "Waste of fuel to keep a helo hovering until the state troopers could motor out. They left the swimmer on the beach with a weapon." Maji's puzzlement must have shown, because she added, "In case of bears. They come out of the hills hungry in the spring. Ruins the evidence."

"So did the swimmer get a lift back with the troopers? And have we read his statement?"

"Hers," Green corrected. "Yes. You're welcome to it, though it won't help. Coroner's report confirms everything she noted about blunt force trauma, time of death based on the body temp, the water temp, and the rise in the tide."

"How long was he out there?"

"Hours."

"Long enough to off-load the gold from the *Arkhangel* onto the *Eagle Song* before calling the Coast Guard for help?"

Kim and Green looked at each other. "If they had a tender, they could have gone to Charlie for help, killed him, taken his boat, off-loaded the gold, and put his boat back in its quiet cove looking innocent. Maybe," Green said.

"They'd still risk the gold being found that way," Kim noted.

"But that's a deferred risk, unlike sinking," Maji said.

"Regs require they have a working tender," Green said. "But then, these guys didn't know to make sure all their valves were closed. So who knows."

"Thumb might have rigged the leak to throw a wrench in the works." If it meant stopping Sirko, Maji knew he'd gladly sink a ship and get in a gumby suit to await rescue.

"No way to know unless he tells us," Kim said, dialing his phone. "Checking on that tender."

"I heard the Coasties towed the *Eagle Song* back in," Maji said. "Do we know exactly who did that?" There had to be a chain of custody log someplace.

"Sure. Coast Guard had a boat out in the channel for marker maintenance, so they sent it over."

"Have the crew on that boat all been screened?"

Green's brows rose and she turned to Kim, who was just hanging up.

"The tender was towed in behind the *Arkhangel* and didn't have to go to salvage. Boatyard manager says one of the Russian guys puttered away in it," Kim reported.

"Great," Green said, sounding anything but happy. "And we have another crew to run checks on now."

"I'm going to touch base with Command again," Maji said. She went to the window and looked out into the black sky, toward where she knew Mt. Edgecumbe sat across the water. Dogpatch confirmed there was no word from Thumb yet.

At the knock on the office door, Maji turned and looked along with the other two. "Enter."

AET Taira pushed the door open and stood at attention. "I'm clocking out soon. Lieutenant Commander Fitzsimmons asked me to see if you needed anything before my watch ends. Or call if you need him to come in."

"Thanks, no," Kim answered for them.

"Aye, aye." Taira turned to leave.

Green stood abruptly. "Wait."

Taira turned back. "Ma'am?"

"Rios needs a ride." She looked to Maji. "We'll be a while yet. You should get some rest."

Maji looked to Taira. "You don't have to walk the dog or anything, do you?"

❖

Taira slowed her Jeep to a crawl on the quiet residential street, and Maji gave her the house number.

"I know," Taira responded, pulling to the graveled shoulder across from Dee's house. "I came by to check on her when she was in the hospital. Ended up talking to Nate instead." She hesitated. "I know we're not supposed to ask you three about...anything, but... what are we doing here?"

"Making sure she's safe."

"Oh. Good."

As they spoke, Dee walked in front of the picture window, backlit by a lamp somewhere deep in the living room. "Jesus," Maji exhaled. She got out and closed the Jeep door quietly, heading for the front door.

"Hey, what are you—" Dee began when she saw Maji on her doorstep.

"Do you have any security here at all?" Maji interrupted.

Dee looked sullen. "Both doors lock."

"Really. Stay here." Maji turned and nearly knocked Taira down. She almost ordered her back to the vehicle, then thought better of it. "You too. Right here."

Maji skirted the little house easily in the dark, guided by light from the windows. At the back door she spent all of thirty seconds breaking in. She crossed quietly through the kitchen and dining area to the foyer. "No fucking security."

Both women startled. Neither bothered to ask how she got in.

"Get inside."

They obeyed, Taira looking around with frank curiosity. Dee closed the door behind them, chagrin warring with hostility on her face. "So? It's my house. I can take care of myself."

"Not alone, on display." Maji waved at the picture windows, then walked over to them and yanked the blinds down. Then she spotted the bottle of tequila on the coffee table. "Is that open?"

"No. And it's not new, either. Charlie put it there three years ago. He said he needed to know..." She turned her back on them.

"You don't need to prove anything," Taira said, reaching one hand toward Dee, then pulling back.

"And you don't need to spend another night alone with a ghost," Maji added. "Let me check you in at my hotel, just till we round the jackasses up. Couple days, tops."

"No." Dee turned back and crossed her arms. "I'll go to Mom's."

Maji shook her head. "Too predictable. Look, there's a couch at my, well, Rose's suite."

"I have a couch too," Taira interjected. Seeing Dee's look of alarm, she added, "No one would expect you to be there. Would they?"

Maji almost chuckled. "You on Lifesaver Road in Coastie housing?" With the *Authorized Personnel Only* signs and a small tight-knit group of neighbors. Not bad.

"Yep. Right next to Jack's place. We could even borrow Jasper. He's very protective." Taira gave Dee a challenging look. "Unless you're ashamed to be seen leaving my place in the morning?"

Dee blinked twice. "No."

Maji took that as a *yes* to the proposal. "Okay, then. Grab whatever you need for two nights."

When Maji opened the door to the hotel suite, she wasn't surprised to find Dev on the couch, reading a paperback by the light of a single floor lamp. "Hey," she whispered.

"Dude. How was your day, dear?"

She took a seat at the far end of the couch from him. Now that he was a regular Army Reserve member and no longer part of Delta, she couldn't brief him on the mission. But at least she had been able to share the Russians' photos, which were on public record thanks to the arrest. She pulled her copy of their passport shots out of her jacket pocket and held the one of Tom between them. "Nice day, mostly spent with nice locals. The two I tangled with got get-out-of-jail-free cards, courtesy of Dmitry. You recognize him, right?"

Dev squinted at the shot of Tom in his cover persona. "Well, I'll be damned. Is that a scar? Crappy haircut too."

"Yeah. I bet he's got some tattoos that don't wear off, since we saw him last."

"Have you heard from him?" Dev asked, then rolled his eyes. "Not that you could tell me. Would be nice to know if there's a tie-in with Doc's stalker, that's all."

"Amen, brother," Maji answered obliquely. "No sign then that Javi's left town, now that he's been made?"

Dev shook his head. "He gave Rose some line about getting paid more the longer he stays and not wanting to tell them she's not interested in the reality TV thing until he gets home."

"Got ears on him?"

Dev nodded. He looked tired. "Dude's reporting in by phone. Just that Doc's still here, so far. Oh, and that she's with you, and where you two are staying."

"Great." For months she'd stayed away from Rose, and within days of their getting together that fucking psycho knew it. Too late to undo. "Did Hannah suggest moving her?"

A creaking behind her caused Maji to turn. Rose stood framed in the bedroom door, in the long T-shirt she used as pajamas. "If I'm endangering Ri, Dev, I want to get on a plane with you tomorrow. Right after my presentation."

"No, that's not—" Maji stopped when Dev poked her with his toe. "What?"

"Think about it, dude," he said.

Maji thought. Did Sirko know her face now, as well as her Army name? The Photoshopped likeness his goons had relied on last summer would be useless now, if Sirko did have a mole at the Coast Guard. And he might hurt Rose just for payback, or just to throw her off her game. "Fuck." She sighed. "Okay, book two seats out in the afternoon."

"Good call, dude."

Thinking beyond this mission, Maji asked Rose, "You up for a bit of acting?"

"Does it involve my not being in love with you again? I have had a chance to practice that role."

Maji nodded. "Maybe a bad breakup." *Temporary and completely fake, please.*

"You want Javi on ice after he calls that in?" Dev asked.

"If he doesn't get on the first plane out—yes." She paused. "Can you do that and keep eyes on Rose?"

He gave her a look to remind her that he had his own set of special skills. "I'll manage."

"If you think I should skip my presentation, I'll forgive you," Rose replied. "So long as you don't get hurt."

Maji never could promise that, so she didn't. "Let's keep this as normal as possible for you." *And anyone else watching to see if you try and bolt.*

"Pretend breakups are not normal."

"Sorry. I meant the give your talk, wow the colleagues, and win tenure part."

Rose did not look convinced. "Are you two about done?" When they looked at each other and nodded, she added, "Then good night, Dev."

Dev gave Maji a look she was happy he didn't translate into words. "I'm in the room next door. If you need me, bang on the wall. If you don't need me, try not to make any alarming noises."

"Dude," Maji replied, annoyed with how much fun he took poking at her for her first serious relationship. Then another thought struck. "We're still clean in the suite, right?"

He nodded. "I swept again. Other than a bag of clothes you should maybe throw out, you're clean. Relax, *'ukhti alsaghira.*"

"Thanks. And good night, *akhi.*" She usually saved the term *my brother* for Tom. But if she was *my little sister* tonight, he could be a sibling too. Tomorrow they'd go back to *dude.*

❖

Rose didn't move from the bedroom doorway until Maji had closed the door to the hall behind Dev and locked it. Much as she liked Dev and hoped to get to know him better someday, she planned to do it by meeting his wife and daughters. Showing off her bare legs and braless top was not part of that plan, no matter how many times he'd seen her in a bikini last summer. Now that they were alone, she wanted Maji less dressed also.

Maji turned and nearly bumped into her, catching the look in her eye as she put her hands out to stop the collision. "Um…"

"Oh," Rose said. "Are you still on the clock?"

Maji took a small step back, frowning slightly. "I need to get online briefly, and after that I'm on call." She paused. "I was just going to check on you and then take the couch."

"Don't be ridiculous. We both need rest. I promise not to keep you up…too long."

"Yeah, but if they call and I miss it, that would be really bad."

"You'll get a phone call?" Rose asked, feeling there was something she was missing still. "Then why not come to bed?"

Maji looked at her steadily for a few seconds. "Have you ever done drugs? Molly, ecstasy, coke, anything?"

"I've had pot brownies. And smoked a little."

"I don't mean buzzed. I had more mind-altering…in mind. Truly not aware of your surroundings."

Rose didn't want to ask what Maji had taken to reach that effect. The thought of her that vulnerable, or that dangerous, was disturbing. "No. I guess not. Does that make me boring? Or just sheltered?"

"Not boring. Never boring. Could you maybe sit down?" Maji looked uncomfortable.

Rose sat. Maji sat across the little table and took her hand. "Tell me, Maji."

"When you want me, and you're within reach, I'm pretty much toast. You kiss me, and I don't hear people come in the room. You touch me, and the rest of the world fuzzes out." She looked away. "I really could miss that call."

"Oh. I…" *I want to come over and see that theory in action. Damn the Army anyway.* "You'd better get to work then."

"I'm so sorry." Maji's green eyes looked heartbreakingly sad.

Rose squeezed her hand. "Don't you dare say things like that and then apologize. Just get your obligations out of the way as quickly as you can."

Maji nodded and fetched her laptop. She set it up on the tabletop and booted up. "You don't have to stay up," she said over the screen. "You've got a big day tomorrow."

"Manage yourself, Sergeant," Rose replied. She stood, restless with the thoughts she was holding back. "Can I get you something? Tea?"

Maji's hands on the keyboard stilled. "Do we have any food?"

"An apple and those nuts-and-twigs bars you like."

"Cool," Maji replied more to the screen than to Rose.

When Rose set the snacks near her, Maji was reading her screen with full attention, only her eyes moving back and forth. She frowned, typed again for nearly a minute at a furious speed, and then looked up. She noticed the glass of water, Clif bar, and apple to her left. "Thanks. I'm nearly done."

"Just do what you need to do," Rose said.

Maji barely seemed to hear her, biting into the apple while she watched something on the screen. Rose slipped off to the bedroom and changed into the silk teddy she had packed in an optimistic moment. Maji hadn't used the word addiction in her drug metaphor, but Rose would have understood if she had. Only the thought that she might somehow endanger Maji by taking a part of her highly focused attention from her work made Rose keep her distance, even now. It might be selfish, but she was not going to give up their last night together. Once Maji walked out that door, who knew when she'd see her again?

Rose heard Maji go into the bathroom, brush her teeth, flush, and wash. She slipped a robe on and waited for her in the doorway to the bedroom, at a respectable distance. When the door opened, Maji seemed a little surprised to see her.

"Thought you gave up on me."

"I tried that once. It didn't work. Are you done?"

Maji nodded and waited in the bathroom doorway.

"Where's your phone?" Rose asked.

"On the table."

Rose picked it up and headed back into the bedroom. She set it on Maji's side, on the bedside table, and turned to see Maji in the doorway, a question on her face. "I turned the volume all the way up and plugged the charger in."

"Thanks."

"Do you want to put your gun in the safe?"

Maji's hand went around to her lower back. "No. I should keep it handy." She handed it to Rose and watched her set it by the phone, still looking puzzled. "Your tomorrow is as important as mine. Why do I get the bed?"

"Because the couch isn't big enough for both of us."

"Rose…"

Rose didn't approach her, wanting to make sure Maji heard her out without lust clouding her response. "Don't argue. Just listen. I go home tomorrow, and you go God knows where. I don't fault you for that, and I don't want you to apologize. But when you have the chance to be with me, whether it's for five minutes or five years, I want one hundred percent of you."

"Okay. But what about…" Maji gestured toward her phone, blushing.

"I will not let you miss that call. I will be your designated driver, so to speak. Trust me."

Maji closed her eyes, nodding. The mix of fire and vulnerability in them when she met Rose's gaze again made Rose reach out.

Maji took her hands and pulled gently until they stood forehead to forehead, the tips of their noses brushing. "Yes."

Rose slipped the robe from her shoulders and was gratified to hear Maji groan, still holding herself back from the kiss seconds away. "I know you'll stop if I tell you to. But unless I do, nothing exists but us. Understood?"

"Yes," Maji rasped. "Yes."

Chapter Seventeen

Maji stretched to reach her phone, pulled it near her face, and clicked it on. No calls, thank God. Maybe she would have heard. Maybe not. The screen's brightness made the room seem darker, despite the soft filter of dawn through the curtains. Five thirty. She should probably get up and get ready.

"No calls," Rose mumbled. "Need more sleep?" She sounded nearly coherent now.

"Whatever you want." Maji snugged back into Rose's front. "Do you need to practice your talk?"

Rose kissed the back of her shoulder. "No. Dee and Dev were my test audience. I'm ready."

"Really? Both of them?" Maji wondered how they liked each other.

"Yes. Dev was very polite, and Dee…she's lonely."

Maji picked up the sympathy in Rose's voice. She was right, of course. "She said that?"

"Not in so many words. But she likes this woman, and she's afraid to even try with her. It's sad."

"A Coastie? Petite Japanese American, pretty and kind of… smart-ass?"

Rose pushed her. "How did you know? Are you bugging me?"

"Nope. I sent Dee to her house last night. Maybe that couch got slept on, maybe not."

"Trickster," Rose murmured into Maji's neck. Then she started nibbling softly on the spot where Maji's neck and shoulder met. "Tasty trickster. I'm not even going to ask."

Rose's hand slipped from Maji's waist down to tease her center, then slid up her belly to the space between her small breasts.

"Rose…"

"Oh. Do you have to go?" She started to withdraw her hand, but Maji caught it and held tight, weaving their fingers together.

"Not until they call. I'm one hundred percent yours, still. It's just…I'll miss you. I'm sorry we—"

Rose pressed their joined hands over Maji's mouth. "Hush. This is not good-bye. I'll get home early and have a chance to catch up before next week's classes. And you'll come visit as soon as you can." She put their hands back on Maji's chest. "Deal?"

"Yes, please. Can I see where you work, and cook with you, and…do other normal stuff?"

"If you insist," Rose replied. "What would you like to do when you visit?"

"I don't know," Maji hedged. "Go to the farmers' market without guns and backup. Use my real name." *Not lie to your friends or put you in danger*. "Not rescue any strangers."

"But that is your normal." Rose nudged a thigh between Maji's legs. "And now I get to help. Don't you want my help?"

Rose's free hand made the sort of help she was offering abundantly clear. "Yes," Maji squeaked out.

"Mm. Try again. Ask me in Italian maybe, or Farsi."

So Maji did.

As she zipped her slacks, Rose heard a sharp rapping on the suite door. "Rios!" a woman's voice called.

Should she answer? Rose looked through the peephole and saw a woman's face. "Just a minute," she called, ready to bang on the wall for Dev.

"What's up?" Maji called through the bathroom door.

Rose cracked it enough to get a peek at Maji's form, naked except for the towel around her long hair. "Someone's at the door. A woman. Tall, very blond."

"Hold on," Maji said, strode out without adding a stitch, and looked through the peephole. The rapping came again. "Hold on!" Maji repeated, this time as a bark. "Let her in," she told Rose as she disappeared back into the steamy bathroom. She left the door ajar.

Rose unlocked the door and pulled it open. "Hello."

"Morning, ma'am." The striking woman's bearing and formality seemed at odds with her jeans-and-sneakers casual dress. She stepped in and waited for the door to close, then extended her hand. "Lieutenant Green, Navy. You must be Rose."

"You didn't call," Maji said as she emerged from the bathroom, stuffing a T-shirt into the waist of her jeans. "Anything on fire?" She headed into the bedroom.

Lt. Green shook her head. "I got a room in town too. Doesn't come with breakfast, though."

Rose noticed the empty plate on the table, the coffee mug by it, and guessed that Maji had fetched breakfast from the downstairs buffet earlier. This time, she'd managed not to wake Rose when she moved. "She may be ready again soon."

"I'm good," Maji answered, emerging with her hands behind her head, the last of her french braid in progress. She wore a fleece pullover now, and socks. "You want some coffee? Or breakfast downstairs?"

Lt. Green shook her head. "I'll grab something at the…" She stopped herself, looking to Rose, the empty bedroom, and back at Maji. "Is there someplace we can talk?"

"Do you speak Arabic?" Rose joked.

Lt. Green tilted her head. "I understand a bit. Why?"

"Never mind." Maji looked to Rose, not with reprimand but apology. "We can head out."

She started to rise, but Rose stopped her. "No. It's okay. Let me grab Dev, and we'll pop down and get you a plate. Will that give you enough time?"

"Yes, ma'am. Thanks." Lt. Green looked surprised but sincere.

"He's just outside the door," Maji added.

Rose looked through the peephole and sure enough, there he was. She didn't ask, just went out and invited him to join her.

Dev was quiet in the elevator, the ride shared with travelers taking their luggage to checkout and beyond. In the empty breakfast room he asked, "Who's the badass blonde?" At her look, he smiled and said, "I was in the hall when she arrived. Your suite is clean. Really."

"I'm sorry. After last summer, I'm a little paranoid."

"Not paranoid if they're really out to get you," he joked as he started to fill plates with some of everything at the buffet.

She found a tray and started loading it also. "Ha-ha. She's a lieutenant. From the Navy."

"Really?" He paused while filling juice glasses. "Well, good."

"What does that mean?"

"Nothing. Only, don't worry about Ri. She's got great backup."

When they arrived back at the room, juggling two overloaded trays, Maji let them in. "Wow. *Tutti a tavola*, eh?"

Rose smiled. "I have a few minutes, if you don't mind company now." A bite before her presentation wouldn't hurt, but mostly she wanted to defer the inevitable good-bye.

"Coffee?" Lt. Green offered.

"Yes, thanks," Rose agreed, setting the table with four plates and the trays in the middle, family style.

Dev grabbed silverware from the drawer. "Sure," he said, extending his right hand. "Dev Goldberg. Army Reserves, here for Paragon Security."

"Once in, always in," she replied. "An honor to meet you, Dev."

"Likewise, I think."

She chuckled. "Think what you like."

While Rose was puzzling over the odd exchange, Maji took her hand under the table. "Safe travels. That's what they say up here, right?"

"Sorry you had to cut your trip short," Lt. Green said. She slipped her long frame into an open seat and accepted the plate of bacon and sausage from Dev. "We do appreciate you reducing Sergeant Rios's exposure."

"Meaning what?" Rose asked.

Maji glared across the table at Lt. Green. "Watch yourself, Lieutenant."

"Sorry. Nothing, ma'am. I'm sure she'll keep her focus on the assignment better knowing you're safe, that's all."

Rose knew that wasn't quite it, but before she could press their guest, the spiky blond head bent in prayer. With a quiet "Amen," Green set to work on her plate. She ate more like Dev and Tom than like Maji. Maybe she was in a rush to get going.

"Anybody going to videotape you today?" Maji asked.

Rose accepted the diversion. "No. This is a pretty low budget group."

"I could use my phone," Dev offered.

Rose stood and cleared her place setting. Between stage anxiety and all the words unspoken at the table, her appetite was dead. "Try, if you like. I'll be ready in five, Dev." To Maji she added, "Don't leave without...before I do."

Maji just nodded.

When Rose returned, Maji was sliding a comm into her ear, its transmitter pack waiting on the table for her.

Rose looked from Maji to the transmitter and back. "Do you need help with the wound dressings before you go?"

"Nah. The skin's healing uncovered now."

"Unless you get it dirty, or wet." Rose looked to Green. "Don't let Ri go in the water."

"Uh, okay."

"Seriously. I know she has your back. Do you have hers?"

Lt. Green pushed back from the table and stood, her full height imposing. "Yes, ma'am. We do."

"You promise?"

Maji raised one eyebrow at her, but kept her tone mild. "She just did, Rose."

"And, ma'am?" Lt. Green looked uncertain for the first time since she'd strode in and taken over the room. "My condolences on your loss. Staff Sergeant Benedetti was a remarkable soldier, and we will see his mission through. You have my word on that as well."

Rose stared at her silently, then noticed that Maji and Dev were both standing at ease, hands behind their backs and eyes trained into the near distance. "Thank you, Lieutenant. Please be careful."

As she should have expected, a single silent nod was Lt. Green's only response.

Rose watched Maji slip her gun into the holster at her lower back and settle the fleece down to hide it. Maji wasn't pretending to be someone else's streetwise girlfriend now. There wasn't the Maji she knew and loved plus this character of Ri here. Today the woman she loved and the soldier she loved were the same person, going off to face dangers unnamed with people Rose didn't know but had to rely on nonetheless. In what world could that ever feel normal? When Maji reached for the door, Rose stopped her with a fierce hug and a quick kiss. "See you soon."

Maji's nod, and the soft certainty in her eyes, was her promise.

Maji felt only a little conflicted leaving Rose with Dev while she went off hunting for hidden gold. If Dev had still been Delta, rather than a private contractor with Hannah, she'd have been happy to trade places with him. He probably wished he could too.

"Lieutenant," Maji said, "I realize you and Kim have point on this mission, but I'd appreciate it if you wouldn't upset Rose."

Green snorted. "If she can't handle the life, she's got no business being married to an operator."

"We're not. She's not been briefed."

"Seriously?" Green took her eyes off the road briefly. "Then what are you doing here?"

"Trying to take a vacation together, like normal people."

Green had the nerve to chuckle. "Good luck with that. She wants normal, you're out of luck."

"I know." And around now, Rose might be figuring that out too. "You married?"

"If you can call being hitched to a SEAL married."

Green's tone didn't invite more inquiry, but Maji couldn't resist. "And she's been briefed?"

"He, Rios. He's a SEAL."

Double wow. "Oh. That's convenient, I guess. What's that like?"

"On the rare occasions we're home at the same time, it's hot monkey sex heaven. Rest of the time, it's like being single and too busy to care." She paused. "If you're looking for advice on civilians, look elsewhere."

"Roger that. No, wait—aye, aye." They crossed the O'Connell Bridge to Japonski Island, headed for Air Station Sitka. "Speaking of which, we need a quick stop on Lifesaver Drive," she informed Green. "I stashed the boat captain there last night."

"I know." Green flicked a glance at her. "We've had eyes on her since the team arrived."

Of course they had. Well, she still wanted to check in. "Good. Let's see if she's remembered anything that might be helpful."

Fierce barking met them at Taira's door before Maji could even knock. But when Taira opened it and spoke firmly to the dog, Jasper sat and wagged his tail expectantly.

"Morning," Maji said. "May I?" She indicated offering her hand to the dog.

"Sure." Taira coached Jasper's friendly restraint as Maji let him sniff her hand and ruffled his ears. "Dee? You have company." To the women on her doorstep, she added, "Come on in."

Dee appeared on the stairs while Taira was lacing up her black uniform boots. Maji wondered where she found military issue shoes that small. She had to get her own uniform tailored to fit.

Dee looked down at them with some chagrin, like she'd been caught out. Her long dark hair was still damp, but she was fully dressed in fresh clothing. "Going to hide me someplace else today?"

"Not if you can stay with people you know nearby. I just wanted to ask if anything those guys said to you had come back. Or if you remembered anything else that might be useful."

"Where is it?"

Taira turned and looked up at her. "Where is what?"

"That's what I said too," Dee replied. "They didn't like that. That's when they stuck me, I think."

Well, that didn't help much. Though it did confirm what she suspected, that Sirko's men didn't know where their payload had gone. Which made her think of Green's disturbing breakfast update on the crew that had towed the *Eagle Song* in. "AET Taira, how well do you know Ensign Morgan?"

"Robin Morgan? A little, I guess. She was a giant squid for the Halloween party. Always brings a casserole to the potlucks. Seems nice. Why?"

Because the ensign had taken emergency family leave the day after towing the *Eagle Song*. And her family had not seen her, nor had they experienced an emergency. "She's missing. Just wondered if she's the type to go AWOL, or if she did, where."

"No." Taira shook her head. "Definitely not. But she did have a boyfriend in Arizona. Maybe if she got pregnant or something…" She shook her head again. "No. She'd still report in."

"Thanks." Lt. Green spoke for the first time. She looked to Maji. "We should go."

Maji gave the dog one last ear rub and stepped toward the door.

"Wait," Dee said. "Is Rose safe? With just that friend of yours?"

"He's got it handled. But if you wanted to hear her talk, I'm sure she'd appreciate a friendly face in the audience."

"I can just walk in?"

Maji nodded. "Security sucks. She's on in…" She looked at her watch and sighed. "About twenty minutes."

"Crap," Dee said and hustled down the steps, lightly bumping Taira on the way. "Sorry, Liv."

Taira stood. "I'll drive you."

"No."

"Come on. I'll stay under the limit."

Dee looked to Maji, then back at her host. "If they're looking for me, I don't want you near me."

"Sweet," Green said. "But unnecessary. We have a tail on you, ready to move if you're in danger."

Dee frowned at her. "Fine. They can drive me."

"Then they wouldn't be an effective tail, would they?" Green seemed almost amused. "Take the ride."

"You'll be late for work," Dee said to Taira. *Stubborn as ever.* Taira grabbed the dog's leash. "No I won't. I'll take Jasper home on my break."

❖

In the office that had become the SEALs' command center, Lt. Kim met their bad news with some of his own. "Command relayed a coded message from Thumb: *Bird wouldn't sing. Wings clipped. Eggs still hidden.*"

So the Russian crew hadn't gotten the location out of her before Ensign Robin Morgan's untimely demise. "Could the gold still be in Sitka, then?"

"Most likely. We think Ensign Morgan hid it, then ran. She caught a flight to Arizona."

"And the boyfriend?"

"Also missing. Didn't show up at work a couple days after Morgan arrived. They might still be running together, but I doubt it."

Maji shook her head. "Wings clipped. Fuckers."

"We're getting her phone logs now, see who she contacted in her last few days," Kim said.

Green frowned. "If we've thought of that, Sirko has too."

Maji hoped their official channels for that kind of information were quicker than Sirko's hackers. She was tired of playing catch-up to this guy. "Could Jack help speed that up?"

"Dunno," Kim responded. "He said he had to go into town and just took off earlier."

"A little squirrelly," Green added. "So I slapped a tracker on his jacket."

"And?"

Green shrugged and looked to Kim, who clicked the mouse attached to his laptop and scanned the screen. "Come look."

The tracker showed that Jack had not gone into town, or even back across the bridge. "What's here?" Maji asked, pointing to a spot where the program indicated he had stopped for seven minutes.

"A little Coast Guard building. Next to the boat dock and launch ramp."

There he must have taken a boat, because the tracker showed him out in the middle of the channel. It looked like he'd passed all the markers until the largest, then paused there, circled it, and stopped at two more points a few miles to the northwest. Hiding something? Or searching? Either way he must be done, because the tracker last showed him circling back to the dock. "Hey, I think he's headed back—"

They all looked up at the knock on the office door. "Enter," Green barked.

"Hey," Jack said. "Sorry for leaving you unattended. Got the parts for the helo. You need anything else before I hit the gym?"

"Nope," Kim said. "Thanks."

"PT?" Maji said, heading toward him. "Can I join you? I need a workout bad." She turned back to the lieutenants. "If you two don't mind?"

"Uh…" Jack began.

"By all means," Green replied.

Jack gave them a smile that looked forced. "Sure. You'll find spare duds in the women's locker room. See you in the gym."

Green frowned at the abruptly closed door. "Can't picture him working for Sirko. Doesn't seem like the type to be motivated by money. Or to get his thrills from cloak-and-dagger."

"They never do," Kim reminded her.

Maji remembered Jack's argument on the plane. "Check on his wife, Tina. Flight attendant, has a place in Anchorage."

"Will do." Kim paused. "Watch your six with him."

"Aye, aye."

CHAPTER EIGHTEEN

The door to the conference room opened just before Rose started her presentation. For a second she thought Maji had made it, but then she realized that the short, dark-haired woman trying to slip in unobtrusively was Dee. She gave her new friend a grateful smile and a little wave. A few heads turned in Dee's direction as she took the chair that Dev offered to her. Bolstered by the support, Rose gave the cue for the lights to be dimmed.

She managed to show all the slides within her allotted thirty minutes, even with a few interruptions. It wasn't her fault that Q&A ran long—this group was genuinely enthused. One of the academics gave a long, rambling statement masquerading as a question and Rose gamely pretended to give his point due consideration. All in all, a successful presentation.

The only surprise, when the lights came back up to full, was Javi. She spotted him in a chair along the back wall, as if he'd slipped in late. He gave her a hopeful smile, and she remembered that she had one more performance left to give.

When the moderator cut off questions, the room cleared quickly, the conference goers anxious to move on to lunch. They wouldn't have time to go far if they wanted to be back in time for afternoon sessions. Since she was flying out in a few hours, Rose hoped a celebratory trip to Ludvig's could be squeezed in. But first it was time to put on a good show for her used-to-be friend.

"So you made it," she said as she approached Javi. "That makes one of you."

"You were brilliant," he said, kissing her on both cheeks. "Why the long face?"

She hesitated, as if choking up. "I told Ri off last night. Since she didn't bother to come today, I guess I was right about her."

"If she hurt you, tell me where to find her and I'll go give her a piece of my mind."

Rose laughed bitterly. "No, you can go have a beer together and compare notes. All anyone wants to do anymore is feed off my notoriety. Or money, which is ironic. It always comes back to money, just like Angelo said."

He reached out to comfort her, but she flinched. "Don't touch me. You're as bad as she is. If you thought I'd inherited gobs of money, you'd have come offering me sympathy months ago too."

"She thought you were rich now? When you live like an adjunct?"

So he'd been watching her for some time, then. Or Sirko's people had. Rose didn't suppress the shudder that thought provoked. "I could have been rich. But why would I want blood money? I gave it away as fast as I could. I don't want to profit from Ang's death, and I'm done with people who do."

Javi's face showed that her message was sinking in. "I really am sorry, Rosita."

"Really? Then tell those vultures to leave me alone. And you— you leave me alone too. Go home. I am, so you might as well too."

"But—"

"I'm done, Javi. Now I have to go clear my stuff out of that stupid hotel and get to the airport. I don't want to be stuck here with that woman one minute longer. Excuse me." She pushed past him, not looking back.

Dee found her a few minutes later in the women's room. "Rose? Are you okay?"

"I'm fine. Sorry if I alarmed you."

Dee took in Rose's return to equanimity with concerned watchfulness. "I could follow that guy for you."

"No need, but thank you." Rose finished touching up her mascara and turned from the mirror to face Dee. "Ri and I are—"

"Fine. Yeah. I get it."

"Oh. Am I a bad actor?" If she hadn't convinced Javi, her efforts were wasted.

Dee gave her a rare smile. "No—you put on a good show. I would have bought it, if I hadn't seen Ri myself this morning. No way did you just break up with her."

"You saw her?"

"Yeah, she stopped by to check on me." Dee looked like she wanted to say more and also didn't want to.

Rose decided not to pry, as curious as she was about Maji's collaboration with Lt. Green. Whatever they were up to, there was nothing she could do to help—except leave town.

They exited the conference center without spotting Javi. Dee kept a hand on Rose's back as if giving her moral support. Dev kept them in his line of sight, discreetly walking in the same direction toward the hotel but often on the other side of the street.

Dee looked around when they reached the hotel lobby door. "Where'd he go?"

"I'm sure he's nearby," Rose replied, heading for the elevator.

"Maybe he's talking to the guy that Navy woman put on my tail. Must be good, 'cause I haven't spotted him yet."

Rose wondered if Dee had met Lt. Green too. "The Navy?"

"That's what Liv said," Dee replied.

"The woman your sister is so set on matchmaking for you? How would she know?"

Dee flushed deeply. "She's in the Coast Guard. They've been out at the air station the last couple days, I guess. Liv doesn't know more than that, 'cause they're not allowed to ask Ri or the Navy folks any questions. So I'm guessing they're SEALs."

Rose would have laughed at that leap of logic, but for what she suspected about Maji's work. "Ah," she said, as the elevator arrived at their floor. She looked down the hallway, and there was Dev coming from the stairwell toward them.

Rose threw her clothes into her suitcase as quickly as she could, not bothering to roll or fold anything. She'd have plenty of time to iron in California.

"Nobody's chasing you," Dev noted.

Rose glanced at both of them. "I want to take you two to lunch."

"Really?" Dee asked. "Where?"

"Ludvig's. I promised myself I'd get back there, and this is my last chance."

Dev looked at his watch. "Is it a popular place? Busy?"

"There'll be a wait at the lunch rush," Dee confirmed. "But I could go put us on the list, have a table when you get there."

Dev nodded. "Might work."

"Just don't stick me with the tab," Dee said. "My budget doesn't stretch to three meals at that place."

"Of course not—this is on me." Rose laid a hand on her arm. "I owe you both a thank-you. And since I don't have a kitchen here, Ludvig's will have to stand in."

"Is their cooking as good as yours?" Dev asked.

Rose felt herself flush as Dee watched them both, looking like she wanted to know more of their history but would never ask.

In the women's locker room, Taira emerged from the showers and looked startled to find Maji rooting through the lost and found bin. "Can I help you?"

"Hey. Jack said there'd be clothes I could borrow in here, to work out in."

"Not in there. Hang on a sec, I'll show you." Taira opened her locker and dropped her towel.

Maji took the opportunity to look around the locker room. When she heard, "Still here?" she walked back toward the now fully clothed Taira.

"Just looking around."

"Well come look in here." Taira showed her a door marked simply *Gear*. Inside, the shelves were stocked with a little of everything in the way of athletic wear, from swimsuits to sweatshirts. *Who needs the gift shop?*

"Swimming?"

"Nah. I don't float."

"Neither do we. Rescue swimmers spend most of their pool time under the surface. Rest of us just imitate them."

Maji hoped Jack wasn't in the pool. That'd be a terrible place to try to talk. "Even pilots?"

"Sure. I went out on a recon once when Jack was copilot, and we got a call for a kayaker in distress, right in the middle of it. Didn't have time to go back to the station and pick up a swimmer, so we flew out direct." Taira checked to make sure Maji was following, clearly enjoying telling the tale. "I put the basket in the water, but the poor guy was too hypothermic to pull himself in. So guess who went in—in his flight suit."

Brave—or stupid? "Sounds risky."

Taira shrugged. "We don't recite the Guardian Ethos to sound cool. It's in the Coastie DNA. I could tell you stories like that all day and never run out."

"About Jack?"

"About lots of us. People who talk shit about the Coast Guard don't know how hard we train or how hard we work. You make it through basic here, you could serve in any branch. Can't say the reverse."

Maji grabbed herself a T-shirt and shorts. Her own shoes would do fine. "Must be nice to have saving lives as your primary mission. Bet it pulls good talent from other branches, like Jack coming over from the Air Force."

"Yeah." Taira stepped out of the little room and closed it back up when Maji followed. "Why are you so interested in the Lieutenant Commander?"

"I'm concerned, that's all. He seems off today. Any ideas?"

"Oh, he always gets stressed right before he hands command back over. It's a lot, being responsible for the whole station when it's not your usual duty post. We have a great crew here, but if anything goes wrong on his watch, it's still on him."

Maji nodded. "Makes sense. When's he off the hook?"

"Tomorrow morning."

"Good. Guess I'll go blow off some steam with him now." Maji headed toward the unmarked lockers to change.

"Take any locker without a name on it." Taira headed for the door. "Oh, and tell Jack for me, I'm putting Jasper back at his house."

"Sure. Thanks for taking Dee in, by the way. She seemed better for it."

Taira pinked up. "Any time. Happy to help."

Maji suspected *happy* was an understatement. She hoped by now Dee knew as much.

Maji found Jack working out alone. He looked fit in his PT clothes, his legs lean but strong like a runner's and his shoulders bulkier than she would have expected. Controlling a helicopter did require a rock solid core but not upper body strength per se. She'd seen Black Hawk pilots handle the controls when they had to hover for fast roping a team to the ground, or maneuver through rough terrain at high speeds. The concentration and motor control were key. And staying relaxed under pressure, like Jack on that rescue video. Maybe it was swimming that bulked him up, or just a love for feeling pumped and looking good in a T-shirt.

Something about the way he was going after the weight rack, though, made her think he was exorcising demons rather than just conditioning his body. The sheen of sweat on his face hadn't reached his perfect thatch of straw-colored hair yet. But the dark spots on his T-shirt said he'd cranked out a few sets before her arrival.

Maji glanced at the Workout of the Day board. Maybe this was just his normal CrossFit routine. She smiled and pointed to the list of exercises in chalk under the heading WOD: Loredo. The list included twenty-four squats, twenty-four push-ups, twenty-four walking lunge steps, and a four hundred meter run. For six rounds, timed. "Whatcha got left?"

"Haven't started. Wanna join me? I can scale it."

"No need." There was nothing on the list she couldn't do, though running four hundred meters indoors would be awkward. "Mind if we switch out burpees for the run?"

Jack walked toward her, swinging his arms in circles, loosening up. "Really?" When she didn't blink, he cocked his head. "Guess there's a first for everything."

"I just need a minute to warm up."

"Good idea," Jack said, sucking down water from a sports bottle. "You lead."

Maji started with jumping jacks to get her blood pumping, and then some kicks to loosen up the hips. After all her joints were oiled and her muscles oxygenated, she scanned the WOD list again, committing it to memory. Checking back would interrupt the flow, and this circuit should run short, fast, and hard.

Jack offered to handle the timer, and they worked through the exercises nearly in sync. Maji took the opportunity to ask friendly, oblique questions, and slowed down a notch to let him catch enough breath to answer.

"You must take time to fit your PT in at home." He complimented her when they rose from the third set of push-ups, and he took a minute to towel the sweat off his face.

"I do as much as I can. Travel's trickier," she admitted. "What do you do for PT when you're out of town?" If she couldn't get him to slip any intel, at least she might get some new workout ideas.

Unsurprisingly, he ran wherever he went, swam wherever he could, and did crunches and push-ups anywhere he had to, including hotel rooms or airports. Maji empathized. "More fun when you have company, though."

"Yeah. I loved to travel with Tina. She's always game to..." He looked away, covering his obvious distress with a few coughs.

"Sorry you hit a rough spot. You get to talk to her since the plane ride?"

"No, I'm giving her space like she asked." Maji noticed he looked away from her again when answering. When they wrapped up the fourth round, Jack said, "You know, I'm going to cut it short today. Want to lead a warm down?"

"You start. I'll catch up in a minute." Maji moved to the chin-up bar and made a little hop up to get her grip on it. Three pull-ups in, she saw Green come through the door, her eyes scanning as she moved.

"Lieutenant Commander!" Green barked.

He straightened up from his toe touches, his face trying unsuccessfully not to betray his anxiety. "Yes, Lieutenant?"

Maji cranked out three more pull-ups during the exchange. At the top of the fourth, Green appeared to notice her. Maji gave a nod and lowered down to start the last few. Or maybe just two. She'd lost some strength the last few weeks.

"Though she be but little, she is fierce," Green said, her eyes smiling.

Maji pulled two more out, with more effort than she would have liked, and dropped to the floor. "Life's better when you're a beast."

"Amen, sister." Green turned her focus back on Jack, who was wiping down equipment. "Hey, Jack. Where's the gold hidden?"

He didn't quite squelch the panic before plastering on a bewildered look. "What?"

"The gold that the *Arkhangel* crew moved to the *Eagle Song* before Coasties towed it in. Where is it now?"

Jack's glance flicked around the room. It was empty but for them, the machines, and the emergency exit a few feet away. "I don't know what you're…" And then he moved.

Nice explosiveness, Maji thought as she sprinted to cut him off, springboarding off a weight bench.

Jack screamed as something made an audible crunch.

Now on top of him, Maji took the opening to pin him to the floor.

"Hey!" Taira called out, running toward them. "Get the fuck off him."

Green pivoted toward her and swept both feet out from under her, catching her by one arm and righting her with it pinned behind her back. Maji hoped that was just caution on Green's part, not an indictment. One traitor was too many already.

"What the fuck," Taira yelled, red-faced and gasping. But she wisely did not struggle against Green, who looked like an immovable object holding her calmly while standing in horse stance to even their heights somewhat.

"Everybody calm down," Green said loudly. "Jack, what broke?"

"Not me, I hope." Shards of wood nearby suggested the second likeliest option. "But my leg hurts like hell."

"Okay, we'll get you to the medic in a minute. First, answer my question. Where is it?"

"I don't know." He squeezed his eyes shut. "I wish I did."

"Where is what?" Taira piped up. "What is everyone after?"

"You want to know, start by cooperating," Green said. "We need to lock the gym and talk—all of us. Okay?"

Taira looked to Jack. When he gave her the nod, she agreed. "I'll kill the lights and dead bolt the doors."

Maji eased off Jack and gave him a hand into a sitting position, taking a knee herself. He rubbed the side of his thigh, and she hoped he'd just taken a hard hit to the IT band. Painful, but only temporarily disabling.

Lt. Green motioned for Taira to sit by them. "We got the phone logs for Ensign Morgan's cell." She paused, as if to give him a chance to confess something. "She called you twice before they found and killed her."

"Robin's dead?" Taira burst out.

Jack pinned his eyes on the floor. In shame? Maji wondered. Guilt?

"Yeah. Thanks to the same guy who had his agents attack Dee. He doesn't take *I don't know* very well." She turned to Jack. "So I hope you've got something we can work with. What about Tina? Do you at least know where she is?"

Jack covered his face with his hands, breathing hard. Crying, maybe. Almost hyperventilating. Maji looked to Green, her question unspoken.

"Airline said she didn't report to work today," Green updated her.

Taira popped to her feet. "Oh, shit. We have to call the cops."

"Sit," Green ordered, rising to her full height.

Taira shook her head. "No, we need the cops. I just went to Jack's house, and Tina was there. She acted weird, and I thought maybe she was taking stuff, you know…" She skipped the predivorce innuendo. "I came to tell you, Jack. Guess I didn't need to." When he didn't raise his head, she looked to Green. "Now what?"

"Now we get her back," Green said, then looked away. "Kim, you read?" After a tiny pause she continued, "Agreed. Out." She looked at Jack. "We're mobilizing a team."

"No!" he gasped, looking up at last. "They'll kill her if I don't deliver."

Green shook her head. "No. They won't. We've got you." She turned her focus back to Taira. "What exactly happened?"

"I went to take Jasper home and saw someone inside, so I knocked. The door opened just a crack, and Tina acted like she didn't know me. Jasper scented something and started barking. Tina said to take him away, that dogs scared her. I thought…" She looked to Jack. "I'm sorry."

Jack looked worse, his eyes almost glassy.

"We'll get her back, Jack," Maji promised. "We'll get the gold and we'll get her back. Breathe."

Green turned to Taira. "Got a stretcher down here?"

"By the pool."

"Go. Bring it in. Now."

Taira nodded and ran out.

"Help us help you, Jack," Green said. Maji bet she did a great good cop in interrogations.

"I don't have it!" Jack said, pounding the floor with one fist. "I don't know where it is."

"What did Morgan tell you?"

"Nothing that made sense," he insisted. "Just two weird texts."

Green crossed her arms. "No PFDs for moths." When he looked alarmed, she added dryly, "We hacked your phone."

"Fine. Whatever helps. But PFDs is the only part I get."

Personal flotation devices, Maji interpreted. "Life jackets?" They both looked at her as if she was wasting time with rhetorical questions, so she posed a serious one. "And the second message was?"

Jack answered, "Rust never sleeps."

"Sounds like code," Maji acknowledged. "But one she thought you would understand."

"Or could figure out," Green added.

Taira burst back in with the stretcher, and they moved the discussion to the medical ward.

CHAPTER NINETEEN

At Ludvig's the server remembered Rose and greeted her warmly. Dev's phone vibrated, trying to dance itself off the table, and he stepped outside with it while they put his order in.

When Dev returned, he gave Rose a satisfied smile. "Javier reported in that you're leaving, and they've got him a ticket on the flight an hour before yours."

"If you need a cab," Dee suggested, "Nate's driving today. He can take you."

"That would be great," Rose said. "Did he drive you today, for the incognito effect?"

"No. Liv did. I stayed at her place last night." Seeing Rose's surprise and delight, she added, "Not like that. Ri asked her, for... security."

"Well, I'm glad you were safe. And now, you said, you have a shadow?"

Dev looked concerned. "Someone's following you?"

"The Navy lady said it was a tail. For my protection."

Rose put on an innocent face. "And Dee thinks they might be SEALs. What do you think?"

"I think if they tell you they are, that's a good sign they aren't."

Dee looked at him askance. "Nobody said who they are or what they're doing, and the Coasties aren't allowed to ask."

"Liv is in the Coast Guard," Rose explained. "What does she do there?"

"She's an AET—that's an Avionics Electrical Tech," Dee replied. "She fixed my depth sounder, just like that. And they go up in the helos too. She helps with search and rescue."

Rose waited for more, but Dee looked embarrassed to have said that much. She wondered if Maji might have been watching out for their new friend's heart, as well as her safety. Rose wouldn't put it past her.

The meal itself took center stage. Dev had the halibut with sautéed mushrooms, Rose the grilled duck breast with pomegranate glaze and wild mushroom risotto. Dee got the pesto gnocchi, because as she pointed out, "It doesn't swim, fly, or walk on four feet around here."

They shared bites all around, with Rose oohing the most openly. Dee seemed almost embarrassed by the way Rose emoted over her food. Dev chewed a bite of house-made gnocchi thoughtfully, before declaring, "Good. But the pesto doesn't compare."

"What's wrong with the pesto?" Dee asked him.

"Nothing. It's excellent like everything here," Rose answered for him.

Dev smirked. "Come on. I may not have been allowed in the house, but I did get to try your family recipe. It's the best."

Rose flushed, not from the compliment but from the recollection of her uncle Gino barring Dev from his house due to his skin tone. "I'm not sorry Gino went to prison. See where his racism gets him there." To Dee she added, "But my grandmother's pesto is really, truly the best in the world."

Dee gave her a knowing look. "So's my grandma's fry bread. But so is everybody's."

"But your mother's really is." Rose laughed. "And when Danny and Kyla say so, I'll back them up."

Dee didn't laugh. "Maybe I should go there tonight. I don't want to put Liv in any danger going back to her place, even if some shadow's got my back."

"Best not to expose your family, either," Dev said. "My hotel room's booked the rest of the week, if you want it."

Dee pushed her empty plate away, face also wiped clean in a way that made Rose wonder what was going on behind the outwardly tough woman's cautious eyes.

"Dev?" Rose sat up straight, feeling unreasonably alarmed. "What did Lieutenant Green mean when she said I was limiting Ri's exposure by leaving town? How could my being here actually endanger her?"

"Well, if she's worried about your safety, it's a distraction. And whatever she's up to, focus is paramount. I'm sure the Navy lady just wants her Army asset on her A game, that's all."

Rose's intuition said that was not all. But there was no point trying to pry anything more from Dev. She hoped Maji really was working with SEALs. "Dev? Are SEALs the best?"

"Best the Navy's got," he said, attempting a joke. At the look on her face, he added, "Best we could ask for. Sea, air, and land, right?"

"Oh, right. Well, whatever they're up to, I hope it's just on land. And quick."

❖

By the time Jack emerged from the medical office with an ice pack, he wanted answers and a plan. Maji followed him and Taira into the temporary command center.

"Your house is surrounded, the neighborhood evacuated, and the strike team is ready to go in on my call," Lt. Kim informed him.

"And we've come up with two potential locations to search," Lt. Green added.

"Great. So get Tina out and go search." Jack looked between the two Navy officers. "Where the hell's your sense of urgency?"

"We have teams headed to the radio station and the industrial park now," Kim reassured him.

Picking up the disconnect, Maji explained, "We need you to give proof to Sirko before we take down the guys at your house. As soon as they stop reporting in, he'll know we're fighting back and he'll up the stakes. Tina will be safe, but other civilians will get targeted."

"Like who?" Maji could almost taste his desire to accept that devil's bargain. "Never mind," he said, shaking the internal battle off. "Let's just tell him he can have it. Gold, right?" Jack looked at his watch. "He could call any minute."

Green shook her head. "And just what does it look like, Jack? Can you text him a photo? No—because we don't even know what the payload looks like yet. But Sirko does, so let's not play games that we can't win."

Well, they had two gold weights, and Maji suspected the rest were in PFD lockers of some sort. They could take a risk and fake a photo. But Sirko was hard to fool and brutal when crossed. Much as she sympathized with Jack, Green was right. "Faster we find the gold, the faster you can show proof and liberate Tina. They won't hurt her as long as she's leverage."

"I'm holding you to that, Rios." Jack looked determined now, focused. "Let's split into two teams. Where are we searching?"

Maji was relieved to see him switch into action mode. But they couldn't let him pilot this mission, so they'd need to put him to other use. "Yes," she confirmed, "we have two teams. Come around and see them, already on task. You can help best from the IC here."

She pulled a chair behind Kim's desk and Jack lowered himself into it, glued to the laptop's split screen.

"Team one," Green said. On screen, two buff guys were loading equipment into a Subaru. There was no sound, but the camera showed they were talking. When they looked toward the driver's door, the camera panned to the driver. Number four, wearing the camera, was probably talking to Lt. Kim via the comm set.

"Where are they headed?" Jack asked, his voice slipping into pilot mode, modulated even in a crisis. Maji hoped that meant he accepted them as his crew now.

"The KCAW Radio offices. Based on 'Rust Never Sleeps' being a classic rock song and on the station playing *The Moth Radio Hour*."

Jack looked skeptical, but focused on the screen of the second laptop on the desk. The view from inside that car was moving considerably faster. "And them?"

"To that old industrial park out Sawmill Creek Road." Maji recalled from her visit with the state trooper that the Russians had searched there already. But maybe they didn't know what they were looking for.

"How can I help?" Taira asked.

"Go find out where Ensign Morgan's team mothballs its equipment," Jack replied without looking up. "And hustle back."

Taira nodded, heading for the door at a jog. "Aye, aye, sir."

Maji motioned Green over to her, as far from the laptops as she could get without leaving the room. Quietly she asked, "Who's watching Dee?" If there was a strike team at Jack's house, and two teams on search, the numbers fell short.

"The Raven Radio team was. But she went to lunch with your girlfriend and her bodyguard. Sirko shouldn't need her with Tina in the bag, but we'll put a guy back on her soon as we can spare one."

Green was probably right, but it bothered Maji that Dev had two protectees and no immediate backup. Soon would have to do. "Right. I'd like to get on your comm line."

"Sure. Listen only for now." Green went back to the desk, opened the other laptop, and typed.

Maji's earpiece came alive, and a steady stream of quiet male voices relayed information on the two searches. She considered going around the desk and watching the two screens to get the complete picture. But they didn't need anyone else hovering. "Thanks," she said. "What else can I be doing?"

Green picked up her laptop and walked toward the door, motioning Maji to follow. In the next office over, she opened it on the little meeting table. "Take a look at the strike team's feed and help me prep them. The more we know, the less likely your guy gets hurt."

Tom. Maji wished there was a way to give him a heads-up about the coming rescue, a cue to get down and stay down at least. "Roger that."

❖

"Thank you for the lift, Nate. I hope we're not taking you away from time in your studio," Rose said. She looked out at the magnificent view, sorry to be leaving prematurely. Next to her, Dev looked watchful. And in the front, Dee was silent. Rose guessed that she and Nate were close enough to be comfortable together without talk. Nice.

"No worries," he replied. "It's my fresh air day. Gotta enjoy them before the cruise ships arrive."

"How busy does it get then?"

"Too busy for me to get behind the wheel," he admitted. "Those people wander into the road like cattle. I set up in the wood shop at the Cultural Center in the park and let them come to me. Safer."

"Don't know how Heather does it, driving that big bus and having to talk to strangers all day too," Dee said.

"Speaking of roadblocks," Dev said as blue and red flashing lights came into sight just over the rise of O'Connell Bridge. "Careful here."

Nate approached slowly as they watched another car being turned around by the police officer protecting the scene. The car drove past them, back toward town. "I know her," Nate reassured them. "I'll explain your situation."

As he pulled up, however, the officer shook her head. "Closed. Fatality."

Nate stuck his hand out the window, and to Rose's surprise, the officer took it. "Who?" he asked.

"Carl Soo," she said, struggling to hold back tears. She sucked in a couple breaths. "And some guy he was taking to the airport. Big truck rammed them and just kept going."

"Hang on," Nate said, letting her hand go with a final squeeze. He went around back to the trunk, returning with a cooler and water bottle.

As he was handing over what Rose assumed was his own lunch, Dev got out and walked past them into the crime scene. Another officer stopped him, took a look at a badge he offered, and then led him around the far side of the smashed taxi. When he returned, he looked stony. "If we go back to ANB Harbor, can you get us over to Japonski Island in your boat?" he asked Dee.

"Sure." She looked at Rose, then back at him, as Nate turned the car and started for the harbor. "As far as Sealing Cove anyway. Can you walk the last quarter mile?"

He nodded without looking at her, his eyes scanning everywhere as they drove. Rose remembered Maji doing the same while on high alert last summer. "Dev. What is it?"

"Javi."

❖

Dee guided the boat smoothly up to the guest dock, letting Dev handle the dock lines while Rose stayed in the cabin. *Javi is dead* kept running through her mind, a loop that wouldn't stop. Out in the cockpit, Rose heard Dee offer to walk them to the airport. *No!* What if someone was waiting for them on this side? Dee should get as far from them as possible.

"No need," Dev replied and landed lightly in the cockpit.

The cabin door swung in. "Fine. Let me grab you a bottle of water, at least." Dee entered. "Hey, you ready? Sorry I couldn't get you closer."

Rose hugged her good-bye, watching Dev push through the cabin door to join them. She felt Dee go rigid, and for a second she wondered what Dev had done. Then she felt the cold of a gun against her own ribs.

"Stay calm and no one is hurt," said the voice behind her. She struggled to place it, familiar but...

Dev nodded, raising his arms. "I am calm," he said, eyes wide and his Indian-accented voice rising in a way that said he was anything but. Rose recognized the subterfuge but hoped the man behind her did not.

"Dee," she said, releasing her hold on the other woman gently, "back up, please."

"Yes," said the man. "Over there together. All three." He gave Rose a small nudge.

Appear to comply. Buy some time. She moved across the cabin, looking in vain through the windows for anyone on the docks who might help. Then she turned and stifled a gasp. *Tom!* Seeing a second man emerge behind him, she lifted her hands in front of her, eyeing the gun in Tom's hand as if she believed he might in fact use it. "You don't need that. Please put it away."

Tom holstered his gun but the other man did not. Tom pulled a handful of zip ties from his pocket. "Hands," he said, showing her with his own how to hold hers in front of her, ready to be cuffed.

Rose mimicked him but noticed that the other man had all his attention on Dev and Dee. So she followed her training and held her hands so that the zip ties couldn't be fully tightened around her wrists. Tom gave her the tiniest of nods and fastened the restraint. "Ow," she cried out for effect as he straightened up.

"You," he said to Dee next, giving her the same demonstration. "Hands."

Dee looked frantically around, no doubt looking for something to use as a weapon, Rose thought. "Please," Rose said to her. "We'll be all right if we play along, I promise."

Dee gave her a dark look and exhaled loudly through her nose, but she also held her hands out.

Tom zip-tied them and turned to Dev next. "You."

Dev looked to the women with chagrin written large on his face. "I am so sorry. I am not a fighter."

Dee quickly masked her surprise, turning it into a look of derision. Good, Rose thought, she understands the *play along* part.

When all three were bound, the other man spoke to Tom in Russian. Tom nodded and began a pat-down of Dev, sweeping his hands down his chest, sides, arms, and legs. He never paused in the area where Rose knew Dev usually kept his gun. She doubted he had taken it off today, but they were flying, so…

Tom moved on to Dee, who raised her cuffed hands to ward him off. He cocked his head in frustration, taking a step back and reaching into his jacket pocket. Despite trusting him, Rose tensed.

When she saw the syringe, she didn't relax much. And Dee went visibly pale. "Awake search or asleep search. You choose."

"Awake," Rose said and met Dee's betrayed look with the calmest demeanor she could muster. "He won't hurt you. They need us, somehow. Don't you?" When he just shrugged, she added, "I'm Rose, by the way. And you are?"

"I know," he said with waning patience. "One doc, two doc, one lady captain."

"Awake," Dee said. She inhaled and drew herself to her full height, lifting her cuffed hands up to allow him access to her body.

Tom made quick work of Dee's pat down and moved over to Rose. He gave her a little bow. "Dmitry." He looked over his shoulder to the man brandishing the pistol. "Petrov. Small English, big gun. No humor."

"Thank you," Rose replied. His search was again perfunctory, and Petrov didn't seem worried that his partner would miss a weapon. She remembered from camp how a good search was to be done, and also how helpful it was to be underestimated by an adversary. Trying to sound meek, she asked, "What do you want from us?"

"Your phone."

Rose gestured to her purse on the banquette seats across the cabin. Tom fished out her phone and scrolled through her contacts. As he held it to his ear, she could hear the muted ringing. Then it went to voicemail.

"Soldier girl is too busy for you?" he said in mock surprise. "Maybe you shouldn't have broke her heart."

"Try mine!" Dev blurted. "Ri is my friend also. Here." He awkwardly tried to fish the phone from his tweed blazer pocket.

Tom removed it and dialed again. This time, Rose faintly heard, "Go for Rios."

"Sergeant. I have a doc, a doc, and a captain. What do you have?" The smug smile Tom gave them as he listened to her response was not a warming sight. "No. You send proof of gold, then I send proof of life. Call when you have it."

He hung up, keeping both phones. "Sit."

Just how far would Tom take this charade, Rose wondered. Would he actually hurt one of them to keep his cover intact? She wanted to help him fool Sirko, but if Dee or Dev was endangered she didn't think she could stand to play helpless. When Petrov growled something in Russian, she glared at both captors and slid onto the bench beside Dee.

CHAPTER TWENTY

I got it!" AET Taira announced as she burst into the room. "I know where it is."

Maji covered the phone, shaking her head at Taira. When she skidded to a halt, mouth closed, Maji spoke to Tom again. "We will have it shortly. You get me proof of life and we'll talk." She frowned at his response and hung up.

"Proof of life," Jack yelled from across the room. "You're bargaining with those...terrorists?"

Maji met and held his gaze. "Not just for Tina. They have my girlfriend and two of my friends now too." She looked to Lt. Green. "That was Dmitry. Not at Jack's house."

Green gave a small nod at her reference to Tom, not revealing anything to the two Coasties about his identity.

"The *Eagle Song* left ANB Harbor. Bridge is down," Kim reported. "No eyes on the vessel yet. Wish we'd put a tracker on the captain."

Maji dialed Hannah. Fuck the firewall. *Pick up*. When Hannah did, she said, "Rose got grabbed. What's her twenty?"

"Please hold." She rattled off a latitude and longitude. "Appears on the map as Sealing Cove Harbor. I'll update Command." Hannah disconnected without any words of comfort.

Maji relayed the information to the SEALs, adding, "Strike team two?"

"Mustering," Kim confirmed.

"They have Dee, don't they?" Taira asked.

"Yes. And she will be all right—Rose and Dev will keep her calm until the strike team can extract them." At least she hoped so. "Now, what did you learn? Report, AET Taira."

Taira nodded numbly, calming her breathing with visible effort. "Okay. Yeah. Ensign Morgan towed the *Eagle Song* to our dock by the ferry landing. State troopers took custody a few hours later, when they got back from the scene with the body."

"You think she took the gold off during that window of opportunity?"

Taira nodded. "Chain of custody report said there were no life vest lockers, that the PFDs were just strewn about." She paused and then resumed with no question in her voice. "We have a storage area right across the street. Holds trailerable boats, buoys, all kinds of gear. And the out-of-date equipment gets *mothballed* there, before going to surplus."

Maji felt her first hint of relief. "Great. I'll call Dmitry, tell him where to send his men. After they report success, we scoop them up and extract the hostages."

With a brief glance to each other, the two lieutenants nodded.

A different man answered the phone on the first ring, asking in Russian who was calling. Sirko knew way too much about her, Maji thought, then answered as expected in Russian. "Rios here. Where is your boss?"

"In a safe place with his friends, of course. And he does not talk to the likes of you."

"Not Sirko. Give me Dmitry."

After a brief pause with a muffled exchange on the other end, Tom asked in Russian, "How do you know my name?"

"You got the others out of jail," she answered. Hearing the echo of speaker mode, she continued in Russian for the benefit of the unnamed comrade. "If you are in charge there, I will tell you where the gold is. Your men can collect it."

"All my men are busy pointing guns at your people," he replied, then paused and repeated it in English, as if she might not have translated that properly. "You and the Coast Guard official find it, show me, and wait for further instructions. You need that in English too?"

"No. I understand," she replied in Russian. "Just give us time to get to it. Don't hurt them."

"Thirty minutes. You call then, wherever you are. No call, one less prisoner of war." He hung up abruptly.

Maji turned to the others. "Jack and I have to go. You heard the rest?"

"Yeah," Jack replied, before the lieutenants could. "They have our people, and you speak their language." He moved toward her with surprising speed despite the limp.

Green put an arm across his chest. "Hey now. We're all on the same team. And we need your credentials to access storage, anyway. Got a boat with a hoist here?"

"I'll drive you to the launch," Taira volunteered.

Green got the nod from Kim. "Go, go," she said.

Maji was out the door before the second *go*.

Rose tried to get comfortable on the barely padded bench that served as seating. What were they trying to get Maji to do? She pressed her zip-tied hands onto the top of the little table affixed to the floor of the salon. It didn't move at all. Not useful as a shield or a weapon. But Tom had let her sit at one end, with Dev at the other and Dee in between. If he gave them some signal to move, say to charge his partner or take cover, they'd have a chance to act.

Petrov started making coffee in the little galley, and Rose noticed Dee stiffen. "Are you making enough for everyone?" Rose called across the cabin.

Petrov ignored her, but Tom did not. "This is not a restaurant. If we feed and water you, soon you will ask for the bathroom and try something when we say yes. Bad news."

"Head," Dee grumbled. At his puzzled look, she added. "On a boat, it's called a head."

"Why?"

"It's where some people do their best thinking."

Rose gave her a smile and a wink. If they stayed relaxed, their chances of using creativity and spontaneity to grab an opportunity for escape improved. "Look," she said to Tom. "I'm the leverage, right? Why don't you let these two go?"

Tom spoke to Petrov in Russian, who answered with a few words and a smirk. "Petrov says that would make playing with you while your girlfriend works easier, thank you." He let that sink in a few seconds. "But I think a little more insurance never hurt anyone. They stay."

Maji was surprised to find Lt. Green right behind them and climbing into the Jeep. As they flew past the sentry post and the airport came into sight, Maji turned to her with a questioning look. Could they at least check in with the strike teams?

"No stops allowed," Green said loudly enough for Taira at the wheel to hear. And sure enough, Jack gripped the passenger door handle as Lifesaver Lane came into view.

Maji put her hand on his shoulder and gave it a light squeeze. "She'll be okay, Jack. Let the strike team do what they do best."

He nodded silently, and the little neighborhood flew by as quickly as the airport had. The masts at Sealing Cove came into view, and Taira slowed to the speed limit.

"No stops," Green repeated. Maji was glad now that Green was along, realizing that if Taira had pulled into the marina she might have been tempted to leap out herself.

Taira let out a frustrated growl in response but swung the Jeep into the turn lane for the little Coast Guard yard and building next to the channel. Maji could see the blue and red lights flashing up on the bridge, at odds with how quiet the town just across the small strip of water looked. No good time for a fatal accident, but now especially sucked. She doubted they could get to the ferry landing faster by water than by land.

Jack requisitioned the boat with barely ten words to the surprised-looking ensign at the duty desk. "Aye, aye" came with a salute and an offer of PFDs on the way out the back door.

"Suit up," Jack instructed and he grabbed a PFD off the rack and pushed through the back door.

Seeing Taira hesitate, Green barked, "You're with us."

Did Green think Taira was in danger of cowboying off to Sealing Cove if left here? Maji wasn't sure and wasn't about to ask. But keeping all of them safely focused on this task was the right call. She gave Taira a light shove toward the door and followed her out, PFD in hand.

As they zipped up the channel toward the ferry landing seven miles north, Maji sucked in the salt air, gathering her thoughts. In the distance, pale gray clouds were gathering. Did Tom have a plane here? Would he take the gold if they let him? And if they didn't, who else could they get close to Sirko? "Green," she called over the roar of the twin outboards.

When Green crossed the cockpit and leaned close to listen, Maji said, "They'd focus better if we told them about Thumb."

"Negative. Command wants him to stay inside, try to get face-to-face."

So no risking Tom's cover. But…"If he doesn't deliver, Sirko will kill him on sight. Or before."

"One thing at a time, Sergeant. Focus on your mission." Green gave her the look of a superior reminding her soldiers of their duty.

"Which is what, at this point?"

"Same as always. Get Sirko." Green raised an eyebrow. "We adapt as needed."

The workboat shuddered as it touched the dock, Taira hopping off to secure the lines. Maji noted that the state ferry was just pulling in at the landing. Maybe Tom planned to use the Marine Highway or the *Eagle Song* for a getaway vehicle.

"If Dmitry leverages me onto a boat with him and his crew, you can still follow me and the gold to Sirko," Maji told Green. "Sirko wants my ass for payback. If we can use that, don't hesitate. Just secure Rose."

"One thing at a time," Green repeated, turning her toward the dock. "Move out."

Taira punched in the code on the console by the chain-link fence, and the gate clicked open. Inside, they spread out and began searching. The lot was not huge, but it was jam-packed with a well-organized chaos of stored items.

In the far corner, Maji spotted metal racks with standard Coast Guard orange fiberglass lockers on each shelf, with *Life Preservers* stenciled on them. On the ground at the base of the rack stood a hand truck loaded with three red lockers, rust at the corners of the metal cases. "Got 'em," she called out.

As Maji tried in vain to get the hand truck to tip back, Green spoke behind her. "Stand aside, Tiny."

Taira and Jack joined them as the blond Amazon opened the top case, confirmed the contents, and put her full weight on the back of the hand truck, tipping it to roll out of the lot and over to the boat.

"Wait," Jack said. "We need to send proof."

Maji opened the locker back up, stood back, and snapped a photo that showed him with the hand truck and its cargo. She waited a half minute before dialing Tom. "Dmitry. Got my text?"

"Bring it back to the station and load it on a helicopter."

Maji blinked at the phone. "The ferry is right here. Why don't I take it on there, meet one of your people in a town with an airstrip? Then the US military won't feel obliged to chase down a stolen multimillion dollar asset."

"You want proof of life? Do as I say."

"Hooah," she said softly, closing her eyes for a second. In Russian she ordered, "Put one of them on."

The voice on the phone next was Dee's. "What do we do?"

"Stay calm. Follow Dev's lead."

"Okay. And—"

Maji heard Dee protest in the background, a smacking sound, and then silence. "Twenty minutes to show me the boxes again, with the helicopter," Dmitry told her.

❖

Dmitry/Tom took Dee below on request, and a few minutes later Rose heard a thump and swearing, followed by more thumps. Tom dragged Dee back up and threw her toward the table. Petrov took his gun out and looked to Tom for permission.

Rose moved between the men and Dee. "Are you hurt?"

"It was worth it," Dee replied, scowling as she slid in behind the table.

Tom barked at Petrov, who hesitated but put his gun back in his shoulder holster. Then he glared at Dee. "Where is your medicine box?"

Rose noticed that his arm was bleeding, and his hand too. When Dee refused to reply, she asked, "Do you mean the first aid kit, Dmitry the bear?"

Tom looked at her in character, puzzled and irritated. "Poking me like a bear in a cage is unwise."

"Oh no," Rose said. "Not that kind of bear. You're like that bear in the Raven story, isn't he, Dee? The one who pretended to be Raven's enemy, when really he was a trickster too." She hoped Petrov's English was as rudimentary as Tom had implied.

"Ah," Dev said. "I love your Raven stories. Yes, I can see that myself. Can't you, Dee?"

Dee looked at both of them like they were idiots, then at Tom, who held his pose while Petrov went below and started searching for the medical supplies.

"Funny that saying you have, *to eat like a bird*," Tom said. "The Raven I know eats like that—like half her body weight each day."

Dev silently nodded at Dee, whose face registered that the pieces had fallen into place. "Shit. Sorry I cut you."

"Bears have thick skin," Tom said. "But I am bleeding on your boat."

Dee looked down as Petrov emerged from the forward cabin, empty-handed but for a towel. "Under the galley sink," she mumbled.

Tom grumbled at Petrov in Russian and started banging cupboard doors open. The third door he tried was under the sink, and he pulled out the red pouch with a white cross on it.

Now, Rose thought, it was four to one instead of three to two. *I like our odds.*

❖

Even for four fit soldiers, the lockers were too heavy to lift and settle onto the boat by hand. So Jack found packing straps, and they guided the hoist to raise and swing each locker into the cockpit. As the last one touched down, Taira started the boat up.

"Wait," Maji yelled just before Taira put the boat in gear. She hopped over the rail back onto the dock, threw the hand truck on board, and climbed on again. She fell back onto the bench as the steel-hulled boat took off, planing down the channel back toward their starting point.

They unloaded and sprinted for the Jeep as fast as they could without tipping over the hand truck. As they ran, the ensign on duty stepped out the front door of the little building. "Hey! You have to sign back in. And return the PFDs."

"Too urgent to stop," Jack yelled back, opening the back of the Jeep. "Crap."

They all looked from the hand truck to the rear bed of the Jeep several feet off the ground. Maji and Taira positioned themselves at the corners of the lockers closest to the Jeep, while Green and Jack took the farthest two. "Shift then lift," Maji ordered. "On my count."

Each of them braced against an upright edge of the locker.

"One, two, shift." The locker moved a few inches, and they each put their hands beneath a corner. "One, two, and—lift."

The God-awful heavy box landed hard inside the cargo area, and the rear of the Jeep sank a couple of inches. "All fingers intact?" Maji asked.

A chorus of affirmatives came back to her.

They repeated the process with the second locker. Maji's back and legs screamed with the strain of lifting that much weight again, and from a lower starting point. All of them panted with the exertion. "Two down," Jack said.

Maji looked at the locker on the ground, as heavy as the first two but flush with the pavement. Even if they got Mr. Useless in the doorway to tip the hand truck so they could get purchase, somebody would get a hernia trying to lift it from there. "Fuck."

"You have a portable hoist?" Taira called to the ensign who stood watching them. He shook his head.

Lt. Green popped the locker lid and dug in, lifting several weights by hand and setting them into the cargo area loose. Maji squatted down and pulled more out, handing them up. Someone overhead took them, and she reached in for more. Then Taira squatted across from her and mirrored her actions.

When the locker was half empty, Green said, "Hold on. Let's try again."

With the ensign tipping the hand truck, the four were able to lift the metal box and wrangle it into the back. Maji slammed the door shut, noting how the Jeep's rear sagged under the combined weight.

They all climbed in, and AET Taira buckled herself in, turning the ignition before all the doors were closed. As the rest buckled in Jack said, "Steady now. Don't break an axle."

❖

Rose weighed whether to try talking to Tom anymore or to stay silent like Dee and Dev. The way he kept looking at his watch and then out the cabin windows finally got the better of her. "Are you waiting for the cavalry to appear, Dmitry?"

"Keep your dreams, lady. Out there I see only some kayakers. Nobody is coming for you, unless maybe your Navy trains harbor seals." He laughed smugly.

Navy-trained harbor seals? As he gave a translated version of their exchange to Petrov and got a smug look in return, it clicked. SEALs. Maji's backup.

Rose flicked a glance to Dev, who gave her a weak but reassuring smile back. She felt Dee nudge her and spared a small smile in her direction. *Four to one, plus backup. Even better odds.*

The phone rang. "Do you have it?" Tom asked the person on the other end. "Good. Take it to the air station."

Petrov asked him a question, and they appeared to debate something. When Tom resumed his watch at the window, Petrov began pacing.

"Petrov," Rose said, lifting her cuffed hands to gesture toward herself awkwardly, "I'm Rose, and this—"

"Don't get friendly," Tom cut her off. "And don't be alone with him. Especially you." He said something to Petrov then in Russian.

Petrov's response, even though she couldn't understand the words, made Rose's empty stomach tighten. Tom spoke more sternly to him, and Petrov rolled his eyes. "We are clear there will be no playtime until our work is done," Tom said. "Still, stay together like good little hostages."

Rose exchanged a look with Dev and then Dee. What did Petrov plan to do when their work was done? However Tom planned to stop him, she was ready to help.

Her determination turned to fear when Tom punched a number into his phone and ordered someone on the other end to come and pick him up. She bit back a plea as she watched him walk out, leaving them alone with Petrov.

Chapter Twenty-one

The phone rang as they passed the marina. Maji answered. "Go for Rios."

Tom's voice growled in her ear. "Stop on side of road. I am coming with you."

"That's not wise."

"Tell the men watching this boat, if I am hurt, all inside die. Clear?"

Maji looked to Lt. Green, who nodded and spoke quietly into her comm. "All clear," Maji confirmed.

AET Taira reached for her door handle, and Maji clamped a hand on her shoulder. She wanted to hop out and head for the *Eagle Song* just as badly, but neither of them could. "Let the strike team do their job, Liv. They'll pick the right moment."

Tom came jogging across the road, dressed in shorts and a flannel shirt, looking like a tourist with an attitude. Maji shoved her door open and squished to the middle of the back seat. He pulled the door shut behind him, settling his sturdy frame at an angle to fit in, pressed up against Maji. "Go," he ordered.

Maji watched Jack blanch, trying to keep his calm with one of his wife's captors close enough to reach back and grab. "Jack," she said, "breathe."

After two beats, Green added, "Try and act normal. AET Taira, drive directly to the hangar."

"Aye, aye."

All the ground crew working in the hangar stopped and looked their way when the Jeep screeched up and stopped under the one open roll-up door. "Hey, Taira, what'd you—" one began, then stopped himself when Jack popped out of the passenger side looking fearsome. The crewman stood to attention, saluted, and barked out, "Lieutenant Commander."

"At ease," Jack replied. In command voice he called out, "All hands present."

There was a scurrying as crew pulled themselves away from their work and moved into a line. They looked expectant and a little concerned. Clearly Jack could take command but didn't flex that muscle too often.

"You are all on break until further notice. Go do your PT, or get a bite, or catch up on your training modules. I'll page you if I need you."

"Aye, aye, Lieutenant Commander," they answered in unison. Then one ventured, "Sir? May I finish my diagnostic?"

"You may not, AMT Ramirez. Dismissed."

They filed out without further comment. As soon as the room was clear, Jack moved on Tom. Tom dodged the blow, and Green stepped between them. Maji spun Taira away when she leaped forward to join Jack in the confrontation.

"Stand down," Green barked.

"Your wife will be fine," Tom said to Jack with no trace of a Russian accent. "You have my word as an officer."

"What the hell?" Taira said.

Tom turned just his head toward her. "Strictly need to know." To Maji he added, "Vouch for me."

"You can trust him," she said. But damned if she'd reveal his identity. They could guess whatever they wanted about him so long as they cooperated.

"What about those guys who have Dee?" Taira asked.

Jack looked unconvinced also. "And Tina."

"They work for the man we're all after," Tom conceded. "But they answer to me, as long as they believe I do too." He cracked his neck and rolled his shoulders. "Now, we really need to work together. Which helo is in the best shape?"

"For what?" Taira asked.

"A trip across the boundary line. With the payload."

"That's way beyond safety limits, even without the gold," Jack said.

"What if we stripped all nonessential equipment out?" Green asked. Before Jack could answer, she cocked her head, one finger up. "Coordinates?" she asked Tom.

He rattled off a latitude and longitude, and she repeated them into her comm. They both looked to Jack again.

"Maybe. We'd need at least one stop to refuel. And I'd still want to weigh what came out, plus minimize the crew."

"Just two," Tom said. "Pilot and copilot."

Jack shook his head. "Just me. I'm not risking anyone else under my command."

"Even you can't hold up alone that far," Tom countered. "I'm going with you. I did some time as a Night Stalker, so you know I can back you up. Besides, my *boss* expects to hear me giving updates as we go. Tina gets released when we cross the border." He looked to Green. "Strike teams ready?"

She nodded. "Both targets covered."

"All righty then," Tom said. "Let's strip a bird."

They got to work unloading all the search and rescue equipment from the Jayhawk that Taira confirmed as the one most recently overhauled and cleared to fly.

"Do we have a second ready, in case a distress call comes in?" Jack pressed.

She nodded. "Affirmative."

With that knowledge, Jack took a deep breath and seemed to focus, identifying every item inside the helo that was safe to take out. Taira helped make sure nothing got loosened that could work its way free and create a hazard while they flew. Green kept a running count as they weighed all the items removed, right down to nuts and bolts.

"Back the Jeep up close to the open bay," Tom instructed Taira as they neared the end of the weight removal effort.

When she had the Jeep in place, Tom positioned Jack in the opening, legs hanging out like a rescue swimmer ready to drop into the water. "Smile for the camera," he said.

Jack scowled and flipped him the bird.

"Perfect." Tom sent the photo off and handed the phone to Green. "You have anybody in crypto can get a bead on where these are going? We think he's in Beringovsky, but it would be good to confirm." He paused and gave an apologetic wince. "And I need to keep it close, in case he calls."

"Oh, is that all?" Green cocked her head again, listening to her comm. "We have a guy on strike team two. We'll pull him off the house."

"No." AET Taira got between them, looking up into Green's face. "I know a guy right here in crypto—a real tech wizard. Let me get him."

"Is he on duty and on base now?"

"I think so. I'll call him." At Green's nod, she went to the wall phone and dialed an extension. When the call ended, she said, "He'll be right down with a laptop and trace kit."

"Thanks, Liv," Jack said. He held out an arm, and she stepped into his embrace.

"What about Dee, Dev...and Rose?" Maji asked.

"They stay put until after we're in the air," Tom replied. "Since Sirko thinks you're acting under duress too."

True enough. In Arabic she asked him, "What if we just sprung them and kept the gold. Would that get one of Sirko's backers mad enough to kill him?"

"That's plan B but it's iffy, given his clout," he answered. "But if we can pull plan A off, we have a chance to shut him down and confirm the kill, plus take out some of his ring. The gold's the only bait we know will get him out of hiding."

"Why couldn't he want something light?" Green pitched in, also in Arabic. When they turned and stared at her she added, "What? This surprises you?"

Taira stopped working. "What the actual fuck? Who are you people?"

"They're Special Forces, OT," Jack said. "Let them drive. Clear?"

She looked conflicted, but nodded. "Aye, aye, Lieutenant Commander."

"About the weight issue," Jack said to Green. Then he stopped and smiled for the first time. "C'mon. Two tours in Iraq and one in the 'Stan, remember? I can't speak well, but I understand quite a bit."

"Okay, then," Green responded evenly, switching them all to English. "What about the weight?"

"She's as stripped down as we can get her. And that's not going to cut it"—he pointed to Green's tally of total weight removed—"after we add the gold and two personnel back in."

"If you get there and some of the gold is missing, you may both be killed on the spot," Green said.

Maji looked at Tom and Jack and wondered if they were all thinking the same as she was—Sirko would have no need for Jack upon delivery, anyway.

"We'll cross that bridge later," Jack said. "As we say here, *You have to go out, but you don't have to come back.*"

Yep. Maji swallowed hard and looked to Tom. "Does Sirko know exactly how much you pulled up?"

"Only roughly. We could fudge maybe twenty percent. He is getting a seventeen-million dollar helo with it, after all."

"Might be enough, depending on where we refuel," Jack said. He sounded like a man with all thoughts of his own survival pushed to some far-distant corner of his brain. Maji supposed he'd been on enough harrowing flights to compartmentalize automatically.

"Get your options lined up and then call your boss," Green instructed Tom. "The longer you keep him talking, the more we can narrow his location down. Tell me when, and I'll have the tech wizard ready."

"You guys handle logistics, and we'll get busy on the gold," Maji said. "Taira, what can we use to secure these things inside the cabin?" The old rusty lockers were not a safe option.

While they collaborated to get the gold loaded and secured, Maji tried to keep Liv from keying in on the quiet huddle of the planning team. "So you're from Hawaii, huh?"

"Can't talk—thinking," Taira replied. "All of this is for nothing if the engines overheat or the controllers melt down. Stripped down or not, these aren't designed to cruise so many hours, touch down for fuel, and go right out again without maintenance." She stood abruptly inside the helo cabin and went to the open door, leaning out. "Jack!"

"Yo."

"Shave ten clicks an hour off your cruise speed, for cooling and fuel conservation." The lack of an immediate response seemed to frustrate her. "Just try it."

"Aye, aye."

"If he's going down for your crazy-ass mission, it's not going to be in the middle of the Bering Sea," she fumed on her return, speaking without looking at Maji.

"It's no crazier than flying into an Arctic storm and diving into the ocean to save the crew of a sinking ship," Maji said. "By the time they cross the boundary line, there will be teams in place to assist. Nobody's letting Jack go without a fight."

"You're mighty calm for somebody whose girlfriend has a gun on her," Taira snapped back.

Maji shook her head. "Not hardly. But this is the only way I can help to get her home safe." Into the quiet that followed, she added, "Dee will be okay too. We've got her six."

"Okay, I get it. Shut up and let me think." Taira looked at the nearly completed task. "I need to check something. Can you finish packing these things?"

Maji looked at the mass of weights left to transfer into the fresh containers. She was tired and sore and hungry. But the hands-on task did keep her fears at bay some. "Aye, aye."

After a bit, Maji noticed that Jack finally sat and took a break, pressing a fresh ice pack to his leg. She exchanged a look with Green, who watched him for a moment and then wandered to a far corner to speak into her comm with Kim.

On her return, Green spoke plainly to Jack. "Change of plans. I'm subbing in as copilot, and Dmitry will take your seat."

Jack straightened up and gave her an openly disparaging look. "The minute they realize it's not me in the helo with Dmitry here, they'll blow you to bits."

"Put me in a flight suit and helmet, and they won't know until it's too late," she countered.

"Not gonna happen. He's barely got the transferrable experience to second my helo. And you—how much flight time have you had in a Jayhawk?"

"What happened to let them drive, Lieutenant Commander?" Lt. Green cocked one platinum eyebrow at him. "It's my call and you will abide by it."

He shook his head. "Respectfully, ma'am, this is my asset, my crew"—he pointed to Taira, then to the hangar in general—"my career. Whatever airframes you two have flown, it wasn't this bird and it wasn't over these waters." He eyed Tom. "And I'm not sending this guy to go out with my bird just to get killed before he completes his mission. We have the best chance of success with the two of us, even as is." He paused as if considering his next words. "I'm not going to get into a pissing contest with you, but I am the only one here capable of getting us all the fucking way over Russian waters in one piece. Especially if we're trying to stay off radar."

Maji watched Tom watching them sort this out. She hoped his experience and stamina would be enough to carry them if Jack's leg got worse or his energy gave out. "What can we do to get you and Tom in the best possible condition?" she asked. The conversation stopped abruptly.

Green looked from her to Jack and Tom. She shook her head, listening to the voice in her earpiece. "Fine," she said softly. Then, louder, she added, "Send that medic down, and a runner to the mess hall. We need dinner for all hands here."

At the break Tom called Sirko and hashed out the final route plan. Sirko forbade him to land in Kodiak because of the Coast Guard air station there. Or Dutch Harbor for the same concerns about US military presence. They settled on a small town on the upper Aleutian chain that had a robust commercial airstrip and no law enforcement capacity. Maji realized two things as they talked and argued. One, the destination was a cargo ship not too far over the International Maritime Boundary. That would make mobilizing a SEAL team easier. Two, Sirko really did appear to trust Tom. And that gave them a decent shot at the long game, finally capturing the most dangerous criminal left running a viable operation.

When Tom hung up, he looked to the cryptotech. The tech's thumbs-up made them all do a fist pump. They all returned to flight preparations with renewed enthusiasm.

Two hours later, Jack and Tom moved around the Jayhawk out on the tarmac, making their final safety checks. The clouds had lifted but the sun was waning. What a long day it had been, to be followed by a long night for these two.

Jack moved away from the prop wash and motioned everyone over. "I've called my second in command in. He'll be on-site in twenty, thirty minutes." He held his hand out to Taira. "It's been an honor to serve with you. Give Tina my love, and…take care of Jasper."

She ignored his hand and squeezed him hard around the middle, face buried in his chest. He held her a brief moment, then thumped her on the back. Taira pushed back and looked up at him, gulping air. "Safe travels."

"And you—" Jack motioned to Maji to come close. When she did he leaned in, and said quietly, "Tell Tina to be happy. Tell her I said so."

Maji bit back the urge to cry, folding her fear and anger into a neat square and tucking it mentally into her pocket. She nodded silently for Jack, looking him in the eye. Then she gave Tom a long hug and shoved him away. "You get the shot, take him out."

Tom didn't look surprised, just somber. "Hooah." Then he smiled. "I have orders to take you with us, bound and gagged." At her look he winked. "But you have a bad habit of getting away. I've even got fresh cuts to prove it. Give Rose my apologies."

"The bridge is back open," Green said. "Team one can medevac if needed."

Tom nodded and made his final call to the accomplices at Jack's house on Lifesaver Road, reminding them to wait for his call to release Tina. They agreed to sleep in shifts. Maji knew that even if they treated her well, it would be a long night for Tina.

When he called Petrov, Tom asked him to confirm the status of all three hostages on the boat. He counted off with his fingers as he listened to the response: one, two, three, okay sign. To a question from Petrov, he laughed and described "the little soldier girl tied up like a present." Then he asked to speak with Dev. "Act relieved to hear this," Tom instructed in English. "He has orders to dispose of you all now. Do whatever you need to, *akhi*."

Go time. Maji backed away from the helo and watched Tom and Jack climb in. As the Jayhawk rolled down the runway toward the liftoff zone, Taira spun toward the air station and began running. Maji looked hopefully toward Green.

"Go, go."

Maji tore off after Taira, catching her before she reached the parking lot. Taira looked ready to fight her, so Maji waved toward the Jeep. "I'm with you, Liv."

❖

Dev smiled with relief at their captor. "Well, that is over. Now we must—"

"No!" Dee yelled and launched herself at Petrov as he started to pull his gun from its holster.

Rose felt herself slammed sideways, "Down," ringing in her ears. On the cabin floor, she worked her hands loose. A foot cracked her shin, and she cried out involuntarily.

When she looked up, Dev had Petrov pinned to the dinette table. "Stay below the windows," he ordered Dee, who was struggling to stand where she had fallen, by the steps down to the forward cabin.

Sniper, Rose thought, then heard the sound of boots pounding down the dock, feet landing on the deck of the boat. Silence followed, but for the grunting of the Russian as he tried in vain to break Dev's hold.

"Yell all clear," Dev told her.

"All..." her voice croaked out. Rose took a deep breath. "All clear," she bellowed. She looked to Dev for next steps, and the cabin door burst open, a helmeted man with a pistol in front of him crouching low.

Dev fell back from Petrov, who reared up and twitched violently before falling across the little table. The snapping sound of the shots registered in Rose's mind as the blood began to pool. She realized she was screaming when gloved hands touched her head and shoulder. "Ma'am. Are you hit? Ma'am?"

Rose uncovered her face and looked at the shooter. She shook her head and looked around. Dev had an arm around Dee, talking to her softly.

He looked up and gave her a reassuring smile. "We're good. You okay, Doc?"

"No," she answered honestly. She felt dizzy and nauseous. Seeing him frown and start to move, she said, "I'm not hurt. Bruised. Dee?"

Dee lifted her eyes, looked past the dead man in her cabin, and met Rose's gaze. "Alive." She looked at the soldier still crouching by Rose. "Can we go now?"

"Yes, ma'am. My team will escort you." He offered Rose a hand.

She shook her head and pulled herself up, wincing each time she moved one of the several places she had banged while falling. At least her head was all right. "I'm Rose," she said when she could look the man in the eye.

"Yes, ma'am," he said and stepped outside, holding the door for her to follow.

Maji leaped out of the Jeep and chased after Taira, who had left it running near the two ambulances and a taxi in the Sealing Cove Harbor parking lot.

"Hey, you can't go down there," a man's voice called after them.

Neither of them bothered to reply. Maji caught up with Taira where she stood scanning the docks, looking for the *Eagle Song*.

"There it is," Maji told her as she watched Rose throwing up over the stern. A man in tactical wear stood with a hand on her back. Not great, but safe at least. And the others?

Seeing another man, dressed for hiking but no doubt also on the strike team, turn and move to block their approach, Maji called out to him. "Strike team, what is your sit rep?"

"Target down, hostages secured," he replied. "Ma'am."

Dee emerged from the cabin, another outdoorsy SEAL behind her. "There she is," Maji said. She was going to add something reassuring, but just then Dee wobbled and the SEAL grabbed her arm. She wrenched away from him.

"Dee!" Taira called out as she tried to dodge the one-man blockade in front of her.

He scooped her up with one arm, getting as far as, "Ma'am, you need to—" before her boot found his groin. He crumpled.

Both men in the boat's cockpit reached for their sidearms.

"Hold fire," Maji barked, lifting both arms high as she stepped over the wheezing SEAL to try to catch Taira before the misunderstanding turned deadly.

"Liv, stop!" Dee yelled, the panic on her face mirrored on Rose's.

Taira broke stride so abruptly she slipped on the damp dock. Close behind her, Maji reached out to steady her. Taira flailed. Maji dodged to avoid being hit in the face, felt her foot catch on something, and pitched toward the water.

Don't inhale. She hit the frigid water sideways, sensing it enveloping her even as all her muscles clenched at the wave of cold. Darkness overtook her and, right behind it, panic. Maji surfaced coughing, trying to breathe and keep her head above water at the same time. Nearby, blurry faces shouted and waving arms reached out for her.

Maji felt herself being pulled forward, banged against the dock's impossibly high sides, and then dragged up onto the flat. She struggled to turn over, to sit up. Her muscles wouldn't cooperate, shaking and jerking. Through the jumble of voices she heard Rose calling her name. A blanket covered her and a body pressed against the length of her. Rose's face filled her field of vision.

"Breathe, sweetheart. Slow and deep."

"C-crying," Maji said, seeing Rose's tears. "Hurt?"

"Not me," Rose answered. "But we need to get you in the ambulance. Let Dev and the EMT help you now. Okay?"

"Y-yes."

Rose woke with a start when Dev touched her arm. "What time is it?"

"Nearly dawn. They have a bed for you too. She'll be out until the sedative wears off. Why don't you lie down?"

Rose shook her head. Maji looked so peaceful now. Watching her thrash in the cold water had been the hardest part of the day. As hostages, they'd been together and ready to act to save themselves. But on the dock Rose had felt helpless and alone, unable to stop Maji from falling in or to help her out again. Green had promised to watch out for Maji; but even SEALs couldn't stop gravity. Rose could live with not knowing when Maji would come home from duty, with logistical inconveniences and even lying to friends about it. But every time Maji left, not knowing *if* she would come home—how could anyone live with that?

For the first time since Maji broke up with her the previous summer, Rose understood why. She would never willingly put someone she loved through the helplessness she'd experienced today. "Dev, were you in the service when you got married?"

"Yeah. I was a Ranger then. But I'd known Mira since we were kids. Why?"

"And when you took the…other job, didn't Mira worry about you?"

"Not going to lie. It was really hard on her."

"I bet she likes having you home on a regular basis finally."

He chuckled. "Some days she encourages me to reenlist. It's not always easy to downshift back to normal life."

Rose didn't reply, and he gave her forearm a gentle squeeze.

Maji woke to an insistent thirst, a dull headache, and every spot she'd banged or scraped vying for her attention. But worse than those, the memory of Rose crying. She tried to lift her head. "Rose?"

"She finally went to get a shower," Dev said. "Spent most of the night there." He pointed to the chair, clearly disapproving. But he also raised the bed so she could sit up and brought her a cup with a straw in it.

Maji sucked down the water with gratitude.

"She's got questions that deserve answers," Dev said. "If you don't marry her, I will."

"Dude, you're taken."

"Yeah, well, if it's not me, somebody will. And it should be you, if she'll still have you."

"Thanks for the vote of confidence."

"Anytime, dude." He gave her a visual scan that felt clinical. That was never good. "How do you feel?"

"Like death warmed over." Everything hurt, right down to the sting where the IV fed into her vein. "How soon can I get out? I still have one day here, right?" *If she'll still have me.*

"I have your phone, dried out and operational, if you want to check."

"Thanks. Hit speed dial for me?" She took the ringing phone in her less bandaged hand as he walked out of the room.

Command center was staffed by a reassuringly familiar voice, Captain Alvarez. "Rios, that was a long nap. What's your status?"

"Not quite ambulatory, and somebody hid my pants. Where's debrief happening?"

Alvarez chuckled. Then she said with a note of sympathy in her voice, "Back here. I've got you on the first flight out tomorrow morning."

Damn. "Anything I need to know today?"

"We should have better intel by the time you arrive, but our sources say the Jayhawk made a safe landing. SEALs took the cargo ship, and Tom got away in the firefight. Stole a lifeboat and headed toward a sub that surfaced a couple miles away."

"And the Coast Guard pilot?"

"Negative. Sorry to bear bad news. Speaking of which, have Dev bring you a paper."

"Roger that. Rios out."

"Hey—we're looking forward to seeing you, Ri. Travel safe."

"Thanks. Rios out." Maji took a moment alone to digest the news. Not a surprise, but still. She'd lost others who had risked their lives to help with a mission, civilians and soldiers both. It never got easier and maybe it shouldn't. "Dev," she called.

He popped back in and gave her a minute to scan the front-page story of the Jayhawk going down on a test flight to Air Station Kodiak, along with its valiant pilot. "There'll be an inquiry, and Fitzsimmons will get some posthumous award, no doubt. If you're good here, I'm going to step out and call Mira."

Maji closed her eyes and listened to the soft pinging of machines in her room, the hum of the fluorescent lights overhead, the sound of voices and rubber-soled shoes in the hallway.

The next time she woke, Rose was gently stroking her forehead, smoothing away the dream Maji couldn't remember but knew she'd been having.

"Shush," she said. "You're safe." Rose looked wonderful, her hair still damp and her fresh outfit a bit rumpled. Circles shadowed her tender brown eyes.

"How are you?" Maji asked.

"I've been better. I'll pull through. Are you up for visitors?"

"From the Navy?"

Rose smiled gently, with a reassuring hint of amusement. "No. Liv and Dee." Seeing the look on Maji's face, Rose said, "They could come later."

"No. Let them in. Stay?"

Rose nodded. "Of course."

Seeing Dee walk in holding hands with Liv lifted Maji's spirits a fraction.

CHAPTER TWENTY-TWO

Rose recognized the look that passed over Olivia Taira's face when she saw Maji sitting in the hospital bed, bandaged and attached to an IV drip. Remorse.

But Liv gave Dee's hand a little squeeze and stepped resolutely forward, straightening her spine. "Ma'am, I've come to apologize. I read the situation wrong, overreacted, and—"

"Freaked out. Yeah. It happens when you care about someone. No matter how good you are at handling a stranger's crisis."

Liv looked at the wall beyond Maji. "It was a bad day all round."

"I heard about Jack. I'm sorry."

Liv cocked her head. "He knew the odds. He was always going to keep going out, until the day he didn't make it back." She frowned. "Still sucks."

"Still does," Maji agreed. "Have you paid respects yet?"

Liv shook her head. "The Navy people were there, so we came here first. I'll go back in a few."

"I'd like to go with you. Would you tell the charge nurse I need my walking papers?"

"Sure." Liv looked relieved to have a reason to step out.

Dee stayed behind, sitting quietly.

"How are you?" Maji asked her. "Really."

"Can't complain," Dee replied. "Least we know what happened to Charlie now."

"They won't get charged, I suppose," Maji said. "The ones that lived."

Dee's face betrayed a hint of satisfaction. "No, but that Navy… Lieutenant Green was real clear. She's taking them in her plane to someplace they won't hurt anybody else—ever."

"And the guy they worked for didn't get what he wanted. Before long, we'll get him too."

Liv popped her head back in. "Sergeant? They want some info on you. That tribe you're from doesn't come up in their database."

"The what now?"

Rose saw Dee smile for the first time since dinner with the family. A lifetime ago. "You're at Southeast Area Regional Health Center. I think your people wanted you off radar, you know, from the local news. This is a Natives-only place. For enrolled members of tribes."

"Oh. Who did the fast-talking?"

"Nate. He was at the marina, soon as they opened the bridge back up. Heard your folks fussing about where to take you. Told them to tell the hospital that you're Mapuche, from down south. I guess the folks here assumed that meant one of those Southern California tribes. There are a lot, and they only keep a list of Alaska Natives on hand here."

Maji shook her head. "Trickster. Well, we'll get that straightened out. Rose, would you fish that card out of my wallet?"

"Sure." Rose went to the little closet and found Maji's things. She held the ID out for Maji to see. "Just this?"

Maji nodded. "They can give it to the hospital administrator. My *folks* will tell them how to bill." Then she looked a little embarrassed. "Could you help me get dressed?"

As they approached the little house on Lifesaver Lane, Maji spotted Lt. Green and Lt. Kim about to get into a rental car. She wondered if the other SEALs had left town already. By sea or air, since land was not an option. "I'll be right there," she said to Taira, Rose, and Dev.

She gave Kim a firm handshake, and Green a nod across the car. "You clearing out?"

"Done as much as we can for now," Kim confirmed.

"At least we set Sirko back a ways," Green said. "We'll see what we get from the two we're rendering."

"Good. I'm being called in tomorrow, so I guess the hunt is on."

"The only easy day was yesterday," they said in unison.

Not in the mood for another pithy SEALs saying, Maji frowned. "Is that what you told Jack's widow? Yesterday sucked for her."

Green shrugged. "We gave the widow the usual reassurances. And a story everybody can live with, even if nobody believes it."

So at least this whole mess wasn't being hung on Jack. He deserved a hell of a lot better. "And AET Taira?"

"She's on admin leave. They'll clear her, of course. Not real recognition for being such an asset, but no blowback, either."

Maji suspected the loss of Jack, and the mystery surrounding what really happened, would haunt the young Coastie. "Okay, then. I'm going in."

"We're off," Green said. "This was a long way from a perfect op, Rios. But it was a pleasure working with you."

Maji nodded. "Thanks for having my back."

When she reached Jack and Tina's door, which already had a black wreath hung on it, Maji paused and listened to the voices inside. "I promised him I would. It's no burden, really. You can visit him anytime you want."

The dog, Maji realized. And on cue, Jasper bounded out to greet her. Taira followed after, leash in hand. She gave Maji a cautionary look as she clipped it on his collar and brought him to heel. "She's a mess."

"And you? I heard you're on admin leave for a bit."

Taira shrugged. "I'm going fishing with a real Tlingit captain. She needs the help right now, and I need the hard work."

"Good. Safe travels, eh?" Maji offered her hand but got a hug instead of a handshake.

"You too, Raven." She was out the door, restraining the dog with voice and leash, before Maji could respond.

In the living room, Tina lay back on the couch with a washcloth over her eyes. The woman sitting quietly in an armchair by her startled at the sight of Maji. "Who are you?"

"A friend of Jack's."

She looked skeptical. "I don't think so. Tina—"

"It's okay, Sally," Tina said. She uncovered her eyes and sat up, putting on glasses. "Would you give us a few minutes?"

Sally looked suspiciously at Maji but took the empty glass from Tina's side and disappeared into the next room. The door clicked shut behind her.

Tina gave Maji a sour look. "They already gave me a bullshit story about Jack being a hero and doing some top-secret flight test for them. And a posthumous promotion. As if."

"No, they can really do the promotion thing. Better benefits, I guess. For you."

"Oh." Tina looked immeasurably tired. "What do you want?"

"I thought I should pay my respects—but I kind of suck at that. Mostly I wanted to see if you're okay, after yesterday's little bit of hell."

Anger perked up Tina's fatigued expression. "Okay? No, I'm not fucking okay. Every time I fall asleep, I wake up sweating, certain I'm...you know. I can't stay here." She looked down. "And I'm afraid to go out."

Maji moved to the couch and took her hand, which was clammy. "You have family here, right?"

"They all knew Jack. And why I left him. Everybody here does."

"Who's Sally?"

"My sister-in-law."

"And how's she been?"

Tina blew her nose. "Really nice. So kind."

"Good. Let them be nice to you, Tina. And get hooked up with trauma counseling as soon as you can. You deserve to be happy."

"Says who?"

"Jack." When Tina stiffened, Maji continued. "I was with him before he went out. I know why he went."

"But you can't tell me. What bullshit."

"I can tell you what matters. First, he wanted to save you. It tore him up that you were here in danger and he couldn't help. But we promised him we'd get you out safe if he helped us."

"Helped you what?"

"Get in the way of one of the worst criminals alive. The guy whose men grabbed you." Any more about Sirko she decided to leave out. "Jack knew when he flew out of here that he probably wouldn't make it back. So he gave me a message for you."

Tina looked torn about whether she wanted to know or not. Finally, she closed her eyes. "Go ahead."

"Be happy."

Tina leaned in to Maji and sobbed. When she came up for air, she said, "Thank you."

"Promise me you'll get counseling. Here, in Anchorage—wherever. But let people who love you help, and see a professional too. Okay?"

"Okay." Tina straightened up. "I promise." Her breathing calmed, bit by bit. "Do you love her? That woman you introduced me to?"

"Oh, yeah."

"Like, you'd fly off the edge of the world to save her?"

"If that's what it took, yeah."

Tina looked away. "I always wanted to feel that way about somebody. I wish it had been Jack. But..."

"You can't be happy trying to be someone you're not. He knew that. Take the blessing, and take care of you."

"I'll try."

❖

Dev stayed a good distance behind them as they walked back to town. Pausing across the road from Sealing Cove Harbor, Rose stopped and looked at the boats bobbing gently in their slips. Hard to believe just a few hours ago the place had been her prison.

"You okay?" Maji asked.

Rose took her hand and kissed the palm. "I love you, Maji Rios. And I'm grateful to Hannah for all the training. But I'll never unsee that man being shot." *Or you nearly drowning.* "Should I be getting trauma counseling too?"

"Probably. It's never a bad idea." Maji looked worried. "How much did you hear?"

"Everything. I didn't realize you didn't know that Dev and I were on the stairs. I'm sorry, I guess."

"No worries. You know more than I could tell you already, anyway."

Rose thought of Tom pretending to work for Sirko. As the O'Connell Bridge came into sight, she realized they would have to walk right past the spot where Javi had died. Did Maji know about that? She stopped. "They killed Javi. Up there."

Maji followed her gaze, then met her eyes. "That's why the bridge was closed?" She sighed. "I'm so sorry, Rose." After holding her tight for a moment, she asked, "You want me to call a cab?"

"No. I want you to catch that bastard. I want him gone." That didn't sound like her, or feel like her. But the fury she felt was too real to deny. "I know that's not your job, but…"

"It's a team effort. And terrible as it seems, you helped." Maji paused. "But we'll make sure you never have to again."

Rose thought about that concept and about the risk to soldiers she knew as well as ones she'd never meet. At the top of the bridge she looked for signs of the accident but found only small bits of glass and some tire marks. "I don't want anyone else giving their life for me."

Dev caught up with them, looking at the area Rose was scrutinizing. "He didn't sell you out. Your friend. We got the rest of the intel last night. Sirko threatened his family. The money talk was just a cover."

"Thank you, Dev," Rose said. Then, as the full meaning sank in, she added, "That's terrible."

"Bravo, dude," Maji said.

"Sorry. I was looking at it from the loyal friend upside," Dev admitted. "Of course, everybody's got a pressure point. Sirko uses that same trick over and over 'cause it keeps working."

Rose strode away from them, down the bridge's incline toward the public library with the best view in the country and to the conference center beyond it. Maji caught up with her but didn't say anything.

"I hate that man," Rose spat out. "If I could stop him myself, I would. I want to keep getting in his way. How do I do that?"

"You stay safe. That's how." Maji sounded angry herself, with an undertone of worry.

What did she think Rose would do, go out and hunt the man herself? No—but Maji would. She'd as good as promised Tina, hadn't she? And what would she do if Rose was endangered again? Javi had capitulated for his family. Jack had flown to his death for Tina. Liv had flipped out when she thought Dee was still being held hostage. And Maji had come running down the dock the moment she was free, so focused on having Rose back that she ended up bruised and scraped and dunked in seawater. Exposed to God knew what on her still healing wounds from God knew where. *Exposed.*

Rose walked on in silence, her thoughts spiraling. A hundred yards from the conference center she slowed down, watching her colleagues chat casually together, the few persistent ones soaking in the weak rays of sun poking through the cloud cover. She felt Maji's hand on her arm, heard her name.

Rose whirled and faced Maji. "You want me safe? Living a *normal* life?" The words tasted bad in her mouth. "Well, I don't want to settle for normal. And I don't want anyone else. But most of all, I don't want to be the reason your life gets cut short. Ironic, isn't it?"

Maji reached for her, but she backed away. "Rose?"

"Leave me alone. Get your bags and go. Don't call me. Just stay away." Rose turned and headed for the shelter of the conference.

❖

Maji strained against Dev's arms. "Don't do it, dude," he spoke into her ear. "Let her cool off."

"I can't just let her walk away. She's scared."

Dev relaxed his hold. "Of course she is. She's a civilian in love with a soldier. And she's new at this. Give her a few hours at least."

"Will you talk to her?"

"If she wants to talk. But if you want my advice...I know how you feel about unsolicited advice."

He did too. But she was feeling desperate now. "Go ahead."

"As soon as she's cooled down, propose."

She squinted up at him. "Seriously? Did you not hear the *go away* part?"

"I did. But also the *I don't want to live without you* part. Dude, give her a reason to believe you'll be there for her."

Well, that brought them back to square one. "How can I?" She thought of Bubbles's miscarriage. Everyone was there for her, except Maji. "I don't even know when I'll be at home, and now she's scared I won't make it home."

"Whatever. All I'm saying is, if she's who you want to come home to, tell her like you mean it."

Maji looked down. Did she mean that? Not that she hadn't daydreamed about coming home to Rose, but would it work? Getting her head out of a mission took a while, and she usually took that time alone. Plus, she'd never done the day-to-day with anybody she was in love with. What if she sucked at it and Rose kicked her out, for good? But...she looked back up at him. "What if she says no?"

"She could opt out," Dev admitted. "And you'd be where you are now. But why would she say yes if you don't show her you're all in?"

Convinced, Maji started to walk past him to go find Rose. Now.

"Whoa," Dev said, stepping out ahead of her. "Go kill some time. I'll text you later." He gave her a gentle shove toward town.

Torn between the craving to go see, touch, and talk to Rose this very minute and the astounding realization that Dev actually knew something about relationships, Maji blew out a breath and gave him a nod. "You want me to pick up anything for Mira or the kids?"

"Yeah. Get some touristy Russian stuff for the girls, you know—those painted dolls or whatever. And some kind of Native art for Mira. You know what she likes."

Maji let him go find Rose indoors and turned herself toward town. At the traffic light, she looked left and right, rudderless. The scent of frying food beckoned from the left, and she let her growling stomach pull her down the shop-lined street. Art and clothing, jewelry, and sports gear called out from the storefronts. The Russian Orthodox cathedral sat oddly between lanes, like an island in the middle of a river. A slow-moving river with little traffic. Maji's brain wandered to Heather and the impending flood of cruise-boat tourists arriving in May. And then the smell of pancit, adobo, and lumpia drew her into a tiny Filipino café.

The scent and taste of her lunch took Maji back to Luzon, to her last mission and the scrapes and bruises still healing on her back and legs. Rose had seemed so calmly compassionate—maybe she'd underestimated how much having the evidence of Maji's work in her face bothered her. She exchanged a few words in Tagalog with the server and wondered if Rose were there whether she would have stuck with English. Because if she used another language not on the short list Rose already knew she spoke, would she want to explain why she'd learned it, how much she'd needed to get by? How many times could she say she couldn't talk about things before Rose felt shut out? If she did propose, and Rose said yes, she could go to Fort Bragg and have family orientation. Would that make her worry more or less?

Maji wandered into the Russian keepsakes store, cruising the aisles like a real tourist, listening to the normal people talk to each other. It was boring, the mundane bickering over where to eat out and the blithe chatter about weather and sightseeing. Why did it never feel boring with Rose? Was it just their newness? If they saw each other for months at a time, would they still treasure those moments like she had these last few days? She took her bag of tchotchkes for the kids and crossed to the little independent bookstore.

In the children's section, Maji found the beautifully illustrated books of Raven stories, the ones by that presenter at Rose's conference. Rose had exclaimed over the sample copies there. Since Dev hadn't texted her yet, Maji sat in a cushy armchair and read all three: *Raven Brings Us Fire*, *Origins of Rivers and Streams*, and *Raven and the Box of Daylight*. Seemed like Raven liked to stir up trouble, but things ended up well for others when he did.

Had Taira called her Raven just because she'd clearly been covert, like a shape-shifter? But Rose had insisted Maji was a Raven too. Maji wanted so much to curl up on a couch and hold Rose and have her explain in her insightful way what the hell all that meant. With Rose, the complicated and messy all got so simple, somehow. Except when she wouldn't let it and pushed Rose away. Like Rose was doing now. She bought the three books and added them to her bag. Rose should have some good memories of this trip.

Chapter Twenty-three

Rejoining the conference felt surreal. Rose had missed only a few sessions, but it felt like she'd left this little world, traveled to a hostile planet, and landed back on earth again—without anyone here noticing. And Lt. Green had asked her, in the hospital room while Maji was zonked out, to act like nothing had happened. That was surprisingly easy when everyone around her assumed she'd taken a break to sightsee. But inside, the dissonance between her public face and her private thoughts kept her off balance. Was that how Maji felt when she came home from...wherever it was they sent her? Was it lonely being part of two worlds, one secret and one *normal*?

Rose accepted an invitation to dinner, insisting Dev join her and her two Scandinavian colleagues. Before meeting up with them, Dev escorted her back to the hotel and checked them into a junior suite. Rose settled herself into the bedroom, not bothering to object to Dev's plan to take the couch, a foot too short for his tall frame. She unpacked only what she needed for the night and leaned on the support of the doorway, surprised to find Dev seated on the couch meditating. Perhaps that's what he did to bring himself back to the normal world. Or just to get through a day without nearly enough sleep.

Rose yawned, and he opened his eyes at the sound. "Sorry."

"All is well," he said. "If you're too tired, we could order room service. But not on my account."

"No." She yawned again. "It's my last chance to see these two in person. I just need enough brain to hold a conversation."

He gave her a sympathetic look. "Anything you want to talk to me about?"

"I don't think you're allowed to tell me the kinds of things I want to know." She spotted the coffee maker on the counter and, missing the full kitchenette of their old suite, took the carafe to the bathroom to fill. "Coffee or tea?"

"Tea, please." He stayed quiet while she puttered with drink making. When she brought him the steaming mug, he said, "I can't tell you what it's like to be on your side of things, the civilian side. But I have been married to someone who is."

Rose took the far end of the couch, not sure she had the energy for anything that involved feelings. But it was so generous of him to offer. "You really do want Ri to be happy, don't you?"

"She's a better teammate that way," he quipped. "But seriously? She deserves somebody special. Be a pity if you were the one that got away."

Rose felt herself flush. Praise from a man who never praised anyone. She wondered what he was like at home, with the ones he loved. "How is it that you have a family and did...the same kind of work?"

He shrugged. "Lots of us do. And I won't lie—it's hard on the wives. They take care of everything when you're gone and have to put up with you when you're home. And even when we're home, you know, there's a piece of us that isn't. Can't be."

"But is your family in any actual danger because of you?"

Dev shook his head. "We take steps to keep who we are and what we do quiet. Even within the military community. Otherwise, they could become targets. What Angelo did was completely off book, and I guess it just shows why we do what we do the way we do it."

Rose nearly smiled. Next thing they knew, he'd be talking about their *thing*, like the Mafia men did. But that reminded her of the reality TV show and how Sirko had used it as a way to track her family, to exploit the prurient interest America had in the Mafia. "Do you think the criminals Ang hurt will keep coming after us?"

"There's no guarantees, but of all of them—and there were a lot—only Sirko really has any resources left to be a threat."

"And do you think he's the only one who knows about Ri and me?"

"That she loves you, you mean?"

Rose nodded. That thought should give her such joy. But right now all she could see was the wreath on Tina's door, the mysterious Navy people driving away after paying respects along with acceptable lies. "That she has a weak spot."

Dev smiled, damn him. "Says who?" When she didn't answer his ridiculous question, he pressed the point. "You think she did anything she wasn't supposed to, wasn't allowed to, or wasn't safe to do, because of you?"

"Well, obviously, I don't know what she was doing with the Navy and the Coast Guard while we were tied up—literally. But I did see her go in the water."

"So you don't ever want her to fall down. She can't slip and fall, because she's some superwoman?"

"Of course not. I just don't want to be the reason she gets hurt."

Dev looked skeptical. "That would drive Mira crazy too. But she knows that the slimmest chance of making it back home to her has kept me alive more than a few times."

"I hate that any of you are in that kind of danger," Rose admitted, looking past him to the gray clouds moving in on the horizon. "And I hate that I don't want you to stop. Ri isn't ever going to stop, is she? Even when she leaves the Army."

"Nah, I can't picture that. You want somebody who looks the other way when there's trouble, she's not the one for you."

❖

Maji walked into the forest and read the stories posted by a few of the totem poles. It was fascinating history and a neat way of storytelling, but she couldn't keep her focus. So she looped back toward the Visitor Center, not sure where she was headed. Everything ached, but the heaviness that made her want to just curl up somewhere also meant she should keep moving. Along the paved path for tourists staying close to the main building were plantings with signs giving their common names and Tlingit names, with information on food and medicinal uses. Deerheart, salmonberry, Indian celery, beach strawberry...Maji stopped reading. Rose would love this. Last summer when she had broken up with Rose to protect her, she was sure it was the right thing to do. Now that the tables were turned, she understood just how bad it felt. She wanted to be mad, but all she could tap was hollowness. When Maji had finally come to her senses, Rose took her back and wouldn't even take an apology. And if Rose could bring herself to give them a chance—again— Maji wouldn't expect one either. She'd just say yes. Whatever Rose wanted—yes.

The sound of chipper voices pulled her back to the overcast day. They were coming from a little building behind the Visitor Center. It had a roof supported by sturdy beams, and half walls on three sides.

At the open front, two gray-haired women talked about the carver working inside as if he couldn't hear them. "I heard they could go on the ocean with those."

"Can you imagine? No, I don't think so. Are you sure?"

"Well, let's go ask the ranger. I want to see the gift shop."

They meandered toward the main building, leaving the man in the red bandana still bent over his work, shaving out the inside of a sizable log. That would be quite some canoe when it was finished. Maji realized the carver was Nate and wondered if he missed the music and lighting of his home studio. Not that the sound of gulls and ravens in the fresh air was a bad tradeoff.

"I heard they could go on the ocean with those," she said to him, mimicking the nasal Midwestern tones of the tourists.

"Can you imagine?" he answered. Straightening up and wiping his hands, Nate gave her a thorough looking over. "You in one piece, then?"

Little swirling pieces. "I hurt all over, but nothing that won't heal." *Hopefully.*

He cocked his head. "Most you can ask for, sometimes. Enough to keep going on."

Her grief was not the only grief, Maji remembered, thinking how recently he had lost his brother, and Dee her best friend. And then there was Javi, and Jack. So much loss—for what? "Thanks for getting me into that hospital under the radar. Hope it didn't get you in any trouble."

He shrugged. "An honest mistake, ennit? Didn't hurt anybody."

"Dee stopped in to see me." Maji considered telling him about her and Liv, but realized she didn't know what was between them, plus it wasn't her story to tell. And besides, in this community he probably knew more already than she did. "She seemed okay, considering. Worth keeping an eye on though."

"Dee's been through worse," Nate said, in a quiet way that made Maji aware he too would tell no tales that weren't his to share. "Said having Rose there made all the difference, though. And that you got the guys that killed Charlie. That so?"

Maji sighed and watched his hands keep moving expertly over the wood, creating shape and form. "You'll never see it in the news. But whatever Dee says, I'd take that as the truth."

He nodded silently as he picked his tools back up. "How's Rose doing, then?"

"Not so good, I think. She's been through a lot, losing family and having assholes with guns after her." Maji hesitated before saying the unthinkable out loud. "She broke up with me."

"Mm." He didn't sound sympathetic, but she knew he was letting that sink in. Well, so was she. After a few minutes of him working and her watching the boats out on the Sound, he said, "You know Raven had a wife, yeah?"

The mythology stuff never quite clicked for Maji, no matter whose culture the tale came from. How could a bird marry a woman? "Was she a human?"

"So they say. Line between the animal people and the two-legged people wasn't so bright back then. And of course, figures like Raven and Bear are something all their own anyway, something more. But you're sidetracking me there."

"Sorry. Where you headed then?"

"Only that Raven was a tough one to live with, always getting up to something, often making the others they had to live with mad."

Nate paused and looked up just long enough to make sure Maji was listening. "But Raven's a hero to us too."

"Why?"

"Well, Raven was kind of a hot mess, yeah? Often hungry, kinda foolish. Easy to relate to unless you happen to be perfect. But Raven managed to make things better for everyone, even while being a pain in the ass. Stealing the sun's admirable, ennit? After all, it was wrong of the man up the Nass river to keep the sun in a box and make everyone live in the dark."

Maji recalled that Raven changed shape twice, took on a false identity, and made a daring escape in order to steal the sun. Foolish maybe, but effective. "So you could admire that sort of chutzpah, but not want to live with it."

"Only takes one to want to, though. And love can make you put up with a lot of bull." He stopped and stretched, reaching for a shop towel. "Want to get some sushi?"

Suddenly raw fish and wasabi sounded irresistible. Unless she could see Rose. Even then, she realized, she'd handle that better with some protein in her. "Let me just check in." She texted Dev, *Safe to come back yet?*

Going to dinner with work people. Hang tight, he texted back. A few seconds later, *Go eat. Really.*

Frustrating as it was to wait, she had to smile. Dev knew her too well. "Sushi sounds great."

Ludvig's was too busy to get in, and Rose realized she was relieved. She wasn't up for the memories of her dinner there with Maji or the evening that followed. The thought of never sharing that kind of evening with her again brought tears to the surface. Arvid and Birgit, engaged in a lively discussion about other dining options, didn't notice. And though he said nothing, she knew Dev did. Much as she appreciated his insights, she was glad they couldn't talk about Maji anymore. If she could just stop thinking about her, the evening might be bearable.

A glass of wine with the fish of the day at the chosen next-best restaurant did help. Rose tried to tune in to the conversation, to fully engage. But fatigue and grief ganged up on her, and she kept drifting mentally away.

"Rose? You knew him, isn't that so?"

Dev caught her eye. "Javier Mendez. The man killed in that terrible auto accident," he prompted.

Javi, protecting his family. "Oh yes. He was a friend."

"So tragic," Arvid said. "In my country, we don't tolerate the driving with the alcohol." The official story, Rose supposed. *How about cold-blooded murder? Do you tolerate that?*

Birgit laid a hand on hers. "So sorry. A terrible loss."

"Rose was so strong, helping the police contact his family, making arrangements," Dev chimed in. "I hope you did not miss your own presentation?"

"No," she said. "That went quite well. It was…earlier."

That gave them all a safe segue back to work topics, with polite questions about her research project, the book Birgit was cowriting, and Arvid's application for a grant.

Rose looked at the empty bed and felt pulled to it. To just dissolve into sleep and forget for a little while the last day. But she didn't want to sleep alone. She wondered where Maji was. Was she alone too? Did she feel this awful?

"I'm going to get changed and bed down," Dev said, heading for the bathroom. "Need anything first?"

She looked up at him, still feeling torn. "Do you think Ri is still in town?"

Dev didn't do a good job of hiding his smile. "I think she's probably in the lobby."

"Oh. Well, please ask her to come up." Rose second-guessed herself. "No, wait. I'll do it." She got her phone out and opened their chain of messages, saw Maji's enthusiastic response to her invitation to lunch at the conference. To join her for a few moments of sweet, precious *normal people* time. *I can't leave things like this*, she typed. *Please come see me.*

After pressing send Rose realized that she had not given Maji their room number. Maybe Dev had given it to her, or…

A knock came at the door. With a salsa beat. Rose laughed with relief.

❖

Maji stood at the threshold waiting to be asked in. Rose looked tired, beautiful as always, and inexplicably happy. Had she changed her mind?

"I wanted to explain," Rose began.

Dev stepped between them, angling to get out. "'Scuse me." Outside, he gave Maji a light shove toward Rose.

As the door closed on him, Rose opened her mouth to continue.

"Wait," Maji interrupted, afraid to hear anything that started with *I wanted to explain*. "Don't give up on us. I know you're scared for me—I'm scared for you. But I can't let that stop me anymore. I can't stop loving you. And if you need some time, some space, anything at all, you can have whatever you need to feel safe. Dev says I should propose to you, like right now." The surprise on Rose's face was not delight. "But I don't think that's fair, to spring a take-it-or-leave-it on you when you know I'm about to disappear again. So you should know, when we've got this jackass in the bag, I'm going to come back—to you. And I'm going to ask you to marry me and never ever have to pretend again. Not about us, at least."

Rose crossed her arms over her middle. "Is that it?"

"That's the best I've got right now. If you give me another chance, I promise I'll do better." Maji ducked her head and turned toward the door.

"Stop."

Maji turned slowly back around. She could tell Rose was just barely holding herself together. She waited, her breath caught in her throat.

"You cannot be out there hunting Sirko while he thinks Sergeant Ariela Rios has me as an Achilles' heel. The only safe Ri for you *or* me is a single Ri." Rose gave her the barest smile, a whisper of hope. "So *Maji*, here's how it's going to go—as far as everyone else is concerned, I have broken up with you, whoever they think you are. I am single and, God help me, I will date as many yawningly normal people as I have to, to make that believable. I may even kiss one or two if absolutely necessary."

"Are you—"

"Ah," Rose cut her off. "Not done yet. When you are done catching that bastard and anyone else *your folks* are sure knows about us, then you come home to me. Whenever that is. Whatever condition you are in." No hint of the smile was left. "Take too long and you may come home to a really pissed-off single mother. Am I clear?"

Maji swallowed hard. "Is that a yes?"

"To what? Marriage? Hell no. I intend to enjoy dating you— like normal people do, or would if they had you to date. And then maybe I'll ask you. And you'd better say yes."

Maji laughed out loud. "For you, it's always yes."

"Good. Then come to bed."

"Uh, I'm—"

"Too injured to wow me. I know." Rose looked less cross, but still exhausted.

"No. Well, yeah. But also, I have to get gone around four a.m. I'm sorry."

Rose cupped Maji's face in her hands. "You will stop saying that. I'll set the damn alarm. And I just want you to hold me. Can you do that?"

Maji nodded. "Yes. Always yes."

About the Author

MB Austin, a mild-mannered civil servant by day, spends her discretionary time writing, training in a mix of martial arts, and working to end violence. She also enjoys cooking, eating, reading, dancing, and laughing as much as possible.

MB's first series, featuring Maji Rios, is inspired by real people, in and out of uniform, who work to make their communities and the world safer for all. And by the people who feed them.

MB lives with her fabulous wife in Seattle, an excellent town for coffee-fueled writers who don't need too much sun. Peek into daily life and upcoming stories at: www.mbaustin.me

Books Available from Bold Strokes Books

Exposed by MJ Williamz. The closet is no place to live if you want to find true love. (978-1-62639-989-1)

Force of Fire: Toujours a Vous by Ali Vali. Immortals Kendal and Piper welcome their new child and celebrate the defeat of an old enemy, but another ancient evil is about to awaken deep in the jungles of Costa Rica. (978-1-63555-047-4)

Holding Their Place by Kelly A. Wacker. Together Dr. Helen Connery and ambulance driver Julia March, discover that goodness, love, and passion can be found in the most unlikely and even dangerous places during WWI. (978-1-63555-338-3)

Landing Zone by Erin Dutton. Can a career veteran finally discover a love stronger than even her pride? (978-1-63555-199-0)

Love at Last Call by M. Ullrich. Is balancing business, friendship, and love more than any willing woman can handle? (978-1-63555-197-6)

Pleasure Cruise by Yolanda Wallace. Spencer Collins and Amy Donovan have few things in common, but a Caribbean cruise offers both women an unexpected chance to face one of their greatest fears: falling in love. (978-1-63555-219-5)

Running Off Radar by MB Austin. Maji's plans to win Rose back are interrupted when work intrudes and duty calls her to help a SEAL team stop a Russian mobster from harvesting gold from the bottom of Sitka Sound. (978-1-63555-152-5)

Shadow of the Phoenix by Rebecca Harwell. In the final battle for the fate of Storm's Quarry, even Nadya's and Shay's powers may not be enough. (978-1-63555-181-5)

Take a Chance by D. Jackson Leigh. There's hardly a woman within fifty miles of Pine Cone that veterinarian Trip Beaumont can't charm, except for the irritating new cop, Jamie Grant, who keeps leaving parking tickets on her truck. (978-1-63555-118-1)

The Outcasts by Alexa Black. Spacebus driver Sue Jones is running from her past. When she crash-lands on a faraway world, the Outcast Kara might be her chance for redemption. (978-1-63555-242-3)

Alias by Cari Hunter. A car crash leaves a woman with no memory and no identity. Together with Detective Bronwen Pryce, she fights to uncover a truth that might just kill them both. (978-1-63555-221-8)

Death in Time by Robyn Nyx. Working in the past is hell on your future. (978-1-63555-053-5)

Hers to Protect by Nicole Disney. High school sweethearts Kaia and Adrienne will have to see past their differences and survive the vengeance of a brutal gang if they want to be together. (978-1-63555-229-4)

Of Echoes Born by 'Nathan Burgoine. A collection of queer fantasy short stories set in Canada from Lambda Literary Award finalist 'Nathan Burgoine. (978-1-63555-096-2)

Perfect Little Worlds by Clifford Mae Henderson. Lucy can't hold the secret any longer. Twenty-six years ago, her sister did the unthinkable. (978-1-63555-164-8)

Room Service by Fiona Riley. Interior designer Olivia likes stability, but when work brings footloose Savannah into her world and into a new city every month, Olivia must decide if what makes her comfortable is what makes her happy. (978-1-63555-120-4)

Sparks Like Ours by Melissa Brayden. Professional surfers Gia Malone and Elle Britton can't deny their chemistry on and off the beach. But only one can win… (978-1-63555-016-0)

Take My Hand by Missouri Vaun. River Hemsworth arrives in Georgia intent on escaping quickly, but when she crashes her Mercedes into the Clip 'n Curl, sexy Clay Cahill ends up rescuing more than her car. (978-1-63555-104-4)

The Last Time I Saw Her by Kathleen Knowles. Lane Hudson only has twelve days to win back Alison's heart. That is if she can gather the courage to try. (978-1-63555-067-2)

Wayworn Lovers by Gun Brooke. Will agoraphobic composer Giselle Bonnaire and Tierney Edwards, a wandering soul who can't remain in one place for long, trust in the passionate love destiny hands them? (978-1-62639-995-2)

Breakthrough by Kris Bryant. Falling for a sexy ranger is one thing, but is the possibility of love worth giving up the career Kennedy Wells has always dreamed of? (978-1-63555-179-2)

Certain Requirements by Elinor Zimmerman. Phoenix has always kept her love of kinky submission strictly behind the bedroom door and inside the bounds of romantic relationships, until she meets Kris Andersen. (978-1-63555-195-2)

Dark Euphoria by Ronica Black. When a high-profile case drops in Detective Maria Diaz's lap, she forges ahead only to discover this case, and her main suspect, aren't like any other. (978-1-63555-141-9)

Fore Play by Julie Cannon. Executive Leigh Marshall falls hard for Peyton Broader, her golf pro…and an ex-con. Will she risk sabotaging her career for love? (978-1-63555-102-0)

Love Came Calling by CA Popovich. Can a romantic looking for a long-term, committed relationship and a jaded cynic too busy for love conquer life's struggles and find their way to what matters most? (978-1-63555-205-8)

Outside the Law by Carsen Taite. Former sweethearts Tanner Cohen and Sydney Braswell must work together on a federal task force to see justice served, but will they choose to embrace their second chance at love? (978-1-63555-039-9)

The Princess Deception by Nell Stark. When journalist Missy Duke realizes Prince Sebastian is really his twin sister Viola in disguise, she plays along, but when sparks flare between them, will the double deception doom their fairy-tale romance? (978-1-62639-979-2)

The Smell of Rain by Cameron MacElvee. Reyha Arslan, a wise and elegant woman with a tragic past, shows Chrys that there's still beauty to embrace and reason to hope despite the world's cruelty. (978-1-63555-166-2)

The Talebearer by Sheri Lewis Wohl. Liz's visions show her the faces of the lost and the killers who took their lives. As one by one, the murdered are found, a stranger works to stop Liz before the serial killer is brought to justice. (978-1-635550-126-6)

White Wings Weeping by Lesley Davis. The world is full of discord and hatred, but how much of it is just human nature when an evil with sinister intent is invading people's hearts? (978-1-63555-191-4)

A Call Away by KC Richardson. Can a businesswoman from a big city find the answers she's looking for, and possibly love, on a small-town farm? (978-1-63555-025-2)

Berlin Hungers by Justine Saracen. Can the love between an RAF woman and the wife of a Luftwaffe pilot, former enemies, survive in besieged Berlin during the aftermath of World War II? (978-1-63555-116-7)

Blend by Georgia Beers. Lindsay and Piper are like night and day. Working together won't be easy, but not falling in love might prove the hardest job of all. (978-1-63555-189-1)

Hunger for You by Jenny Frame. Principe of an ancient vampire clan Byron Debrek must save her one true love from falling into the hands of her enemies and into the middle of a vampire war. (978-1-63555-168-6)

Mercy by Michelle Larkin. FBI Special Agent Mercy Parker and psychic ex-profiler Piper Vasey learn to love again as they race to stop a man with supernatural gifts who's bent on annihilating humankind. (978-1-63555-202-7)

Pride and Porters by Charlotte Greene. Will pride and prejudice prevent these modern-day lovers from living happily ever after? (978-1-63555-158-7)

Rocks and Stars by Sam Ledel. Kyle's struggle to own who she is and what she really wants may end up landing her on the bench and without the woman of her dreams. (978-1-63555-156-3)

The Boss of Her: Office Romance Novellas by Julie Cannon, Aurora Rey, and M. Ullrich. Going to work never felt so good. Three office romance novellas from talented writers Julie Cannon, Aurora Rey, and M. Ullrich. (978-1-63555-145-7)

The Deep End by Ellie Hart. When family ties become entangled in murder and deception, it's time to find a way out... (978-1-63555-288-1)

A Country Girl's Heart by Dena Blake. When Kat Jackson gets a second chance at love, following her heart will prove the hardest decision of all. (978-1-63555-134-1)

Dangerous Waters by Radclyffe. Life, death, and war on the home front. Two women join forces against a powerful opponent, nature itself. (978-1-63555-233-1)

Fury's Death by Brey Willows. When all we hold sacred fails, who will be there to save us? (978-1-63555-063-4)

It's Not a Date by Heather Blackmore. Kade's desire to keep things with Jen on a professional level is in Jen's best interest. Yet what's in Kade's best interest…is Jen. (978-1-63555-149-5)

Killer Winter by Kay Bigelow. Just when she thought things could get no worse, homicide Lieutenant Leah Samuels learns the woman she loves has betrayed her in devastating ways. (978-1-63555-177-8)

Score by MJ Williamz. Will an addiction to pain pills destroy Ronda's chance with the woman she loves or will she come out on top and score a happily ever after? (978-1-62639-807-8)

Spring's Wake by Aurora Rey. When wanderer Willa Lange falls for Provincetown B&B owner Nora Calhoun, will past hurts and a fifteen-year age gap keep them from finding love? (978-1-63555-035-1)

The Northwoods by Jane Hoppen. When Evelyn Bauer, disguised as her dead husband, George, travels to a Northwoods logging camp to work, she and the camp cook Sarah Bell forge a friendship fraught with both tenderness and turmoil. (978-1-63555-143-3)

Truth or Dare by C. Spencer. For a group of six lesbian friends, life changes course after one long snow-filled weekend. (978-1-63555-148-8)